FOCUSED

ജ ൠ

For now we see through a glass, darkly;
but then face to face: now I know in part;
but then shall I know
even as also I am known.
1 Corinthians 13:12 (King James Version)

FOCUSED

By Julie B Cosgrove

**Cross  Words
Press**

Cross **Words**
Press
Fort Worth, Tx

FOCUSED

Cover Designs by Gina Jenkins. @ metroebs@gmail.com
Bluebonnets photo taken by James Cosgrove, Blanco TX
Eyeglasses courtesy of Microsoft Royalty Free Clip Art
Author photo by Burden Studios, Burleson, TX

This is a faith-based book proclaiming glory to the Triune God, Father, Son and Holy Spirit. Opinions stated in this book are the author's based on her Christian faith and interpretation of Biblical Truth. They are not necessarily the views of the publisher.

Unless otherwise indicated, all Scripture quotations in this publication are taken from the Holy Bible New International Version®(NIV) Copyright1973,1978,1984

ISBN:978-0-9849844-1-1 Paperback
Printed in The UNITED STATES OF AMERICA

21 20 19 18 17 16 15 14 13

Dedicated to —

Anne, who insisted that I write this.
Gina and Kenny for the late night graphics session.
And to Gail, Sandy and Robi who added
so many right suggestions.

Acknowledgments

I have used my own life experiences as a jumping off place for this story, but in no way are the names, characters and/or events meant to be anything other than a fictionalized account. I am blessed to own Texas Hill Country acreage, left by my maternal grandfather and great uncle, along with the ever-growing members of my family. Friends who have walked down the path to the riverfront in the quiet of the morning as the mist rises from the ripples have told me they have felt a little closer to God there. It is always an honor to share that with them.

Like my main character, Christina, experiences of city, small town and Texas Hill Country have shaped my life. Our upbringings and life events tend to do that. So I wish to make it very clear that it is not my intent to show any negativity toward those of privilege and high social standing, nor likewise to those who have never experienced that way of life. I simply acknowledge it was not a lifestyle I chose, and for good or for bad, that choice became one many inspirations for this story.

My hope is as you follow Christina's tale, you will begin to see anew your own life's journey and what a blessing each of you are to others, even in the seemingly mundane of your everyday world. If you live in an empty nest, realize it is not really empty. God dwells in the center. You don't need to try and fill it with anyone else or anything else. Change is life, and

God knows how to help you handle change because He is the only constant.

I thank my sister Anne who told me I should write, Alice and Clare, my spiritual cheerleaders and the examples they have had on my life, North Texas Christian Writers for their tutelage, advice, support and critique, (especially Gail, Sandy and Robi) and KLOVE.com and The Journey 88.3 for the background music online that kept the reason for telling this, well, in focus.

Finally, but foremost, I thank my Lord for the people and events He has brought into my life. To Him alone be praise, honor and glory.

Julie B. Cosgrove

Prologue - The Litmus Test
1985

Oh, why did I insist on coming here?

Christina's hands dripped with anxiety. The heirloom serving dish slipped out of her grasp and clunked onto the cedar log table. The take-out fried chicken wobbled as the sound ricocheted against the wooden walls of the summer cabin where her ancestors once ate, slept and loved. She raised her shoulders to her ears and grimaced.

Her mother scowled. "Must you be so clumsy? I don't want your grandmother's china platter chipped."

Must you always criticize me? She clamped her lips into a taut line and swallowed her true response, just as she did every time. "Yes, Ma'am."

Christina watched her mother scoop the carton of coleslaw into a lead crystal bowl. It seemed appropriate. She felt as if she'd been born for a plastic tub life but shoved into crystal from the get-go. She never did quite fit into her mother's idea of what a daughter should be. As a child, she'd often wondered if she'd been adopted.

Ticks from the old mantle clock perched on the rock fireplace vibrated into the kitchen and pounded in her ears. Finally, her mother's voice broke the stifled hush that hung between them.

"So, Christina, how long have you known this Jeff of yours?" One eyebrow arched as she clumsily dried a dinner plate. A two-carat diamond ring bulged under her yellow Playtex glove. She always insisted on the dishes from the cabin's kitchen being washed before using them. Pity her latest maid-cook didn't accompany them this trip. Christina sighed and dunked her bare, ring-less hands into the hot suds. They were used to it. Her apartment had no dishwasher.

"A few months. But I really like him, Mother. *Really* like him."

Christina noticed Jeff and her father through the screened window. They walked down the rock path. Lazy daisies peeked between the stones, in danger of being crushed by their cowboy boots. Her father stared straight ahead. Jeff talked with palms clasped behind his back. His posture seemed as stiff as a scarecrow's. His fingers twitched. She wondered why he appeared so nervous? It was just her dad. Everyone felt comfortable around her dad. Easy going. Not like her mother.

"Okay, true." Christina dipped another dish into the soapy water. It splashed her *Save the Dolphins* T-shirt. "I agree that Jeff's not socially conscious of how he looks. He's happy in plaid pants and a striped shirt if they're comfortable and relatively clean." Out of the corner of her eye, she caught her mother's sneer.

Christina went on to defend him. "He may be rough around the edges, Mother, but he more than makes up for it with his strong work ethic and morals. He's honest and kind and," she nodded with emphasis, " . . . and gentlemanly."

Her mother remained silent.

Christina wiped her hands on her cut-off jeans. The tennis bracelet, a gift from her sorority little sister years ago, cast minute rainbows upon the bubbles. She squared her shoulders. "He may not be in your circle of influential friends, Mother, but Jeff can look someone in the eye no matter what their social standing and make them feel appreciated and important. That's why I love him. That's why I want to marry him." To her shock, the words now blurted from the secret confines of her heart actually made sense.

"I know, dear. And, we think you have made an excellent choice." Her taunt mouth relaxed, almost into a smile.

Christina's balloon of rebellious pride for daring to date outside her mother's social circle popped. It slid into the suds along with the sponge. "You . . . do?"

"We, your father and I, admire Jeff, too."

"But, you don't know him."

Her mother sighed, then set the plate on the counter. "We know more than you think. Upon hearing of your courtship from your sister, we hired a private investigator. A few days ago, the P.I. reported back to us. He told us Jeff Willis didn't have any dirt on him worth digging up."

Christina's eyes and mouth widened at mother's words. "How could you?"

The woman looked away. She fingered the choker of pearls at her neck. "He told us Jeff served his time in the Marines, right? We know he was injured in Lebanon. Spent months stateside in the hospital and received the Purple Heart for that. Shot in the hip, I believe."

"Yes, I know." When she saw her mother's eyebrow arch again, Christina added, "He, uh, told me all about it. It, ah, still catches now and then."

"I see." Her mother looked down to take the next rinsed plate her daughter had placed in the drainer.

Christina noticed her smirk. *Please don't let her see me blush. Surely she and Dad . . . maybe not, it was the 1950's after all. Oh, never mind.*

"Anyway. . ." Her mother emphasized the word to regain her daughter's attention. "We learned he'd been an A student at St. Paul's, a respectable school from what I hear, even though it is Catholic."

Christina rolled her eyes. She knew her mother was snooty-proud about her British Protestant roots. *But, Mother, but come on. Just because your maiden name is Winslow . . .*

"Oh," she pointed the plate at Christina's face, "and he said Jeff was an Eagle Scout. Your father liked that."

"He worked to put himself through college, too. Graduated with honors with a B.S. in structural engineering from U.T. in Austin. I guess your spy told you that as well."

"Yes, well, we knew he was in construction of some sort." She sniffed and tilted her head as she rubbed the plate dry.

To Christina her gesture meant even though he's decent enough, he's not an attorney, bank officer or a doctor, my dear. Not our class.

"We asked the P.I to dig a bit further, but he couldn't uncover any police record, except for a few speeding tickets. Even your father's had a few of those."

Christina felt her cheeks heat. She turned away and counted to ten, slowly.

Focused

Her mother placed her latex-covered hand under Christina's chin, gently twisting it back to face her. The glove smelled pungent, straight out of the package. "So you see? Now we know your Jeff is an outstanding young man."

Christina's eyes narrowed. *How dare she think I'd be stupid enough to date any guy who wasn't.*

The woman shifted to face her daughter full on. "You had the foresight to know in your heart he would make a good husband."

"And he will." Her voice had an edge to it.

"Your father and I should have trusted you more, honey." She placed her hand on Christina's back with motherly tenderness, a rare act for her. "You're a grown woman. We just didn't know his family and we were concerned. That's all." She returned to her duty of wiping dishes.

"He loves it up here, you know." Christina's eyes took on a mischievous glint. She raised her forefinger for effect. Jeff had passed one of the family litmus tests as to whether a beau was worth dating or not. He loved the Texas Hill Country.

Christina leaned into the sink to get her mother to look at her. "And, Mother, " she held up a second finger. "He loves God." Test number two passed.

"We know." Her mother nodded in the direction of the window. Outside, the two men were shaking hands and smiling.

Now, Christina understood. She squealed and hugged her mother, dripping suds down the back of the lady's linen sundress, recently acquired on a shopping spree to Neiman Marcus in Dallas.

Julie B Cosgrove

Later that night, on the door stoop to her apartment, Jeff brought out the black velvet box, down on one knee, per proper tradition.

Chapter 1   Steamed
Twenty-four years later

Christina locked herself in the bathroom for the first time in her married life. Above the rush of the shower, she heard a fist bang against the door. She jolted at the sound. *Go away. Please, just go away.*

"Hon, you okay in there? Coffee's ready."

Her mouth opened to answer, but couldn't form the words. There were too many she wanted to say to him and she'd regret them all later if she did.

Eyes closed, head propped against the back tile, she pressed her spine into the corner of the shower stall, wishing the water would drench her inside out and send the hurt down the drain with the swirl of soap bubbles. Things, which might seem little to anyone else, had built up like plaque in her emotional arteries, clogging any rational thoughts from reaching her heart.

Another loud knuckle rap. "Okay, then. See ya tonight. I made raisin toast. Your favorite."

Julie B Cosgrove

Raisin toast. As if that would make up for everything else. Today, the thought of greeting Jeff with a cheek smooch before he traipsed off to work thrust bile into her throat. She'd done that every day for the last twenty-four years. And, why? Because, growing up, she'd seen her mother air kiss her father's cheek to launch him into the world of business each morning? Silly, empty routine. Besides, when did she ever do anything like her mother? She'd always gone to work as well. So, why didn't Jeff ever smooch *her* goodbye?

She masked her gulped sobs in the spray of steamy water. Her chest ached as the weight of her world pressed against it. Everything once precious seemed obscured by a black veil of loss.

Loss over her dad with an intensity she told herself a grown woman shouldn't have. She even missed her mother, even though they had rarely seen eye to eye. Loss of her grown son, Josh, now in an apartment of his own. With work and college classes, he rarely came around unless he had a mound of dirty laundry. Or needed cash. His schedule was so different from theirs. She'd saved his brief messages on her phone to listen to when she became lonely for the sound of his voice.

Most of all she missed the closeness she and Jeff once had. It had slowly dissolved, blending into matrimonial patterns like sugar in Southern sweet tea. Now, instead of his arms, this shower stall was her refuge. And she hated tight places.

* * *

Focused

Jeff heard the shower running . . . still. What had it been? Fifteen minutes? His wife had always been a long tub soaker, he knew that. But when it came to the shower stall, she'd be in and out in less time than any private in the Marine Corp. She always hated tight places.

So why in the . . .? He shook his head. Who knew.

Every morning for the past umpteen years Christina had greeted him, robe sashed around her, hair still a bit disheveled, with a smooch to send him off to work. Not today. Was this one more routine hitting the can now that their son had flown the coop? Who knew? Lately her moods were as changing as Texas weather. Hot, cold, muggy, icy.

Jeff hissed under his breath. "I am not a mind reader. If I've done something, tell me. Woman, you're driving me nuts."

His hand reached for the door knob. Then it froze. The thought of busting in and pulling back the shower curtain to ask her what the heck was wrong made him cringe. Wouldn't be pretty. She hated surprises worse than tight places. Besides, he wasn't in the mood for an explosion and didn't feel like dodging the shrapnel she'd launch in his direction. So he knocked instead. No answer. Not even when he told her he'd made raisin toast, her favorite.

Last night, Christina left the den in a huff. He didn't know why. Just as well, though. He hadn't been in the mood to hear her jabber on about this and that. The vise clamp around his cranium had been a killer and the mindless noise on the TV hadn't helped to ease it.

She'll cool down by tonight. But one whiff told him the scrambled eggs he'd left sizzling in the skillet weren't cooling down. They were burning. He dashed down the hall, grabbed the pan handle with a towel and turned off the flame. Ruined. He flicked on the vent.

Darn that woman. Christina used to fix breakfast for him and Josh every morning, when Josh was around. Now he had to fix his own. He hated cooking.

Jeff took a swig of the brewed caffeine to wash down the nagging thought that he really didn't matter to her now. *Sure, she's mourning her dad, and in a way Josh. But dammit all, I'm still around.*

He shoveled as much of the rubbery brown eggs as he could into the trashcan then tossed the skillet into the sink. He snatched one of the slices of raisin bread from the toaster, now ice cold. That and a cup of coffee would have to suffice.

Soft fur rubbed against his calf. Small blue eyes peered up at him over long white whiskers in a black mask. Heart softened, he picked up the purring feline and nuzzled its fur.

"At least one female in this house loves me this morning. Don't you, Precious?"

That cat rubbed her jowl against his freshly shaven cheek. It almost qualified for his morning smooch. His mood melted.

"I love you too, Baby. But I gotta go, now."

Jeff punched the automatic garage door opener with his fist. A brisk March breeze swirled the last of the winter leaves into the garage in a haphazard waltz. He slid into the bench seat of his truck and

Focused

backed out into the world of traffic and another hectic day at the office. His Styrofoam coffee cup, still perched on the hardtop, made it four blocks before sliding off into the gutter. A new record.

* * *

Waterlogged, Christina remained in the shower until she was sure her husband had left. The last of the hot water had left as well. *Enough. I have to get to work. This shower pity party isn't going to pay the bills.*

One hand turned off the water as her other grabbed a towel. She proceeded with her weekday ritual of dressing in the business casual and hosiery already lain out on the bedroom chair the night before. But first, she had to remove her marmalade cat from on top of them. Another ritual.

"Momma's Okay, Fat Cat," she told herself more than her furry companion. So named for his girth and ability to outdo any garbage disposal, the male feline was her favorite. He lay on her stocking feet as she sat at the vanity.

Christina blinked her eyes wide to thwart any tears from ruining her freshly applied mascara. Pupils rolled to the ceiling, she willed her emotions back into her stomach. Maybe her avoidance had steamed Jeff as much as it had the bathroom mirror. Or at least made him think about what he'd done. The click of her heels down the hall emphasized each syllable in her thoughts. Then, at the kitchen door, she halted. The range vent whirred on high speed.

What has he done now? She stared at the sink. Her favorite skillet rested in slimy water. On top floated brown gunk she assumed had once been scrambled eggs. Her arms clutched around her chest in a pretzel as she tapped away her anger with her foot. How hard was it to cook eggs? Perhaps she had spoiled him by doing everything for him all those years. She certainly didn't have time to scrub it clean now. Jeff wasn't the only one who had to get to work. She added it to her growing list of things to do before she hit the sheets that night, exhausted as usual.

She grabbed the last piece of raisin toast, filled her commuter mug with coffee, hopped in her seven year old Accord, and headed for the accounting clerk job she had held for the last fifteen years. It was the last place she wanted to be. Surely there was someplace she could go, one door she could open without stress tumbling out like junk from an overstuffed closet.

"Another day, another dollar," her dad always said.

Today, Dad, it's more like ten cents after taxes. Dad. Had it really been two years since the funeral? A whiff of memory, mingled with the damp March air, allowed just a pinch of grief to filter back into her heart. It had been overcast and gloomy that day, too.

Then it happened. One ray of sun poked through the gloom. When Christina reached the intersection to turn east towards work, a quote from her high school literature class marqueed across her brain. "Go west, young man, go west." On a whim, she made a U turn. She dug her cell phone out of her purse, called in sick for the first time in years, and without a bit of regret, just kept driving.

Chapter 2   The Escape

Bluebonnets, Indian paint brush and wine cups poked from the prairie grass in the medians along the highway, a true sign of spring's arrival in Texas. The smog and clouds dissipated with each mile. It turned into a gorgeous day—the kind that made adults feverish and persuaded children to play hooky. Not even her anguish could stop its lure.

Christina toyed with the small gold cross around her neck, dragging it back and forth on its chain. Her conversation with Jeff last night, if it could be called that, still burned in her heart. She reached for her cell phone to call her sister. The dial face said 8:05. She should be up by now. Carrie answered on the third ring with a groggy, "Hello?"

"It's me. Gotta minute?"

"Sure. Just getting my coffee." A long yawn. "You sound like you're in a tunnel. Where are you?"

"In the car. On the road." Christina heard the breakfast chair scoot across the floor in her sister's kitchen, then her voice, more awake and serious.

"Okay, I'm sitting down. What's up, Sis. Jeff? Josh?"

Tears formed again in her eyes. She sniffed them back. "Jeff. We had a non-fight."

"And that would be . . .?" A spoon clanked round and round in a coffee cup.

"Well with Josh off on his own, there's no ball games, Scout meetings or high school band functions to rush off to after we get home at night."

"But, that's kinda nice, right?"

"Not really. Every evening we sit in the den in front of the TV. He's in his recliner and I'm on the couch. You know, our conversation time used to be rare and precious. Now, it's dwindled to a few remarks about work and the weather. Is it like that for you and Paul?"

"At times. It took us a while to settle into not having the kids around." The sound of her sister inhaling deeply was next. "Mmmm. What did mankind do before coffee?"

"Woke up grouchy I guess. Anyway, each night I feel like we sit in silence despite the noise coming from that boob tube. Same shows, week after week, all his choice, of course. Jeff says it helps him unwind. I hate it."

"Then go do something else."

Christina checked her rear view mirror, then switched lanes. "But, if I leave the room it irritates him. So I bring in magazines, crosswords, my Bible study, mending."

Focused

"Ah. Playing the dutiful wife role?" The slurping of coffee came through the phone.

"I guess. It keeps the peace, ya know? Still, night after night he stares at that darn TV. Once, a century or so ago, he had told me he couldn't take his eyes off of me." She gulped back a sob.

"Uh-huh., know whatcha mean. Yuk. Forgot the creamer." The chair legged scooted again . "So, what was the non-fight about?"

Through the earpiece, Christina detected slippers shuffling across the kitchen floor. She kicked her heels off and stretched her toes over the accelerator pedal. "My glasses. I was doing some sewing and couldn't focus. I told him I didn't know why I let that optometrist talk me into bifocals. Three years and I still can't get used to them. I tossed them onto the couch and tried to thread the sewing needle by squinting. Do you know what he said?"

"No." More spoon clinks.

"He muttered through the sports section in front of his face, 'Then get a refund.' I knew he was irritated. He has a way of snapping the newspaper when he turns the page."

"They all do that. Universal male sign."

"Anyway, *Wheel of Fortune* was on the TV. He looked up and said, 'Buy a vowel, lady.' As if the contestant could hear his advice." Christina slammed on her brakes when a big rig in front of her stopped. The height of his truck prevented her from seeing the traffic light turn red.

"So?"

"He talks to the TV, but won't even look at me. He doesn't care, Carrie."

9

Christina could hear her sister sigh, and then take another slow gulp. "Come on, Sis. You don't mean that."

"Yes I do. It's true. I told him I can't get a refund. It's been way too long now. He snaps his paper again and says, 'Ah, the Bears won.'"

"So?" Her sister's voice resonated with growing impatience.

"I got upset, Okay? I jammed the needle through the button of his shirt I was mending and pricked my finger. I threw it down, stood up and said, 'Darn it!'"

"Oh, you'll burn for that one." Carrie's tone of voice began to mimic Jeff's sarcasm.

Christina swatted away the barb. "He didn't even see what I'd done. He told me to calm down and just go get another pair. A new pair is way too expensive. We can't swing that right now. Carrie, you know what he did?"

"Tell me. It obviously upset you."

The light must have turned green. The eighteen wheeler inched up the hill. Christina looked in her side view mirror to see if she could scoot around him. "He puts down the paper and says, 'Then live with it. Either way, your choice. Then he punched the volume control on the remote—I felt my temper rising with each green notch on the volume bar—and told me, 'While you're up, I could use a glass of ice water. Now hush. The show's coming back on.'"

"He said that? What did you do?"

"I got his precious water and slammed it down next to him. I wanted to dump the glass in his lap." Christina turned on her blinker and swiveled her

10

Focused

head. The driver in a white pick-up behind to her left waved her to go ahead. She waved back.

"I'm sorry, sis. Maybe he'd had a bad day?"

"Lately, they all are. I'd had it. I stomped out of the room. I dug my nails so deep into my palms, they still hurt."

There was silence on the other end. Then her sister's voice returned. "What happened this morning?"

Christina shifted the cell phone to her other ear. "Nothing. I stayed in the bathroom until he'd left."

"That solved a lot." The sympathy in her sister's voice evaporated.

Christina's ears felt hot. The volcano inside her bubbled. Again. "You just don't understand. Gotta go." She flicked off the cell phone and threw it onto the seat. Her foot pressed harder on the accelerator.

Christina peered through the windshield at the Farm-to-Market road that stretched out ahead. *Well, the heck with you, Jeff . . . and the office, and tax season. I'm sick of all of you.*

She was tired of being ignored and feeling useless, sick of the day in and day out lifestyle that kept her world trapped in a rut. She was weary of compromising, of swallowing down the hurt and anger time, after time, after time just to avoid conflict and keep the status quo peace. Wiping her eyes with the back of her hand, she flipped on the radio.

A blast from the past selection. Steppenwolf's "Born to be Wild" screamed over the airwaves. He sang about getting out on the highway. Convinced the DEEJAY selected it just for her, she pressed her stocking foot down further on the pedal and locked her elbows. With her head back and the breeze whipping through her collar-length ginger hair, she zipped down the Texas Hill Country back roads, windows down, tunes blaring. The song made Christina feel thirty-five years younger. For the first time in eons, she felt free. Goodbye routine, do-for-everyone-else life.

Her cares swooshed off the back of her car like colored smoke in a wind tunnel experiment. The vibration of the airstream in her ear and the music numbed her brain to everything other than driving. The scenery, once so familiar, zipped by her as she sped around the curves. Mile after mile of wildflower-hugged posts in fenced fields lay ahead, dotted by an occasional oak or clump of mesquite and cedar. No buildings, no traffic lights, no bumper-to-bumper cars.

She slowed to a stop at the end of State Highway 290, and then stared at the mossy colored humps of the Texas Hill Country. They beckoned her. Her deepest and fondest memories, fuzzy and warmed by time, emerged from a cold dark place in her heart. As she inhaled the crisp countryside air, all the city smells left her nostrils. For a brief moment she sat, car idling, arms hunched forward on the steering wheel and breathed in. That is, until she noticed a rusty red Chevy truck growing larger in her rearview mirror.

I wonder how far this tank of gas will get me? Christina flipped on her right blinker, dropped her accelerator foot once more and zoomed ahead down State Highway 281 towards Johnson City . . . and beyond.

* * *

Focused

As he drove to work, Jeff pushed away the thought that his wife's moodiness had anything to do with him. He just couldn't see it. *Women. Go figure.*

Maybe last night she'd just been on edge because of work. He certainly had been. Christina worked for an accounting firm and next week the April frenzy would begin. It did seem to be getting her goat more this year. He remembered her whining about someone being out and she doing all the work. Sure, that's all it was. Besides, he had his own problems and they hadn't gone away after he locked his office door last night.

As soon as he walked into work, he noticed three people waiting for him, holding papers and quizzical looks. Great way to start the day. He unlocked his door, set his briefcase down, pointed to the apprentice who appeared the most bewildered, and motioned him into the office. "Morning, Jim. Whatcha got?"

"The new stadium addendum. I can't make heads or tails of it. "

"That's Bob Weaver's isn't it? Did ya call him?"

"Yeah." The young man shuffled his weight and set the rolled plans down in a chair. "Left a message. Twice. It bids at Two."

Jeff turned away before his face revealed the headache settling into his left temple. And to think he'd only been there five minutes. Feeling the intern's eyes at his back, he flipped on the monitor and watched its soft glow filter onto the desk. He ogled the blinking white hourglass telling him cyberspace was

13

coming to life. It mesmerized him for a second or two, draining his brain of the present.

Why had he accepted this management job? Because he was over fifty and that was what a man was supposed to do. It meant he'd climbed the rungs, made a name. Besides, it qualified him for the pension fund. As if he'd ever be able to retire.

A fisted cough broke his trance. Guessing he couldn't stall much longer, Jeff sat down in the office chair. It creaked back in a slight recline. Two fingers motioned to the antsy eyes of the perplexed youth. "Let's see it."

"Yes sir. Thanks." The kid nearly jumped over the chair in eagerness as he unrolled the plan over Jeff's keyboard, jostling yesterday afternoon's leftover coffee in his office mug, its rim stained with a film of coddled milk and caffeine oil. *Just Do It!* The faded red slogan on the mug yelled in silence.

Through the door Jeff saw the rest of the small pack had hung around. Were they waiting for his expertise or one of the warm bear claws in the bakery box Midge set on the break room table next to the gurgling coffee pot? Probably both. Was he the only one who actually did the work around here?

He wondered, if he got up and left, would he be fired?

Chapter 3   Okay, I'm In

Three hours later Christina stood in a doorway waiting for her eyes to refocus from a cloudless day to the darkened room. The cedar planks of the cabin creaked and groaned, seeming to question the presence of this sudden off-season occupant.

As well it should. Why did I end up here of all places?

Here, where she spent many a summer night listening to the rhythm of her parents' snores, subconsciously in sync after many years of marriage, float across from the sleeping porch at the other end. Never again. They were both gone now. The strange silence blared in her ears, clashing with her memories of children's laugher, Big Band music streaming from the old turquoise clock radio, and her dad rocking in his chair. A cold splash surged up her spine and into her tear ducts.

A Blue Jay cawed as it swooped past her. She jolted, which released the screen door she'd been holding open with her backside. Its hinges screeched closed behind her. The vibrating *boing* of the spring echoed into the room. It seemed as if the house, eager for someone's return, pushed her inside.

Okay, Okay, I'm in. Christina set her purse on the table and ventured further into the stillness. She crept across the living room into the bedroom where she once slept peacefully as a child, careful not to disturb the past which clung to the dusty walls.

Her reflection in the oval mirror revealed a middle-aged woman with an inkling of gray in her hair. And with deep dark circles under her eyes. *Ugh, do I really look that bad?* She rubbed them to remove any smudged mascara, a futile attempt.

Christina plopped on the cot and peered at the soot-covered face staring back at her. The sun-faded quilt released a slight musty odor, a familiar fragrance from her childhood. The four-room cabin always held that smell before being aired out each summer, as had been the ritual for almost two-thirds of a century—that is until lately. It had been at least two years since she or anyone else had set foot in this place. Closer to three. She supposed her parent's void was as painful for Carl or Carrie as it was for her.

A glance at her watch made her gawk. Already 10:25? Her mind held a vague memory of the last few hours. She remembered turning west and calling her sister, who could've cared less, about last night. She recalled the wind in her hair and feeling carefree. But what else?

"I could have ended up in a wreck. What on earth was I thinking?" Christina asked out loud to her mirror image.

The reflection didn't enlighten her. Her brain answered, though. Maneuvering for the last few hours

16

on autopilot, not having to think, but just …doing for once. And it had felt wonderful.

"Okay," she said to the mirror. "Sure, there's been times, driving the same route to work and back, day in and day out, I've zoned out only to realize I'd traveled several more miles than I thought." Christina rationalized everyone did that. She often thanked God for taking over the wheel at those moments. "But never," she whimpered to her dust-covered twin, "Never for over two hours."

Was she losing it? Had all those emotions she'd swallowed down finally fermented into an intoxicating madness? There had to be a rational explanation for this conduct. She shook her head as one would a Magic Eight Ball, expecting an answer to float up. It didn't.

Christina slumped over the edge of the cot, resting her elbows on her knees. She kicked off her two-inch heeled pumps and traced the braided throw rug's ovals with her stocking toes. A breeze outside rustled through the sapling oaks. It whipped dust particles which gleamed in the sunbeam through a crack in the door. They danced like microscopic fairies above the cedar planks. She could hear the ancient Cyprus trees creak as their limbs rubbed together in the wind.

This summer place always captivated her heart. Not the Federal style two-story residence in the posh, tree-lined neighborhood where she had been raised in San Antonio. Not the ranch- style house in Allensville where she and Jeff had raised Josh and lived for the last twenty-one years. This rustic cabin from her mother's side of the family, nestled in the Texas Hill Country on a cliff overlooking a languid emerald river is what she'd always thought of as home. It had been a refuge from high society's scrutiny during her childhood and repose from the ordinary working housewife existence of her adulthood. She realized how much she'd missed being here, perhaps more than she missed her parents.

Like a warmed beach towel just off the clothesline, a feeling of familiarity settled around her, full of edited memories that included only the good times. Not just good times, the best. Not like now.

Hill Country rivers were always cool— visitors said cold— fed by underground springs below the surface beyond the sun's warmth. On a hot summer day when temperatures could soar into the lower nineties by midmorning, the sixty-eight degree river invigorated the soul. As kids, Christina, Carrie and Carl often washed their hair while swimming. And a cool dip right before bedtime guaranteed a better night's sleep on sultry summer nights.

Looking back on it, Christina marveled how her upper class urban parents could purposely desert their lifestyle every summer for a crude cabin with no TV, no air conditioning, and especially no maids. That all came later, after her dad's law practice became prestigious and they hosted more weekends in the country for their social crowd. A cedar garage with the servant quarters were added at the back of the property, as was a separate guest house. In fact, the hot water heater hadn't been installed in the cabin until then, during her preteen years. That's when her parents had the bath modernized as well. Up until then, she and her sister refused to use the shower in the cabin. It had Daddy Long Legs bouncing in the rust stains that drooled towards the drain. It reminded them both of a scene from Alfred Hitchcock's *Psycho*. Besides, when you swam all day long in a crystal clean river, who needed a cold-water bath?

That thought curled her lips in a long overdue smile and led her mind to the first time her mother considered her old enough to carry the bowl of boiled water for her father's shave. She must have been six or seven. She remembered her mother telling her to be very careful. Her mother handed her the metal basin. Even through the pot holders, Christina could feel the heat. Sensing her mother's proud eyes following her, she tiptoed the sloshing bowl into the bathroom, determined to pass this milestone with flying colors. Mouse-like, she inched over the threshold and watched out of the corner of her eye as her father leaned into the metal medicine cabinet's mirrored door, chin cocked, face frothed and razor in hand. With tongue tip stuck out between taught lips, she set basin onto the toilet seat. When he reached down to take it, he winked at her with a twinkle in his Irish eyes. She knew she'd done a good job.

Christina, warmed by that memory, now racked her brain for others. Had they all been that pleasant? Surely not. Life wasn't like an episode of *The Waltons*. Still, over all of those summers, she couldn't recall any harsh words or hurt feelings penetrating the cedar walls. They must have been erased as easily as an edited paragraph in Microsoft Word. Highlight the thought, right click the mouse, choose cut and poof—blank it out.

Julie B Cosgrove

So, how do I blank out the hurt and anger I feel now? Her hand crunched the quilt. *I miss ya, Dad. You'd know what to say.*

Christina rolled onto her back and sank into the old springs of the cot. The indentation from years of use by various sized bodies left a cocoon effect. She snuggled into the recollection of simpler summer days.

Except on Sundays, only two modes of dress existed then: a bathing suit under shorts and P.J.'s. The locals had nicknamed the three siblings and their friends the River Rats. Together they combed the hills for imaginary treasures and conquered villains like the heroes in the comic books they were rewarded for good behavior during weekly trips into Riley's General Store.

Christina eyed the stack of yellowing Archie, Disney and Marvel comics in the wicker bin. They must have been good a lot. Or, her dad's soft heart caved into his kid's pleas. That seemed more likely. Oh, how they tried to manipulate him. Her sister, Carrie, was the openly devious and clever child. Carl, her older brother, acted more aloof. But Christina's innocent blue-eyed smile masked a quiet defiance. A typical Daddy's little girl. Yes, her dad had been wise. It was he that manipulated them without crushing their individuality. As a parent, she could see that now.

She grabbed the top comic and flipped through it. She wondered if they are worth anything now? Nah, probably not. Definitely not sellable on eBay. Christina sat up and tossed a Cinderella comic across the floor. Total garbage. Prince Charming. Love ever after. What a joke.

Focused

She rolled her eyes and plopped back on the cot in a huff. In her twenty-five years of marriage, she had never felt as empty as she did now.

From off in the distance came the mournful cooing of a dove—steady, monotonous, soothing. It called out for its mate.

Chapter 4   The Old Red Rocker

Christina stared at the red wicker rocker perched in the corner of the bedroom. Her eyes fell to the cobwebbed left front leg. A smile etched the sides of her mouth. She pointed out that leg to Jeff on his first tour of the cabin twenty-three years ago while they were courting—when she'd been gaga over him. She closed her eyes and let the memory seep into her mind.

"See that rocker? That's Dad's favorite chair. When we were kids, he used to sit there and read to us every night. One day I came up from the riverfront to get a Coke and found a Mexican rat snake wrapped around that front leg." Her outstretched finger twirled in its direction.

"You did?"

"Yeah. I was eight. Maybe I'd just turned nine. Boy, did I scream bloody murder."

"I bet." Jeff crouched on his boot heels and peered at the rocker leg, as if it might still be possible to see where the snake had slithered.

"Dad came running to my rescue. He hollered to my brother, 'Son, get the garden shears from the shed so I can whack off its head.'"

Jeff grinned at her attempt to imitate a man's voice. She felt her cheeks warm and swallowed hard. "Naturally, Carl came running. We always came when Dad called."

Jeff straightened up and turned to her. "He chopped it off right there in front of you? Your father?"

Christina nodded. "Carrie and I cowered behind the door watching as Dad unwound the headless snake from the rocker. I swear it seemed ten feet long. He took it out onto the rock porch. Laid some newspapers in the sunlight and set the pieces on them."

"Why?"

"An old wives' tale from the Revolutionary days says a headless snake wiggles until sundown, trying to rejoin its body to its head."

"That's right. That's why they carried that flag showing a chopped up snake representing the colonies. I remember that from 7th grade U.S. history."

"He wanted to prove it was false. That's my Dad. Never miss a chance for a nature lesson."

"I see."

She could tell by the tone of Jeff 's voice he really didn't. Christina sighed and sat in the rocker. She ran her fingers over the wooden arms, then cocked her head. "His passion has always been to teach us to observe what most people never notice."

Jeff shook his head. "Like?"

Focused

"Like where different birds choose to nest, or an abandoned skin of a katydid locust dangling under an oak leaf. Or how to spot a doe with her fawn camouflaged in the tall brush. Things like that."

"Valuable lessons."

A giggle bubbled in her throat. "That's not the end of the story. Everyone from nine months to ninety years in our family knows it backwards and forwards. The day the little sisters finally got even with big brother." She moved her hand as if reading it across an imaginary marquee.

Jeff smiled. "I'm all ears. Tell me." He leaned back against the door jamb to the bedroom.

Christina nodded and began to gently rock. "Later that day Carrie cornered me. She whispered in my ear, 'I bet Carl put that snake in the house. He knew one of us would come back up here to go potty or get a Coke.' She figured he wanted to look like a hero to the girlfriend he'd brought for the day."

Jeff's eyes glimmered. "Most of us do, ya know."

Christina gave him a sweet smile. "I wanted to tell Dad. She told me she had a better idea. She crept over like an Indian brave to the snake's body. It already had flies all over it. When she picked it up, they buzzed around her."

Jeff raised his left eyebrow and interrupted the story again. "Pretty gross. Carrie wasn't a bit squeamish?"

Christina shook her head, then continued with the tale. "Carrie was always the bold one. She took the dead snake and wrapped it around the tire to my brother's VW. The passenger side. She made sure the

25

headless part was tucked out of sight, so all he'd see was the rattles. I sat there watching, twisting my hair. A nervous habit I had that my mother always hated."

"You still do that you know, like when you are trying to solve the crossword puzzle in the newspaper. Sometimes, you do it in church when the rector's sermon is a bit too intellectual."

"I do?"

He nodded, "Which, I admit, it can be at times."

Christina knew she blushed. She saw a loving twinkle in her beau's eyes.

Jeff shifted his weight against the wall. "I interrupted you. Please, go on. What happened next?"

"Okay. Where was I? Oh, yes. When Carl opened the car door for his girlfriend, he screeched like a hoot owl, ruining the macho male image he tried so hard to achieve. Carrie and I watched through the bedroom curtains unable to stifle our laughter."

When she finished her story, Jeff was laughing as well. "So, tell me. Is it common for ya'll to bring the people you date up here?"

"It's one of the little tests the three of us learned to perform. If our current beau loves God and the Texas Hill Country they're worth dating in my dad's eyes. That's why Carl brought up his girlfriend."

Jeff grabbed her hand to help her from the old red rocker. "So, is that why I'm here?"

"Could be." Christina winked. "We better finish the tour before I see if mother needs help with dinner. Looks like her maid no-showed."

Much to her delight, she could see Jeff fell in love with her summer place from the moment he set

Focused

foot on the property. He was a true nature lover, just like her dad.

Christina looked at the old rocker, now laced in cobwebs, and wiped a tear from her cheek. The memories of the times her dad sat there, once so tender, now ached inside her. So did her memories of the day her dad met Jeff. She had been so much in love back then, so ready to fight for her man.

She thought she'd made the right choice. She was so sure. She'd even prayed about it.

Then, Christina heard a rustle outside the cabin bedroom. A skitter through oak leaves whiffed up the aroma of damp earth, as homey a sound and smell as sausage sizzling in breakfast skillets. Some furry little soul rummaged for a tasty morsel. She'd seen enough of them in her lifetime, and not just up here.

It was not uncommon for a city dweller to have a stray raccoon, opossum or rodent saunter to their back porch to sniff the dog food. How many times had she crouched quietly with her dad and siblings under the bonnet of the fig tree waiting for the pair of iridescent buttons in the dark to turn into a nose, whiskers and tiny paws creeping towards the bounty that beckoned in the plastic blue bowl? Countless times. It was one of her family's favorite form of entertainment on warm nights.

Just because hunting was a Texas tradition, it didn't mean hunters were heartless. Christina and Jeff's fathers often rescued orphaned or injured critters and taught their children how to care for them. Many healed enough to be released back into the wild. This shared respect and fondness for God's creatures great and small became a major ingredient that bonded Christina and Jeff as a couple, along with his unpretentious Texas charm and old fashion manners. He'd bow a hatless head for a funeral procession out of respect for the dead and the living and open doors for a lady. Like a fly to paper, she'd stuck like glue.

She remembered her dad and Jeff joking one summer about this place being their wives' dowry and the reason they'd married them. *Maybe that's why he and Dad always got along so well. Maybe that's really why I married Jeff.* Probably, she acknowledged. But the revelation didn't bring her any comfort.

Unfortunately their fathers never met, except in Heaven. Jeff's dad died in a hunting accident while Jeff was in Lebanon, two years before he and Christina met. Her dad passed away from a major coronary three weeks after Josh's graduation. That year, Christina mourned the loss of two of the three men in her life — her son to manhood and her dad to the grave. Now, she felt Jeff slipping out of her grasp as well.

Were they just holding on because of their vows, the binding words said before God and man over two decades prior? After all they were both Texans and a true Texan's word was still considered his bond. A strong, warm handshake and a square look in the eye sealed any deal. Had that bond begun to disintegrate after her Dad died? The adhesive of their marriage certificate seemed to be loosening. It oozed down, leaving a sticky trail of tears on the walls of her heart.

Christina sat down with the next thought. Only now did she realize that she and her mother both married men who preferred the great outdoors and deer blinds to opera houses and tea rooms, wooden rockers to Queen Anne wing-backed chairs perched on oriental carpets. So, in fact, had her grandmother. It was, after all, her grandfather who built this rustic cedar dwelling. Perhaps it was in the genes on her mother's side of the family to be attracted to less socially refined, outdoorsy men. Did it stem from the rugged, pioneer Texas spirit which once flowed under the rustle of her ancestors' petticoats? Could she really blame it on that? Hadn't God chosen Jeff for her and vice versa? It was what she always believed. So why did the choice feel so wrong now?

She didn't know the answers. She felt her dad might have known. But he wasn't sitting in the old red rocker for her to ask.

Chapter 5   Cover the Bases

Something in Jeff's mind pushed its way to the surface ahead of the facts and figures in front of him. It resembled his wife's voice, but he could not quite hear her words. Why had she stomped out of the room last night and locked herself in the bathroom today?

He wondered if his stepfather ever had times like this with his mother. Surely they did. He could call and ask him, but the first thing out of his stepfather's mouth would be the reminder that Jeff's choice of a wife had been someone way out of his league. No one in Jeff's family ever betted on it lasting this long.

The Missouri–Pacific tracks divided the city into class zones, making Jeff's boyhood house literally "on the other side of the tracks", yet no more than two miles from Christina's house in the more upscale zip code. Even though Jeff was five years older, he and Christina shared many of the same memories. But they never met as children. He went to inner city Catholic schools, she the posh Protestant parochial amidst an oak-lined avenue. Their worlds were the distance between Venus and Pluto.

Jeff threw down the pencil and rubbed his eyes. The numbers in front of him blurred and faded to black, pushed away by the underlying tension present over the past few months like a slow, gurgling lava of emotions that pushed through the foundations of his marriage into the cracks left by unsaid words and strained silence. Perhaps last night, the volcano had begun to erupt. There was a time they'd stay up to the wee hours jabbering about nothing at all, and everything. *Was it that long ago?*

Bob leaned against the doorjamb of Jeff's office and knocked. "You on a diet or something?"

"Huh. No. Why?" Jeff peered over his reading glasses, barely raising his head from the plans rolled out on top of his executive desk.

"Well, you didn't grab one of the bear claws Midge brought."

The desk chair creaked as Jeff adjusted his position. "Didn't you see the line waiting out there to get in here? I feel like getting one of those 'Take a Number' dispensers like they have at the DMV." He leaned forward and tapped his pencil back and forth on the legal pad trying to find a rhythm. It had evaded him all day.

Bob pushed off from the opening, uncrossed his leg and took a step in, his hands in his pockets. "Well, it's now half past lunch. Wanta get outa here?"

Jeff shuffled papers back into stacks, then logged off. "Yeah. Sure. Where are we eating?"

Bob knitted his brow and leaned his hands on the back of one of the customer chairs in front of the

Focused

desk. "It's Tuesday. Where we usually go on Tuesdays. You sure you're okay, man?"

Jeff's answer was a quick peer over his glasses before he grabbed his jacket and exited to tell Midge he was going to grab some grub.

The two walked around the corner to deli. The chalkboard announced: *Today's Lunch Special: Corned Beef on Rye* .

Grabbing his tray, Bob chose the banana pudding, and a table near the window. Jeff followed.

"Okay. You're way too quiet. Spill." Bob shuffled in his seat and leaned his arms on the table, making it wobble. The matchbook, jammed under one leg in an attempt to steady it, flipped into the aisle. Jeff kicked it back with his toe.

"It's... heck I don't know, Bob. Christina's been super moody."

Bob cupped his hand to the side of his mouth. "That time of the month?"

"Huh? No. Uh, uh. This has been building for two or three. More. She seems to be getting worse. It's like watching Mount Vesuvius rumble, wondering when it will explode." He stabbed his fork into the potato salad.

"She has been through a lot of stuff, Jeff. Lost both parents so close together. Josh growing up and off on his own ..."

"Yeah. And work's been a bear for her." Jeff rubbed his forehead a minute and then looked across the table. "I've been working almost every weekend. Hey, I guess I've been a bear, too. "

Bob raised an eyebrow then bit off a chunk of Rueben.

"Right." Jeff nodded. "Did I ever tell you how we met?"

"No. But something tells me you're going to." His friend winked. "Go ahead. Lay it on me."

"It was on the bus. I rode it downtown to work to save on gas. I'm sure she did because parking was slim to none. The first time she got on, I couldn't take my eyes off of her. She had on a tailored suit and high heels. She oozed pure class. So did the perfume she wore. I could smell it when she passed by my seat. Yet there was a humbleness about her, ya know? No high nose stuck in the air."

Jeff took a bite of sandwich and swallowed. Then, he continued. "When the bus jerked away from the curb, she wobbled backwards. She grabbed the bar above my head. I grabbed my breath. I instinctively reached for her waist to steady her."

Bob leaned in. He looked interested in the tale. "Did she slap ya?"

"No," Jeff laughed, "though I half expected her to. She mouthed a thank you. Then, she reached down to stick her left heel back into her opened-toed sandals. Her toenails were polished in a soft pink, matching her manicured fingernails. I saw that small gold cross she wears slip from her inside her lace blouse. It dangled right above her cleavage. I felt like a pool of primal goop, dripping off the seat."

Bob raised his eyebrows in rapid fire. "Uh, huh."

"For the rest of the week I watched for her bus stop. She'd get on and maneuver to the back, not once acknowledging me."

Focused

"Your gallant, but gentlemanly act ancient history, huh?"

Yeah, well, still, I couldn't forget her. I finally got up the gumption to sit at the back of the bus where she sat everyday reading her novel. After two weeks of casual talk, I considered asking her out on a date."

Bob laughed. "Not a fast mover were you?"

Jeff shrugged. "I needed time. Ease into it slowly. Win her trust. She didn't know me from Adam. Anyway, I'd saved enough to be sure I could take her to the movies, then afterwards to dinner at a candle-lit restaurant—you know, the kind with real table cloths, soft music, and appetizers which would cost as much as the movie tickets and snack bar?"

"Uh, huh. Funny what we'll do when the heart takes over. They sure know how to play us, don't they?"

Jeff agreed. "When I asked her, I know I sounded just like Porky Pig. I never dreamed she would actually accept. But she cocked her head, thought for a few seconds, then said, 'Okay. When?'"

"And you fell on the floor in shock, right?"

Jeff looked out the window, smudged from lack of cleaning. "You know, I recall the two of us walking to my car after the movie, though for the life of me I can't remember the movie's name or plot. Doesn't matter. It was a date flick anyway. The kind I now usually tune out as soon as Christina tunes into one on Cable."

"Oh, yeah. Mary watches those, too. When I let her." Bob winked.

Jeff's gaze returned to his friend. "Yeah, every once in a while we gotta let them have the remote, right?"

"Keep's the peace. Happy wife, happy life."

"Yeah. I wouldn't know, lately." Jeff looked back outside. A couple walked arm in arm. The guy looked smitten. "I do recollect something seemed to click between us on that first date. After the movie, we talked about childhood memories, astonished that we shared so many. I knew then I'd be asking her out again soon. And," Jeff raised his finger, "I'd have to ask the boss for a raise."

Bob laughed. "You always did aim high, my friend."

"I asked her if she remembered the time the train trestle caught on fire near the golf course. It was a big deal. Fire engines from all over came. We all ran to watch."

Bob nodded. "I remember that when I was a kid, too. It was on the news. All that black smoke looked like a tornado."

"The smell of that burning pitch. It was rancid for days. You know what she said? 'Mother had to get the curtains and rugs cleaned before her dinner party.' Boy, I felt the classes clash. Man, I thought. Maybe this was a mistake. Almost took her home instead of the restaurant."

"What made you change your mind?"

"I got in the car and clicked my seat belt. She clicked hers, touched my shoulder and said, 'Did your school ever go on the field trip to Rainbow Bakery?' That convinced me."

Bob looked vague. "Because . . .?"

36

Focused

"Because she was obviously trying hard to keep the conversation going. It was like saying, 'I want this date to go on.' Just mentioning it brought back the taste of hot bread with melted butter and jam they'd hand out to each class at the end of the tour. She gave that giggle girls always do when they flirt and said, 'I'm getting hungry now.'"

"So you took her to the restaurant and the rest is history, huh?"

Jeff, lost in thought, didn't pick up on his friend's hint. He continued, "I parked the car in the last stall in front of the restaurant. Luckily not in a puddle, or I would've seriously considered pulling a Sir Walter Raleigh gesture with my jacket. Then, I noticed the valet swaying back and forth in his epaulets. She pretended not to notice I didn't know he was supposed to park the car. Pure class."

Jeff stopped, took a bite of his lunch. Mouth half full, he went on, "I got out and rounded the fender to get her door. A bit of lace slipped from under her hem as she twirled her legs to the pavement. Just like a ballerina. When I offered her my hand, her grasp felt soft and warm as dove's breast."

Bob's eyes glazed over. Jeff chomped some more. Then he laughed. "Here's the funny part."

Bob sat back, arms folded. "Okay. Go on. What happened?" He swished his spoon around the banana pudding bowl, then not catching it all, scraped his fingers along the sides and licked them.

"The waiter pulled out her chair before I could. He waited politely for her to settle, then he comes and pulls out mine, too. Can you believe that? Then, the guy placed a napkin in my lap. I flinched. She looked at the menu and again . . ."

Bob finished the sentence, ". . .pretended not to notice."

"She chose a lesser priced dish, but not the cheapest one listed, knowing that might offend me."

"The girl had style, all right. You married a good one."

"Yeah." Jeff eyed Bob. "What do ya think? Flowers?"

"Can't hurt. Cover the bases, man." Bob set the bowl back on the tray.

Jeff pulled out his cell phone. "Know a good florist?"

Bob jerked his head. "How long's it's been since you bought her flowers, dude?"

Jeff shrugged.

"Try West Avenue Florists. They do a good job."

Jeff Googled it on his smartphone, found the number and ordered a dozen peppermint carnations. A voice said she'd check to see if they had any in stock. He cupped his hand over the mouthpiece. "Used to be her favorite. Guess they still are. I'll pick them up tonight on the way home."

Bo gave him the thumbs up sign.

Then Jeff heard the voice confirming they did have them. He gave his credit card info. "You're open 'til six, right?" He clicked his phone off. "Think I'll just walk in the house with them, and maybe with dinner under my arm, too."

Bob winked. "Might do the trick."

Chapter 6   Feathered Nests

Christina felt a cold stone settle in the pit of her stomach. When she said those vows all those years ago, she thought she'd never feel alone again. But now, that was exactly how she'd been feeling. Her thoughts echoed back to her in hollowness.

Rising from of her stroll down memory lane, she felt thirsty. She wondered if there might be a cold Coke in the fridge, leftover from past summers. Grasping the handle, she didn't feel a vibration. *Of course. The electricity's turned off. Duh.*

Now she hoped no one had left anything behind. She sure didn't want to open the door, just in case something green and growing lurked inside. The thought made her shiver in disgust. But, having nothing to whet her whistle only enhanced her thirst. Why hadn't she stopped off on the way and gotten something to drink?

She wondered who might be home. Neighbors in the Hill Country always kept the back door unlatched, the coffee pot on and cold Coca Cola in their icebox, as refrigerators were still dubbed, even though it had been sixty years since the last one appeared in the Sears catalogue. She recalled seeing one on the Owens's back porch as a child. Rusted around the edges, it had a round cage on top, as if a flying saucer had landed on it. It even whirred the way a five year old could imagine UFO's sounded. When she stood on her tiptoes she could barely touch it. She stopped trying when Bud Owens told her the little aliens would get her and bite her finger.

In her grandfather's era, everyone went to the neighborhood Lone Star Ice House daily to buy the blocks of ice needed to keep their iceboxes cold. The stores also sold reasonably priced things to go in them such as milk, Cokes, eggs and cheese. People still talked about "running down to the icehouse" for something even though most of the places didn't survive the national chain convenient store invasion. But the old terms stuck. Things were slow to change in this part of the country, and for Christina, that wasn't necessarily a bad thing. It was a comforting stability in a too fast-paced spinning world fueled by cyberspace and stress.

Christina hopped onto the kitchen counter, dangled her legs, and stared at the green speckled linoleum floor, laid when she was a toddler. The Owens were the closest neighbors, just down the road over the creek. They might be home, but she hadn't seen them in years. She hadn't been in their house since the Bud incident. Ancient history. But even if it had been a month of Sundays and then some, they were the type of folk to be excited to see you and ask you to sit a spell at the kitchen table so they could catch up on all your news. Texas hospitality ruled, no matter how deeply you had gouged their son's ego back in high school.

She wished, over the years, her own backdoor had been more hospitable for her neighbors in Allensville. But Jeff liked his house to be his sanctuary. Always had.

"I need peace and quiet when I get home, not a bunch of people chattering." His voice echoed in her mind.

She slid off the counter and walked over to the dining table, made by a local craftsman long ago. Folk in the Hill Country lived hard, laughed heartily and acknowledged God as the center of their lives. No Bible thumping, just a quiet resolve that showed in their eyes and their lives whether it was Sunday in the pew or Saturday night at the Steppin' Out Dance Hall. In this part of the world, where you can experience tornadoes, drought, floods and fire ants on a yearly basis, you had better rely on God. You definitely couldn't rely on Mother Nature.

Sitting down with one leg tucked under her, she traced the notches in the wood of the cedar table, shined with half a century of accumulated polish. Maybe instead of relying on God, she had relied on Jeff too much over the years. Just as she had relied on her father. The first man in her life was dead. Could she even contemplate life without the second? Then her nest would really be empty.

Guilt over being slothful and self-indulgent crept into her soul. Why was she on this stupid nostalgia trek? What good did it do? So, Jeff was not the same man. Maybe she was not the same woman. Big deal. People change.

Life had grinded them into another shape—steadily, slowly, day after day, as a stream molds a pebble. She glanced at the small pudginess where her hourglass waist once was. *Another shape is right. Neither of us would fit in our skinny high school jeans now.*

She allowed another thought to surface. Feathered nests after a while no longer fit, like twenty-five year old jeans. They need to stretch. She wondered from where that tidbit of wisdom originated. Was it from a book she'd read, or perhaps an original thought? God inspired? Hardly.

Christina rose with a sigh and tiptoed through the closed cabin as if to not awaken its hibernation. Sunlight outlined the long canvas awnings rolled down and fastened to the sills. They were designed to keep the weather out of the screened-in porch. She unlatched one of the canvas awnings and pulled the ropes, rolling it to the top. A welcomed breeze floated up from the cliff, cooled by the river below. It drifted over her face. When the wind picked up, the other awnings billowed slightly and then flattened with a "slap". Back and forth, in and out. The porch inhaled and exhaled the generations surrounding her.

Christina looked at the old ceiling fan and noticed a delicate cobweb dangling between two of its blades, a sure sign of an abandoned and shuttered summer cabin. She resisted the urge to jump up and find the broom. No, the cabin didn't need to be pristine and perfect anymore. Her mother wasn't around anymore to inspect it, or her daughter's life.

Focused

Why had her mother been so overly critical? And why had Christina spent so many years jumping through hoops to try and win the approval she could never get? Even now, the hurt stuck in her craw. So what if I can't call my husband perfect? Or our son. Whose were? Dad had his faults too, didn't he? Nothing in life is perfect.

She shrugged and sat down on the chair positioned to view the river. At least the ceiling fan was off. Lately she had developed an aversion to them. She hated how the path of the blades reflected right between her bifocal lines: dark, light, dark, light flashes that threw her focus a little off balance. She yanked them off her nose and peered at the smudged lens.

She fogged them with a blast of her breath, then rubbed the smudges away with her blouse. "I am always adjusting these darn glasses," she addressed the arachnid delicately suspended between the blades, the only other occupant as far as she knew. Upon hearing her growl, she noticed the spider skitter into the shadows for security.

Glasses were first stuck on her nose in third grade. Along with her good grades, the specs had earned her the label of "nerd". But she never had so much trouble with a pair until these. The half moons were too large, cutting right in the middle of her irises. She constantly repositioned them on her nose, trying to find the right focus. At work she found it troublesome to see the computer monitor, nodding her head up and down like a Bobble-head doll on the dashboard of a car.

Once again the familiar anger began to emerge—one which raised its internal head a lot lately though she never considered herself to be a fretful or short-fused person. Still, at times she screamed like a banshee inside, just like that painting she saw when they went to the Museum of Modern Art in New York when she was thirteen. The distorted girl, mouth open, swirls of life and discontent streaming behind her while she remained caught in suspended animation. Christina could relate.

"Am I kicking myself because the darn things cost almost four-hundred dollars? I accepted them knowing full well they weren't made quite right," she addressed the spider. "Spine of a jellyfish. Why didn't I speak up that day?"

Like the mirror, it didn't answer.

That day, she'd peered back through the new glasses at the sales clerk on the other side of the optical desk, hesitant to say anything.

She could hear her mother spouting off one of her platitudes, "Don't make waves and chance upsetting the clerk. She might end up not liking you and then what type of Christian witness would you be? Besides, it might get around town that you were rude. We have our reputation to consider."

So, at the time, Christina convinced herself it would just take awhile to adjust to bifocals. She signed the credit card receipt, then dashed out of the building.

Why had she put up with the wretched things and resigned herself into believing it was her lot in life not to see well? Penitence for making a poor choice and spending way too much money? Some morsel of inherited parental wisdom surfaced. Something about being thankful for what you had and the starving children in China?

44

Focused

She shook her head again, but the mental Magic Eight Ball still gave no poignant response.

Jeff's remarks surfaced instead. "Buy a vowel. Get a refund. Your choice. Ah, the Bears won. Glass of water."

Christina sighed, then peered out over the tops of the cedar trees. Down below the cliff, she could see the emerald green river. Wavelets sparkled like tiny water sprites in a glass-surfaced ballet.

In her mind's ear, memories of laughter, the splashing of water and the "thunk-thunk" of the old diving board bolted to a tree stump resounded up the cliff from the riverfront—summer sounds as natural as the squirrel's chatter or the sharp cheeps of the purple finches darting in and out of the trees.

Lazy river. Not a care in the world. It just kept softly drifting by.

Chapter 7   Glasses in an Hour

Christina needed fresh air to clear her throbbing head. She turned and grabbed the handle to the time-warped cedar door, yanking it loose from a deserted mud-dauber cone. As quiet as possible, she opened the screen door enough to slide through without making the rusty spring vibrate with several declining pitches of *boing, boing, boing.*

Outside, she asked herself why she did that. No one else was around to hear it. Habit. Pure habit. In her teen years, Christina often snuck out of the cabin to bask in the subdued world of darkness during the wee hours of the morning. Late at night there was an undisturbed and peaceful freshness. No intrusive human noises like during the day. No laughter, blaring radios, or car sounds from the highway a mile away. The only sounds were crickets, frogs, and sometimes a rustle through the leaves of an armadillo rooting for grub worms.

She recalled the time a doe walked by her, unaware of her presence because the breeze carried her human scent in the other direction. The doe carefully stepped along the rock path in front of her. Christina sat still. She barely breathed. She could almost reach out and pet it. It made her feel so close to God, as if He walked alongside the deer, smiling at her.

Now, she sat on the same rock stoop in her stocking feet. She wiggled her toes. A few peeked through the runs caused by the cedar floor. The rock, shaded from the sun's path by the tall trees that surrounded the cabin, felt cool.

She whimpered like a child in search of her favorite stuffed animal."Where is that closeness now, God?"

Was God pushing her in a new direction? Perhaps she just felt tired of the way she was living her life. Maybe she wanted to make it into a God-thing. Had she veered off the path or had she tromped down it so long her horizons became as out of focus as her bifocals?

Perhaps I should just go home and stop thinking. Christina stood, brushed the leaves from her bottom and stretched. Did she hear thunder? Surely it wasn't a heavenly answer. One glance confirmed dark clouds building over the treetops to the west.

Time to go. She slapped her hands to her thighs and blocked the tears. Christina locked the screen and bolted the door. She walked through the cabin, then turned to scan the main living area. It held so many years of memories. She shrugged, slipped on her heels and stepped onto the front patio to jerk the front door closed. She wiggled the old key in the lock until she heard the familiar click, closed the screen door and bent over to put the key back in its hiding place under the rock covering the water shut-off valve. Then she stopped dead in her tracks.

"My purse," she hissed.

As she chided herself for the jog down memory lane which left her so absent minded, she again retrieved the key, again wiggled it in the lock, again opened the cabin's front door and snatched her purse from the table. With an under-her-breath curse, Christina stomped back out and slammed the door shut. The cabin shook with her temper.

The sound vibrated over the silent hills. How often in her youth had her mother yelled for them not to slam that door as they dashed out? Suddenly a rush of cold heat spread throughout her body. The weight she had been carrying on her shoulders slid down her back and shattered onto the stone patio beneath her feet. She clumped to the ground and heaved sob after sob.

The mourning dove cooed in the distance, still in search of its mate.

Chapter 8 - The Decision

After the bawling stopped and the stomach pangs subsided, Christina dug in her purse for a crumpled piece of Kleenex. She blew her nose and dabbed her eyes with the corners of the tissue before she straightened to brush the dirt and leaves from her bottom—again.

She hated to cry. It felt so self-indulgent. Yet she was usually sympathetic and ready to comfort anyone else who cried with a hug and a box of tissues. Why was that?

With a cleansing sigh, Christina waved the question away. *Not now. Not another soul-searching trek.* Instead she chose the more tangible path off the property and back to her life.

Her tires popped down the gravel road. It signaled someone coming or leaving the property better than a watchdog. The sound alerted a grazing cottontail which bolted into the heavy brush for camouflage. She inched her car over the cattle guard then accelerated onto the road that led back to civilization and reality. Her tires spewed the last bits of gravel in farewell.

Twenty miles later, she reached the intersection to the highway. She squinted to see if any cars were coming...What? *I'm squinting?*

"Darn!" Christina slammed the heel of her hand on the steering wheel. "I left my glasses back at the cabin on that cot!"

She pulled over to the side of the road. *I have two choices. I can either turn back around and go back to the cabin and all those memories again.* That thought made her eyes sting. She blinked back the tears.

Or, I can do what I've put off doing for three years—get new glasses.

Something inside of her warned her not to head to the cabin. She didn't know why, but the feeling was strong, even for women's intuition. So, for the second time in a day, the normally routine-laden woman made a spontaneous, off-the-cuff decision.

She recalled one of those "get your glasses in one hour" places at the new mall. Several summers back when she dashed into JC Penney for new beach towels, she saw it a sign for its grand opening celebration.

Okay, that's what I'll do. Proud to have a plan, Christina already felt more in control. She'd paid off the VISA credit card last month. That firmed her decision.

She chose to ignore her and Jeff's steadfast rule to never spend over one hundred dollars on anything other than medical care or groceries without discussing it together first. It guarded them from whimsical buying sprees which might enlarge the credit card balance beyond their monthly budget.

"Until he went and bought that humongous new power saw," she spouted through clenched teeth as she noticed more traffic in the side view mirror. "Well, if he can spend three hundred dollars on that, I can spend four hundred on proper glasses so I can see what he's made with the stupid thing. Besides, this is medical care . . . sort of."

She was talking to the air again. That disturbed her. She turned on the radio.

The deejay said, "It's 1:04 and already eighty-six degrees... up next on the hit parade . . ."

No wonder her stomach rumbled. She switched on the blinker and headed for the blue exit sign. On it were two symbols of gas stations and one of a drive-through restaurant which beckoned to the tired and hungry highway masses. Two cars ahead of her had the same idea. The place was packed. She drove around the back, past fly-swarmed dumpsters which spewed the aroma of several days' worth of business. Her tires hit three pot holes before she spotted an open stall. She pulled in and parked near a door that had a silhouette of her gender. Her bladder overruled her stomach. First things, first. Hopefully, they keep their facilities cleaner than the dumpster area.

The car door wedged against the menu board with a thunk. She scraped her back on the door frame when she inched out of her car seat and slid through the narrow opening. The mega-ton, extend-a-cab truck on the other side of the menu board blocked her path. She had to walk around the back of her car, then two more cars before she found space enough to inch to the sidewalk, then back track to the Ladies. She felt every eye on her watching as she slipped into the door.

Upon return, Christina noticed the mega truck was gone, thank goodness. She slid back in, then leaned forward to squint at the choices. Pride and a throbbing back forbade her to get out again to stand inches away and stare at the darn thing in order to read it. She doubted if she'd fit between the menu board and her closed car door anyway. Maybe twenty years ago.

She told the voice at the other end of the speaker, "Can I please have a grilled cheese, tater tots and small limeade, please." Did she really just say the word please twice? *May as well tattoo "Woman always trying to be sweet and polite" on my forehead.*

"Do you want to double size it for only a dollar more?" The youthful pitch came through the speaker amidst the din of voices and clattering kitchen noise.

"No thanks. Not today." Her tone reflected a forced smile.

"How about our cherry vanilla shake? It's on special this week."

With a limeade? Yuk. "Uh. No...thanks." She replied, glad the voice couldn't see her shudder in disgust.

"That'll be five dollars and ninety-six cents. We'll have it out in a minute."

We? How many of you does it take to carry my order out on a tray?

Christina chided herself for her short temper and sarcastic thoughts. The girl was just doing her job. The order taker, after all, wasn't the one playing hooky.

Focused

As she waited for the chipper carhop to deliver her food, she brushed her hair and applied a splash of cologne. With spittle fingers, she wiped away the smudge of mascara under her eyes, a residual sign of her tearful outburst.

She looked at a pimpled smile holding a tray. The aroma of the tater tots floated through the car window.

"Here you are. That's five ninety-six, please." The carhop lilted as she clipped the tray onto the car window. She smacked gum through her required employee smile.

Christina returned the same fake smile and tipped the teen a dollar. In return, the gum smacker handed back four cents in change and one of the peppermints the drive-through always gave out with their meals. Then, she thanked her customer and skated away to deliver the next order.

A thundering "boom-tat-ta-boom" resonated from the radio as a car pulled in next to Christina's subcompact. Out of the corner of her eye she saw the occupant's head bobbing back and forth to a beat he assumed everyone else desired to hear as much as he did. At first it irritated her. Then, she noticed the gum smacker skate to the driver's window. She had a huge grin and love-struck eyes.

"Am I getting old, or what?" As the middle aged, half-blind woman chomped on her sandwich, she recollected hearing her mother knock on the door to her teenage flower-power poster-filled room. She could see herself sprawled on the bed bopping her head to the beat. She heard her mother tell her to turn it down now. Not everyone in the neighborhood wanted to hear what a whole lot of love Led Zeplin, or whoever that is, insisted on yelling. If she didn't she'd be grounded. That meant she wouldn't be allowed to go to Sarah's swim party at the Club where that dashing Eddie Powell would be.

The now-turning fifty Christina mused. Eddie Powell. He was the one who jumped at anything in a skirt and whose parents later bribed the District Attorney not to file statutory rape charges. If memory served, he was the D.A. now and in a middle of a scuttle bug about having an affair. *I don't think you'd find him so dashing today, Mom.*

Christina crumpled the wrapper and stuffed it in the tater tot pouch. She signaled to the carhop, who roller-skated over.

"Have a nice day." The girl twirled on one skate, unclipped her tray and sashayed away.

Yeah. Sure.

The mall was one more exit down which meant she could stay on the access road and pray she didn't run into a cop along the way, literally. Christina chuckled under her breath. She couldn't help it. Punning came naturally to her. Her dad had been known for his witticism and puns. It became a game around the dinner table of who could say the most before they all fell over groaning and her mother raised her hands in surrender.

She checked for bits of food in her teeth via the little mirror on her visor and plopped the mint in her mouth. The voice of her mother echoed in her brain."No sense having lunch breath when some poor eyeglass clerk has to be up close and personal to fit your new frames."

Focused

Yes, mother.

Christina pulled out onto the access road and, a half mile down, turned into the entrance to the Bluebonnet Mall. It started to sprinkle. She was lucky enough to find a parking space near the door to the eyeglasses factory, with its own outside entrance, thank goodness. Entering the store, a blast of cool air hit her in the face. She looked around a room filled on both sides with glass shelves offering hundreds of styles and shapes of frames. There were only two other customers present.

"Mom. Those are dorky." A teenager slumped and twitched her foot back and forth under the optical desk.

"Well, there are several more here you can try. The pink ones bring out the color in your cheeks." The mother held up a pair.

"Everyone at school will laugh." She rolled her eyes, and looked away.

Christina tried not to stare. The girl reminded herself of her own reactions to her mom at that age. The same timeless scowl blared across her face. Maybe all teenage girls acted that disrespectfully to their mothers. Christina thanked God she bore a son.

"You need to see the blackboard, dear." The mother's voice strained.

"Can't I get contacts?"

The whine fell on deaf ears. "When you get a job and earn the money, then we'll talk."

Christina strolled over to the women's frames until the clerk, who had the patience of Job, finished helping them with their selection. Once the mother and daughter moved to the checkout counter,

Christina whispered, "Those look really cool on you. Good choice."

The girl beamed. Christina smiled back, then looked at the mother who mouthed "Thanks".

Ringing up the sale, the clerk winked at Christina and told her, "I'll be with you in a second."

No problem. Take a breather. I'll wait.

Christina's nod of understanding conveyed her message. Feminine telepathy.

Just then, another clerk appeared from the back room and walked over, hands clasped in front. "Now, what can I do for you?" She had a trace of mayonnaise on her upper lip.

"I lost my glasses." Well sort of. But you do not want to hear the whole story, right? "But I kept the prescription." Christina rummaged through the sections of her wallet. "Ah, I knew I had it. Here." She held out the crumpled piece of paper with faded ink.

"It's over three years old." The clerk peered at her through half-rimmed glasses perched on the ridge of her nose. She reminded Christina of her junior high principal.

"I know. But I need them to drive home. Please." She was immediately sorry she'd said that. *Please don't call the cops, okay?*

"I'm afraid you'll need an exam." The clerk replied. "But our doctor is free right now."

Free as in available or he won't charge me? Christina nodded and followed the clerk.

Thirty minutes and one hundred eighty-five dollars later - obviously he had not been that kind of free - she handed the clerk her new script.

Focused

"Great. Now what type of lens did you have? We have several materials and tint shades."

"My old ones were glass and they were supposed to transition into sunglasses. But I often found they never turned back to clear very quickly." *And I felt everyone thought I was on drugs or concealing a black eye.*

"Why don't you consider our newest tint? It reduces the glare from computer screens as well as that halo affect from lights at night. Blue eyes are always more sensitive to that. And they come in plastic, so they are light weight."

"Really. I didn't know that. How much?" *Maybe this is a serendipity after all.*

"And we can coat them while you wait. Only thirty-four ninety-nine a lens." The eager clerk grinned.

So, you mean it's really seventy bucks. Clever ploy. Christina nodded. "OK. Thanks. Let's do that."

"Good. What did you have in mind for frames? We have some nice ones on sale starting at under two hundred dollars…"

The cash register cha-chinged in Christina's brain.

At 2:05 p.m., a smug Christina dodged raindrops back to her car wearing her new invisible lined bifocals with glare resistant tint. She compensated by picking out frames on clearance, which were so similar to her old frames Christina doubted anyone else would notice. Pleased with her frugality, she slid into the front seat and clicked her seat belt. No more adjusting the things on her nose. She could see straight ahead, up, down and off to the sides. And everything seemed so crisp and clear, even in the rain. Why didn't I do this years ago?

An earsplitting clap of thunder vibrated across the mall parking lot and bumped into the hills. She jolted and dropped her keys onto the floor mat. A second clap drowned out her curse as she unclicked her belt to reach underneath her legs to see where they fell. Then, as if God had turned on the tap full blast, the deluge burst open.

Chapter 9   Faded stitches

A strange chill hit the back of Jeff's neck as if someone was breathing mouthwash down his collar. It made him twitch, then turn to look behind him.

All he saw was the credenza. Books, soccer coach trophy, the framed picture of a buck peering through the brush that his wife had stitched in crewel work while she was recovering from a broken leg. How long ago had that been? Josh was in elementary school then. When it happened, Jeff made a deal with a coworker to cover for him so he could leave early and get his son from day care on the days Christina couldn't find a church friend to pick him up. It took a good two months of rehab before the doctor agreed to let her drive again. The whole time Jeff had dreaded it, afraid his boss would need something at the end of the day and he'd be gone. It never occurred to him to ask. That would have been a sign of weakness. Bosses don't need to know about your personal life. What made me think of that now, for Pete's sake? He rubbed the back of his neck, then jerked it to the side and let the pop resound in his ear. The achy tension temporarily oozed away.

Years of afternoon sunlight through the office window faded the colors of the stitchery. It reminded him of his wife. In the past few months her colors had been slowly fading, as if some force sucked out her life's energy with a straw. A cloud loomed over their lives, turning everything dull and washed-out in a grayish glare, like the world on an overcast day. Was it all her doing?

Okay. He admitted to himself the promotion to manager a year ago had taken its toll. What at first seemed an honor for years of a job well done, weighed him down with too much responsibility. Weekends shackled to this desk. Pressures she just could not understand made his neck hurt and his temper short. How could he talk to her about it? She'd parrot back some Scripture as if she could erase his stress off the chalkboard of life and replace it with parables neatly written over it in the chalk dust.

A memory of how he had raised his hand in third grade and volunteered to come to the front to solve a math problem flashed in his mind. He felt so proud. He and his Dad worked for hours on decimals before he understood them. Mrs. Whitaker in her tight proper bun simply grunted a half approval and quickly erased it—along with his ego. After that, the teachers marked him as a quiet but smart child who rarely participated in class. His mother figured it was a phase.

Why can't women understand the pressures we have? Jeff tapped his pencil on the legal pad in front of him, again. At times sitting at this desk was better than sitting in his recliner and feeling the coldness that hung

Focused

just above his head at home. At least here he had
control, well somewhat. Figures, measurements. Those
he could understand, sort out, calculate and determine
the end result. Not like his wife's emotions as of late.
What he dealt with at work added up. It was tangible.
Logical. Well, except for these drawings in front of him
by some idiotic architect. So obviously straight out of
grad school, trying to impress everyone with his
rendition of the new high school addition. His figures
were not making sense. No way would that roof be in
spec. But, Jeff's job was to clean it up so the company
could build it. And to think this kid, the creator of this
mess, little mister junior-junior in the architect firm
whose seal was on the lower right hand corner,
probably made twice what he did.

    He thought of his lunch conversation with Bob
about how he and Christina met. They dated three
more times that week, talked for hours on the phone in
between, then went out again the next weekend, twice.
Six weeks later they ventured to the cabin to meet her
parents—the day he received her father's blessing.
Driven by pure, blinded love and determination, he
endured the long parental cross-examination, sweating
bullets until he saw the twinkle of approval in her dad's
eyes.

    Jeff leaned back in his office chair. His desktop
screen saver depicted stars streaming towards him. He
had always been a Sci-Fi freak. It began when he'd set
the alarm for 3 a.m. so he could get up with his dad to
watch the space capsules zip by. They'd wave
frantically as if the astronauts could see them. He
remembered Christina told him once she used to do

that with her dad, too. Another memory they shared, like so many.

On her dresser in their bedroom was a faded photo of her as a little girl dancing with her dad. Cute, button-nosed, blonde, blue-eyed angel. He could picture her in her baby-doll pajamas, holding on to her dad's hand, staring into the heavens waiting for that tiny man-made light to move across the sky. Even at four years old she would've stolen his heart. He was glad he and Christina never had a girl. If she'd had been anything like her mother, he would've locked her away in a nunnery by the age of twelve. How did her dad do it?

Jeff looked at the clock on his computer's tool bar. It said 3:30. Popping his neck one last time, Jeff hunkered down and willed his thoughts to return to his scrawled figures on the yellow legal pad angled in front of him. He shook away the past and concentrated on the present . . . and their future. If he wanted to keep a roof over her head he had better get back to this proposal. If he could work undisturbed for just a few hours, maybe he could finish it by Friday and not work this weekend. Maybe he could take her back to that restaurant in San Antonio, if it still existed. Saturday night, he'd say he wanted to go into the city for a bite, just for a change of pace. Let her get in the car, turn towards the highway, then surprise her when they kept on driving through Austin. It'd take close to two hours to get there from Allensville. Maybe they'd talk about old times on the way. *Yeah, maybe.*

One of the younger staff tapped on his door, arms full of plans. He had a lost expression on his face.

Focused

Uh, oh. Then again, maybe not. Looks like this is going to take awhile. Jeff motioned with his left hand, "Come on in, Tim. Whatcha need?"

* * *

Josh, who had his mother Christina's blond hair and his dad's blue eyes, scanned the parts manual for HP laser printers. The customer on the phone wasn't making the drive all the way out there unless he was sure they had the drum he needed for his 2005 model. *Smart man. Let your fingers do the walking, bro.* "Yes, sir. I am still looking it up. Thanks for your patience," he said into the receiver lodged in his shoulder blade.

"Hey, don't you have family that lives near Kerrville?" Mandy leaned over the counter and swayed her shoulders back and forth to an invisible beat, definitely not the one playing on the store's Muzak speaker.

Josh cupped his hand over the receiver. "Yeah. Sort of. A cabin. Used to be my grandparent's." He held up a finger for her to hold that thought. "No sir, I don't see it in stock right now. We can place it on rush order and it will be here in forty-eight hours. Is that okay?" He rolled his eyes. Mandy giggled and kept swinging her foot.

After a minute or two, Josh convinced the customer and forwarded the call to the ordering department to process the credit card purchase. He turned to Mandy, now drawing on the glass case with her finger. It was a very slow night. "Why?"

"Huh?" Nobody home behind her big brown eyes.

"Why did you ask about . . .?"

"Oh, yeah." Lights on. Recognition. " 'Cause its flooding real bad. It's on the TVs." She stopped swinging her foot long enough to pivot her shoulder towards the other side of the store. Various size rectangles flashed images of light and color. Six showed the basketball game. Three more, a commercial with a squirrel, but four showed a weather man pointing to a red and purple blob on the radar.

Josh closed the three-ring binder. He walked across the sea foam colored linoleum to the buckskin indoor-outdoor carpeted area that designated the Entertainment section. Legs spread in an at-ease position and arms crossed over his waist, he listened as the weatherman explained the colored blotches overlaid on the area map. Little white jagged-lined graphics depicting thousands of lightning strikes overlaid on it. He felt his manager's garlic-bread-for-lunch breath on his shoulder.

"Switching departments on us, Willis?"

"No sir. It's just that I have family..." He pointed at the screen that was now flashing "FLOOD WARNING".

"He does," Mandy chimed in, as if that added weight to the excuse for leaving one's designated work area without permission.

The weatherman's brows knitted and his hands swirled around the purple blotch spreading east, absorbing the map like Kool-Aid spilled on the carpet. More warnings flashed in a marquee scrolled at the

Focused

bottom of the frame. "Residents are advised to move to higher ground immediately," he urged.

Something grabbed Josh's mind with urgency. Why he didn't know. No one had been up there in years. Still . . .

"Just a quick call, Sir. May I.?" Josh turned to garlic-toast mouth. "I'll take my break while there's no customers on the floor."

"Do it. Five minutes."

Josh walked back to the break room, flipped open his cell and punched "M". No answer. He tried again. No luck. He exhaled into his employee polo shirt and pressed "D" for Dad.

"Jeff Willis."

"Dad. Have you heard about the floods in Kerr?"

He heard his dad's office chair creak. "No. Heard a flash flood watch a while back. Had to turn the radio off. Big bid due. . ."

"Dad." He raised his voice, then stopped. Not respectful. "Sorry. Didn't mean that. Work's got me on edge. I've got a splitting headache."

"Contagious. Had one all day."

Josh heard the aggravation in his father's voice. At least the lecture about respecting your elders seemed diverted.

"Heard from Mom? I've tried her cell twice now."

There was silence. The chair creaked again. A throat cleared. "No."

Josh didn't like the tone behind that answer. "You Okay? Is Mom Okay?"

Julie B Cosgrove

The sigh at the other end disturbed him. He gripped the cell phone tighter and swallowed. Something was not right. His psyche told him that, even if his brain didn't. "Dad, what's going on?"

The chair creaked again. He heard a pencil tapping. "We are both just swamped with stuff now. You know her. She's busy. It's nearing tax time and someone is sick or something. It's probably buried somewhere deep in her purse."

"Yeah. That's what I figured. Still, I . . ."

The chair squeaked, louder. "Son, gotta git. If I hear anything, I'll give ya a holler. But no one's up there, ya know."

Click.

Josh stared at the glow on his cell phone. He tapped it off then shoved it into the back pocket of his regulation khaki Dockers.

Parents.

Chapter 10 The Crossing

Jeff stared at the proposal. If he finished it tonight, all he had to do was enter it into the bid program in the morning, and pray the thing didn't reject his findings.

His eye caught the framed photo on his desk of him, Christina and a teenage Josh sitting on the diving board. Behind them, her parents posed for the camera. The Guadalupe River glistened in the background.

It had been ages since they 'd been to the cabin. He figured the memories were too raw for his wife. Maybe for Carrie and Carl as well. None of them had been there in a while. Their mom passed away a year ago this June, their dad eighteen months prior to that, both sudden and unexpected. No Richter scale could have forecast the earth shattering effects, or the aftershocks on their lives.

Her mother drove in from the cabin to see her doctor the day she suffered the fatal stroke. Christina called to apologize, saying they couldn't make the visit over the weekend, again. Jeff never heard the excuse, but suspected the raw-edged memories of her dad served as culprit. Her mother said it was just as well because she'd been feeling a little flu-ish off and on for a few days. Christina phoned back twice that weekend and finally convinced her to call the doctor first thing Monday morning. She did. That afternoon, the doctor's office notified Christina they were admitting her mother to the hospital. Twelve hours later she was gone and the love-hate relationship screeched to a halt.

In a last ditch effort to gain approval, his wife took on the chore of planning every detail of the funeral, from the hymns that wouldn't offend anyone to the catered food from her mother's favorite bistro. She wanted her mother, even though in Heaven, to finally be proud of her. Perhaps it worked. At last, her mother's friends admired her stoic daughter.

But when the casket closed, so did his wife's desire to head for the Hills. He missed it almost as much as he suspected she did. At least the cabin was sealed tight. Nobody's been there lately. Besides, it's on a bluff anyway. The place, once his wife's lifeline for rest and relaxation, now lay abandoned in the pouring rain. What a shame.

* * *

Even with the wipers on full blast, Christina could barely see the red taillights of the truck in front of her. As the rain cascaded down her car windows in filmy sheets, enveloping her in an opaque shower curtain. Flashes of lightening did little to illuminate the

Focused

highway. Claps of thunder shook her car. She lost the satellite radio signal.

A sudden bolt jolted her memory. *Oh, no! I forgot to let down the awning on the porch. The place will get soaked and everyone is gonna know where I've been.*

Christina grimaced. How stupidly absentminded. She could feel the heat rise in her cheeks as she gave herself a mental tongue thrashing. That's where the entire psychobabble trek down the yellow brick road led—short term memory loss due to emotional overload. Why did she even step foot on it?

She steered her car two lanes over and took the exit ramp, hoping there wasn't another car beside of hers. She couldn't see them through the downpour if they had been there. Saying a fast prayer, then U-turning under the overpass, she climbed the other ramp to get back onto the highway in the opposite direction. Water rushed down, blocking her attempt.

She felt like salmon swimming upstream. In her head she heard the monotone droll of the commentator on a Cable nature show, "…And now we see the undaunted drivers edging their way up up, up the ramp against the torrential blah, blah, blah."

It took her an hour to inch the twenty-five miles back to the cabin. Traffic crept the entire distance like one big school zone. Even at a snail's pace, the rain made it difficult to see the road's curves as it snaked next to the meandering river bank.

She stopped at the crossing. The river resembled chocolate milk. The gushing water churned up silt. The two-lane road, marked by a center yellow line lay underwater. At the far edge of the bridge waves lapped a few inches below the two foot mark on the

Julie B Cosgrove

Texas Highway Department's flood gauge pole. *Good, not that deep yet.*

Christina breathed a quick prayer and patted the dashboard. "You can do this," she said as much to herself as the car. She slowly rolled her vehicle into the rising murk. Her headlights bounced off the leaves and debris which swirled on the surface of the water. A slight jolt as her front tires left the blacktop and grabbed for the concrete bridge's surface made her gasp. *Thank goodness I have new tires.* She felt sheepish that she argued with Jeff when he insisted she buy them.

Just ease your car across, steering away from the current. Christina talked herself into driving through. *Steady, now...slowly, keep the gas pedal even.* She recited each step from past- learned country wisdom. Water pushed against the sides as the coupe crept across the low bridge. Her car froze as if in fear. The whir of her tires told her they were no longer gripping the road. She patted the dashboard and pressed her foot back and forth on the accelerator pedal. *Come on, Baby. You can do this.*

The water level rose half way up her car door. Debris flew by her, swirling in the current caught in her car's headlight beams. The pressure made her car wobble. A broken limb bobbed up and down, streaming towards her car. The rushing sound of gallons of muddy water filled her ears. A minute seemed like ten. Something caught her eye. She turned to see the limb reach the bridge.

Lord help me. That thing is as long as my car!

Its branches reached out a boney hand to grab her. Her heart pulsated in her fingers as they tightly

72

grasped the wheel, in beat to the pounding in her soul. Christina pressed her foot further down on the pedal, praying for her tires to gain traction and lift her out of the murk.   *Come on. Come on. Do it now!*

Finally the tires obeyed. Her car surged forward. The pressure against the doors let loose its grip. Her coupe jerked up the other side out of the swirl.

Christina glanced in her rearview mirror and saw the limb sail behind her. It twisted on one of the concrete pylons marking the low-water crossing then continued downstream. It bobbed for air. Bits of leaves, twigs and a piece of rope trailed in its wake.

Made it. We made it.

Christina put her car in park and rested her head on the steering wheel. For the second time today she felt like blubbering. How on earth did I get into this mess? A Bible verse scrolled across her mind.

> *"When you pass through the waters, I will be with you: and when you pass through the rivers, they will not sweep over you." Is 43:2*

Had the hands of angels pushed her out of the swirling waters? Were there celestial fingerprints on the back of her car now being washed away by the storm? Christina breathed a heartfelt thank you heavenward then sat a moment in the white noise silence of the gurgling, swirling stream behind her and the steady pellets of raindrops on the hood of her car.

Finally, she breathed again. Getting her mind and her car in gear, she applied slight pressure to the gas pedal and eased the car onto higher ground. Two miles later, she reached the cattle guard. The muddy sludge muffled the popping sound of the gravel as she entered the property. The rain was not letting up. She parked the car. Now or never. Christina pulled the collar of her blouse up over her head and made a dash for the cabin. The oak saplings provided little canopy against the downpour as she wiggled the key into the seventy-five year old lock.

Unlock, key. Darn you.

She stomped her foot hard, splashing water inside her shoes. *Great. Just wonderful.* Finally the moisture-swelled cedar door gave entrance for its owner.

Drenched to the bone, she rushed to the open screened window. Luckily, the rain blew in the other direction across the deep cedar eaves which jutted two feet out from the screen. The furniture was only slightly damp and the few raindrops which had made their way through sat beaded on the lacquered slat floor.

"Thank you, Lord!" She hurried to lower and latch the awning just as the wind picked up again and thunder rumbled over the hills. The awning billowed as she struggled to push the toggles through the grummets.

Here it comes. Round two. Christina decided to sit and catch her breath for a minute. She dropped into a wicker chair with a Mexican rendition of poppies painted on the back. When she removed her muddy heels, her soaked knee highs sucked cold against her skin. The right leg of the hose tore as she tugged. She

Focused

wadded them up in a ball and threw them across the room.

What's next? Christina rubbed her bare feet back and forth on the hemp woven porch rug. Almost as good as a massage, it warmed her cramping toes.

She jumped when lightening cracked and stark whiteness blasted through the flaps.

Wow. What a test for her new glare-free glasses. Before her brain could register if her specs passed with flying colors, a rattle of the thunder shook the cabin and vibrated through the pier and beam floor under her feet. Again. And again. The wind howled. Water rushed off the eaves and splashed onto the caliche dirt outside. She became encased in a roaring waterfall. The saplings bent to the ground and bounced under the pressure of the wind and water like playground teeter-totters as . . .

The phone rang?

Chapter 11   Are you there?

The phone is ringing?

She dashed for the ancient black receiver and stubbed her toe on the hemp rug. The phone had a rotary dial wheel. In the center, a faded round paper revealed a smudged four digit number of 9267. At one time that number was all neighbors on the trunk line needed in order to connect them to the Winslow cabin. Christina plopped on the bed, phone cradled on her shoulder, and rubbed her big toe as she fought tears once again.

"Hello?"

"Miz Christina?" A crackly voice came over the wires. Vaguely familiar. But from where?

"Yes?"

"I thought that was you I saw sittin' on the stoop earlier when I was down checkin' the trotline. It's Mr. Owens from across the way. Remember?"

She closed her eyes and breathed a sigh of relief. *Thank you, Lord for Hill Country folk.* As with most rural residents throughout the USA, the families here seemed more tolerant and accepting of people than their big city counterparts. In the country, families relied on each other instead of police and emergency responders. Obviously, there were no grudges over what happened between her and their son in high school. Neighbors were still neighbors and she was thankful this one remembered the phone number.

That's why Christina had preferred coming here in her youth. She'd trade these folk any day for the high society city friends of her mother's with their fancy cars, expensive designer clothes and lavish parties. A more laid back lifestyle existed in the Hill Country, which the hustle bustle, want-it-right-now, don't-waste-my-precious-time city dwellers often found frustrating and mistook for laziness. But, these were salt of the earth people, not afraid of hard work or life's hard knocks. It was in their nature to check on neighbors and offer a hand.

"Oh yes. Of course. How are you? I know we haven't been up here a lot since…"

"I know. All of ya'll River Rats are grown and have families and work to do." The old man's Texas drawl showed no ill will. "Listen, is your husband witcha? The river's a risin' mighty fast."

"It…it is?" She laid down the phone and peered through the flaps. A flash of lightning revealed the river below. The swirling milk chocolate had risen half way up the bluff carrying with it tree limbs, a canoe, and God knew what else.

She sat back down and picked up the receiver. "Sorry, Mr. Owens. I was trying to see the river. Mr. Owens? Hello?"

She tapped the buttons on the phone's old fashioned console. Nothing. It was dead. No Mr.

Focused

Owens, no hum, no obnoxious "If you'd like to make your call again…"

Great. Now what? Christina sat, hands clasped between her knees as she listened to the drenching rain hammering on the tin roof above her. *Not much I can do until it stops.*

With no sunshine, the cabin darkened considerably. She shivered in her wet clothes. She reached over to click on the lamp. Click. Click. Nothing. Was the power out? Christina slapped her forehead. No. Never turned on. *Like the fridge. Right.*

She grabbed her soaked shoes and eased through the cabin. Old memories aided by split-second bursts of lightning through the windows helped her navigate around the furniture. She still managed to bang her toes twice more before she made it to the small bedroom.

Why is this cabin out to get my feet? She groped for the little flashlight in the bureau, and prayed the batteries weren't corroded. A faint stream of light emerged. *Now we're talking.* She tapped the side and the light grew stronger.

Christina tugged open the old bureau drawers one by one in search of clothes left behind by long ago visitors. That's where she remembered her mother kept them in case another visitor needed them. She decided she qualified. Each drawer gave off a whiff of old varnish and time-aged wood. In the third one she spotted folded cotton. *Okay, good.*

Christina fumbled through the folds. She eyed a white T-shirt that read "Don't Mess with Texas" in faded red and blue print, obviously purchased when the highways displayed the slogan years back to keep the littering down. Later promoted in song by Willie and the Boys, it seemed appropriate enough. Maybe the river would obey the time-honored motto. She grabbed some unisex orange and yellow drawstring surfer shorts in the next drawer, slipped into the bathroom and propped the flashlight in the sink.

A bang just outside the bathroom window made her jump out of her skin.

One of the shutters had come unhooked. It flapped in the wind against the cedar planks. She dashed outside around the back of the cabin. The rain stung her cheeks. Her hair clung to her face as she pulled the shutter and re-latched it.

Back inside, she wiggled out of her drenched blouse and skirt then dried off with an thread-bare avocado green towel. She tried not to think how long it had hung there. It smelled a little sour.   Then her heart leapt. There sat an old baby powder tin on top of the commode tank. The holes in the top were etched orange with rust. She blew off the oxidized dust, then rubbed it with the towel. It left sienna and russet splotched streaks that, if it had been on canvas, might have sold for mega bucks as an unknown Jackson Pollock.

Dowsing herself with the fragrant softness, she melted onto the toilet seat. That helps, even my aching toes.

She thanked whoever in the past had left it behind. It must have been ages ago. She couldn't remember the last time she saw baby powder not bottled in plastic. It must have been when Josh was a baby over twenty years ago.

Focused

A sheepish grin pulled at her mouth as an idea began to form. Maybe she could sell it along with the Archie comic books on eBay after all. But, then, she'd have to get approval from Carrie and Carl. And it would take at least a month of emails and texts back and forth to decide whether or not to do it and how much to price it. Decisions were never made quickly on her side of the family when it came to money. She placed the tin back. Too much hassle.

Then another thought pushed its way to the forefront of her mind. Did God, who is Almighty, Eternal and All Knowing, know she would like to have something comforting like the familiar smell and soothing softness of baby powder right now, right here when she was cold and alone in this old cabin? Had He put it in someone else's head decades ago to leave it behind so, in the middle of a storm outside which mimicked the one raging inside her heart, she could have one tiny ounce of creature comfort?

That sounded absurd. But, she thought, God's supposed to know before we ask and He knew us before we were even knitted in the womb, right? The Psalms said so. Would the Lord of the Universe care that much about her microscopic needs in comparison to everything else He had to handle? They seemed petty compared to the starving children in mud huts or the cancer victims in the wards nauseated from chemo, or the . . . she willed herself to stop thinking of examples before she got really depressed.

Changing into the dry finds, she crept back to the cot. The wind's howl became louder and the thunder more constant. Momentary flashes pulsated through the cracks in the cedar door and the shutters in undecipherable Morse code symbols. Rumbles echoed in response over the hills, rattling the glass globe on the ceiling fan above her head. The drumming of rain on the roof deafened her to any other outside noise.

Please, tell me you are here, Lord. Please tell me the baby powder was a sign. I'm alone in this cabin for the first time in my life—and scared.

* * *

Josh returned to the computer department where two months prior, after a year of employment. he'd been promoted to assistant manager. Josh puffed up like a bantam rooster when he received the news until he realized it meant he got all the hassles and blame but none of the glory. Still, it paid for his apartment off campus. And his Mom's eyes had glistened with pride when . . . his Mom. A maternal nudge told him to try her again. Some residual umbilical cord tug no doubt.

Nah. His dad's right. His mom often had her cell in the bowels of her handbag which she slid into her bottom desk drawer at the office. She only carried the phone in case she got a flat tire or something and often didn't use it for days on end. If he needed money or something, Josh knew to call and leave a voice message at home or email her. Texting was not her style. How many times had he chided her for not checking her cell phone for messages? Each time she'd give him the puppy dog hurt look. The one that melted his resolve just as it did his dad's. Females. They knew all the tricks.

Focused

It wasn't worth calling her at work. Her boss didn't like employees getting personal calls. The only exception to the rule had been when he was younger. Raised a latch-key kid, Josh was required to check in when he got home from school. Allowed two minutes max. "Hi, Mom. I'm fine. No, I won't let anyone in. See ya in a few. I promise to not play video games until I've done my homework." Same conversation for six years from junior high until he graduated from high school. Thank God those days were gone.

Mandy cornered him. "Did you get anyone?"

Josh shook his head. Mandy's eyes widened.

"I'll try later tonight on my dinner break. Maybe by then Mom will be home."

"You sure?" She didn't seem very convinced. Mandy was a wimp when it came to bad weather. She always assumed the worse.

Josh placed his hand on her shoulder. "It's okay. The cabin's on a bluff and the water hasn't reached that high since the early 1900's when the flood changed the course of the river. I heard all of the stories as a kid. The great 'hundred year flood, they called it."

Mandy grabbed his arm. "How long ago?"

"I don't know. It was 1909 or something like that."

Josh ignored the chill that hit his shoulder blades. One hundred years ago. He shook off the thought. No way.

Chapter 12   Boat Bottom

Christina's thoughts screamed in her heart, barely audible over the rain. She took off her new glasses and wiped away the raindrops with the Don't Mess with Texas T-shirt. Sitting semi-yoga style with legs crossed under her, she gathered the quilt around her shoulders, holding the ends tight to her chest. *Lord, please still this storm.*

Last Sunday's reading was the passage about Jesus' disciples caught in a storm. How fitting. Except they were together in a boat, she in a cabin all alone. To occupy her mind, she played the scene in her head. If she'd been in that boat, which disciple would she have been? Not the disciple to stand and scream out asking where in the world Jesus was as the storm tossed the boat. Nor would she have been like Peter climbing out to walk over the waves to reach Jesus. Christina decided she'd have been the unnoticed one silently scrunched down in the bow, not out of fear of the storm as much as afraid of upsetting the Master no matter what she did. So she'd do nothing, except maybe pray, right? *Like now.*

Suddenly, simultaneously with a streak of lightening, a bolt of clarity made her sit up straight, and stare open mouthed at the cedar notched wall in front of her. It all came into focus, clear as the world through her new glasses.

She blurted out, "That's just like me, isn't it! That's my life."

A small voice deep inside, yet outside of her, whispered. "Yes, when you don't feel Me nearby, it is."

All her life she'd done whatever was needed to keep up appearances and keep things status quo so everyone would think she was good and not gossip about her. A life without risk as she cowered in the bottom of the boat and tried not to rock it, she'd worried about pleasing others. First it was her mother's society friends, then her parochial girl's school and college mates, then her coworkers, then church family, the parents of Josh's crowd, Jeff's coworkers, her coworkers . . . the list went on and on. She worried if she ever truly pleased Jeff, the man who was supposed to be her soul mate.

Now, the harshest realization of all dawned on her. Through all that worrying and try to please, her focus had never been on the Master— the one who could calm any storm in her life.

This revelation gave Christina a momentary wave of vertigo. Her heart clawed at her chest, a heavy pain pushing in. By not trusting in God to handle the reactions of others, her life became like her old ill-made glasses, settled for. Afraid she didn't deserve better, she convinced herself that putting up with less

Focused

defined her punishment for not being good enough. Why? Because she always felt less—less pretty, less rich, less qualified, less worthy.

"But I want to give you joy in abundance, child." God's voice tapped on her soul.

And all this time, she thought she was trying so hard to be good. But her focus remained on herself and not on God. Contrite, she felt herself shrink into a little girl. Alone in the darkened room, she continued the conversation with her Creator.

She'd always been afraid if she didn't agree with...oh, whatever it might happen to be, she'd find the alternative too costly, or worse than what she already had. She'd upset people, or tarnish her image in their eyes. That was the reason she had put up with those old glasses. . . and a lot of other things. Her mother's platitudes echoed one by one in her memory banks.

Mind your Ps and Qs. Don't upset anyone or they might just gossip about you and ruin your family's reputation.

Then another one. Think before you act.

And another. Never risk upsetting anyone or it will be your fault.

Or worst of all, what if she found out what she secretly wished for was not really what she was supposed to have in the first place? Another cliché suddenly appeared cross-stitched in her psyche. Be careful what you ask for. It was better not to wish for anything.

Then the biggest home-spun cliché of all surfaced from the Magic Eight Ball in her brain. Be grateful for what you have.

Julie B Cosgrove

She voiced her thoughts upward. "Well. After all, that's what all good Christians should do and be, right? Grateful for whatever it is You bestow on us?"

"Do you hear Me?" The small voice tapped once more.

But, the familiar self-criticizing voice inside her spoke louder. "You have never gotten over the dread of ridicule. How stupid you are. You're still cowering to the proverbial 'they'."

All these years, she had fooled herself into thinking she had escaped the grip of high society's gossip and life in a goldfish bowl, as she and Jeff called her mother's translucent for- all-society-to-ogle lifestyle. Christina believed she had escaped their clutches. She moved away and chose to follow her faith and her heart instead. She'd saved herself for marriage, wed a "commoner" and become a working housewife and mother, a very unpopular choice during the free love 1970's. Back then she felt like Christ's warrior against the evils of her generation's stumble into casual sex and drugs. What fervor she had back then.

Now, she felt like a sniveling coward. She'd created her own goldfish bowl to fill the void, striving to always keep the waters clean and clear for peering eyes that saw the little gold cross around her neck or the decal on the back windshield of her car. She was no different than her mother. She could now feel her face squished against the side, pushing to get out.

"The Truth will set you free, child."

Had she also shoved her family into that goldfish bowl? Was that why Josh wanted out of the house so fast after high school? She assumed it was because he was an only child and felt the need for independence.

Surely, Jeff would have said something long before now. Surely, he wouldn't have put up with it all this time, would he? She asked her inner-self, which suddenly felt like a stranger in the room beside her. In her mind, she saw the look on her husband's face as she fretted over a Thanksgiving recipe, or wrapped the Christmas presents just so. He'd tell her to chill, that it wasn't the Queen coming, just her Mom and Dad. She could hear his voice, "Besides, nothing you do will ever be as good as if she did it, right? That's what you always think. So why try?"

She threw herself into a fetal position on the cot. Why didn't I see this before? That old negative inner-self which had been locked inside of her broke free and left on a clap of thunder.

The still, small voice spoke out. "He who believes in the Son of God shall be free indeed."

Christina's world became fuzzy, similar to the first few minutes it takes to get used to new glasses. She felt as wobbly as a toddler, unsteady in this new concept. Could she really take this leap of faith into a new world of "let go and let God", as the old bumper stickers they once sold to raise funds for church camp proclaimed?

"Don't worry. I'm right here. Leap. I'll catch you."

Christina sat, cross-legged, grasping her knees. She rocked back and forth as her mind tried to wrap around all the voice of God said. The thunder rumbled. She ran her thumbnail over her tongue then tapped it on her front teeth as her thoughts came into focus.

What a wakeup call.

Huddled in her Hill Country refuge, the recollection shivered over her. Midlife crisis was a dirty word in her mind, an acceptable excuse to justify a stray into temptations or a self-centered attitude.

No, she would not agree to let this revelation be only that. This was much bigger. That voice told her so. She knew the voice from long ago, though busyness had filtered it out for a long, long time.

Yes, she had found Him again, here where she always did, nestled in the Texas Hill Country way from the din of her life. Was that why she felt compelled to drive all this way?

Christina still did not have a complete answer. But now she knew it wasn't all Jeff. It wasn't just the stress at work. It wasn't hormones. It had to be God tapping on her shoulder. She heard His loving words in the crevices of her mind. Could she really be loved without being good? Had the Lord of the Universe stopped whatever else He was doing, just to calm her and tell her she was loved? Her, of all people. And what had she done to deserve this? Nothing.

That's the scariest thought of all. And yet, it was the most comforting.

She was worn out from thinking. Curling up on the cot, cocooned in the musty quilt, she sank into a deepened warmth and fell asleep. Her new glasses lay beside her, reflecting her finally peaceful face.

Chapter 13   Shining Armor

Light shined in her eyes. Christina bolted awake. Sunlight?

She sat up in bed, astounded by the quietness except for the soft drip of rainwater off the eaves. As her ears tuned in, she heard a squirrel's chatter somewhere in the distance. A cardinal sang out "Teacher, teacher." The world seemed back to normal.

She peered out the side door like Lucy out of the Wardrobe into the ice world of Narnia. Droplets cascaded in slow motion from the branches of the old oaks when a breeze rustled through them. When she stepped out onto the patio, she heard the whooshing as the river rushed to drain the flood and re-establish its banks. Tiptoeing closer to the edge of the wooded bluff, she peered down into the dirty swirls trying to drown the sapling trees bent by the fury. She couldn't see the dock or the diving board. They were still underwater. Cyprus limbs wobbled back and forth, tussled by the current. Half of the path down to the riverfront remained submerged. An inner tube bobbed, lodged on limb, then broke loose and sailed past with debris of grass, twigs and some child's brightly colored swim toy trailing behind.

Christina watched, helpless to change what nature unfolded in front of her. The water table still rose up the sides of the bluff. She had no food or water. She tried to remember the few times her family had been stranded by flash floods, reassured each time that only once in recorded history had it ever seeped into the cabin.

That was over a hundred years ago, right? She racked her memories. When the flooding stops, how long is it usually before the river recedes? At least a day. Maybe two. *And no one knows I am here.*

She dashed around the cabin to her car, hopping on one foot then the next as acorn caps dug into her tender citified feet. When she reached the car, her heels sank into the cool caliche mud. It gushed between her toes. *Gross.* She shook a foot and splattered the sides of her car with tan globs. Christina opened the door and dove for her cell phone in the belly of her bag. "No bars. Dang." She stomped her foot and splattered mud onto her calf.

Her thought process froze. No, she wasn't going to be angry like that anymore. She was going to trust. It was going to all work out. She shoved the phone into the surfer pants' pocket and ran her fingers through her hair. Then she heard a slight popping of gravel.

Whoever my knight in shining armor is, bless him. Right on cue. She cupped her hands to her eyes and watched as an old red pickup edged towards her car. It stopped. The door creaked and she saw a pair of work boots and jeans appear beneath it.

Slamming the door, the now recognizable Mr. Owens swaggered over on his old bowed legs. He touched his cowboy hat with a finger which showed a half moon of black under the nail. "Howdy, Miz Christina. It shore has been a month of Sundays."

Just what she thought he'd say. "Yes it has." She smiled as courteously as she could, resisting the urge to run into his arms and blubber like a small child.

"Didn't wancha to think I done hung up on ya."

"Huh?"

"Blasted phone went dead."

"Oh, oh. Yeah. Mine too". She reached in her pocket and showed him her cell. He does know what a cell phone is, right?

He nodded. "Creek's gone down a bit. Once we could see my truck could make it across alright the Missus told me to come check on ya." He craned his head. "Woo doggie, that river looks mean." He reminded her of Jed Clampett on the Beverly Hillbillies, or vice versa.

"Bless you," she smiled deeply. "How is your wife anyway? And Bud?" May as well ask out of courtesy. "I heard he'd moved to Houston?"

"Dorothy's fine. Ornery as ever." The loving twinkle in his eyes showed he was kidding. "Bud moved, yes. Went and fell for that first grade teacher over in Center Point and when she got an offer to be the principal of a day care several years back, they took off. Left lickety-split. Now she's done left him after all them years. Met some idiot at a convention."

"I'm sorry. I didn't know. You hear from him often, I hope." The blank look on the old man's face made her clarify. "Uh, I mean Bud."

The man nodded. "Oh yeah. Since she left, he's been around a lot more. Of course during deer season I know I'll see him lots." The codger chuckled and spat onto the ground. "How's your youngin'? Full grown by now, ain't he?"

"Josh? Yeah, he's close to twenty. Off on his own, mostly."

Mr. Owens reared back and laughed. "They do take a while getting out of the nest, don't they? 'N just when ya least expect, back they'll come."

An awkward moment passed. She wasn't sure what he meant. "Uh, you want to come in?" Christina motioned towards the cabin. "It's dusty, but dry."

"No, no. Better get on back. River looks like it'll stay up pretty high through the night." He glanced around the property. "You alone?"

"Yep. All alone."

He eyed her cautiously. "You got any vittles here?"

"No. 'Fraid not. Not a good Girl Scout." Christina lowered her head like a penitent in confession.

"Uh, huh. Thought as much."

She looked up and noticed Mr. Owens gave her choice of wardrobe a once over. "Oh, my clothes got drenched. This was all I could find…"

"Never mind. Listen, why don't ya come on over for supper. Wife's fixin' a brisket. There'll be plenty."

Focused

"Wonderful. Tell her thanks. Sorry I can't bring anything. I'll have to give you a ...rain check?" She cringed at her own pun.

Mr. Owens spun on his boot heels and waved over his shoulder, whooping with laughter.

Christina watched him climb back into the truck. As he got in, the seat springs groaned. The rusty old truck door squeaked its complaint. As she sheltered her eyes with the back of her hand, she waved as he took off back down the gravel path and over the cattle guard. He always was one of her favorite people up here. He knew everything about everybody, and was nice to them anyway.

"Thank you, Lord, for Mr. Owens," she breathed.

She tiptoed barefoot back to her car and rummaged through her purse for a brush, and lip gloss. Wiping the dust from the mirror in the bedroom with the backside of the soured Jackson Pollock towel, Christina fluffed her collar length hair and pulled both sides away from her face, then secured them with two bobby pins she pilfered from the Mexican pottery bowl on the highboy. She didn't think the boy painted in the bowl with the donkey by the cactus would mind.

She splashed on some cologne and ran the gloss over her lips. Not too bad for going on fifty. With a few hours of sunlight left, Christina laid her blouse and skirt out on the rock retaining wall overlooking the bluff. She sat for a moment. This patio was where she'd seen the doe, where her family had spent many an evening grilling hot dogs in the outside fireplace and sharing stories of their daily adventures. Memories crowded in again, but she shook them away.

Julie B Cosgrove

What was gone, was gone. In the closet underneath the beach towels—there they were—and deflated life vests and inner tubes, she found a pair of flip-flops. They almost fit if she scrunched her toes.

Out of politeness, she waited for another half hour before she locked up and headed to the Owens. Because of the mud and the fact the creek might still be running a little high, she decided to take her car the half mile up the road to their place. She'd dashed over on foot to get Bud Owens to come play countless times in her childhood. They even had a crush on each other in high school. That seemed eons ago. Well, actually it was. Time did have a way of standing still here. She'd have almost felt Josh's age again, if it hadn't been for her aching toes and chronic back pain.

When she arrived, she pulled her car to the side of the house. She walked up the plank porch that wrapped around the front to the kitchen. As accustomed, she headed for the kitchen screen door. Only strangers and bill collectors used the front door.

"Come on in, or the skeetters will get ya." She heard Mrs. Owens' voice through the screen as the aroma of slow-cooked brisket and onions fluttered into her nostrils. Her stomach growled in response. *Feed me, Seymour.*

The rusted springs whined as she opened the door. "Didn't have a thing to contribute…"

"Don'tcha worry about a little ol' thing like that. Paw told me the flood done caughtcha off guard."

"Like a 300 pound rusher to a quarterback. Heh, heh." Mr. Owens called from the living room. He was sitting in his same old chair scratching his border collie.

Focused

"That can't be Duke?" Christina pointed. She remembered how Bud would cuss when Duke swam out to them and try to climb on their inner tubes. Then he'd always apologize for his potty mouth.

"Nah, one of his last pups' pup. Though ol' Rex here's hardly a pup, ain't ya, boy? He's almost ten now. Duke's been gone near on twenty-one years now, right Momma?"

That confirmed it. Time did have the illusion of standing still in these hills. Embarrassed she turned and asked Mrs. Owens what she could do to help.

"Set the table if ya don't mind. Ya know where the plates are in there, right? Same place as always. Forks and knives are in the drawer." Tearing lettuce into a large wooden bowl, she nodded towards the chipped blue paint cupboard with heart cutouts on the doors.

The younger woman nodded and placed three avocado and gold patterned plates, rims slightly chinked, onto the gingham mats. The chicken paper napkin holder with matching shakers maintained a permanent residence on the Lazy Susan. They had as long as Christina could remember.

She gave it a spin for old time's sake. The Tabasco sauce bottle wobbled. Christina grabbed to steady it, then glanced into the kitchen. Mrs. Owens, bent over her task, whistled a familiar country tune. Thanks goodness she didn't see that. Then as if she felt the younger woman's eyes on her, she looked up.

"Oh, you need to put out four. Bud's here." Mrs. Owens paused from her chopping. "He was outside a little while ago checking on the hens."

"Uh oh," Christina cursed under her breath.

Mrs. Owens smiled and returned to her chopping board.

Christina stared at the gingham and breathed a prayer. *Please Lord, tell me this is not a set up. Couldn't possibly be. We're both married now. At least he was. I still am.*

She subconsciously rubbed her thumb along the gold-banded set on her left ring finger. She went to the cupboard to grab another plate. Just then the screen door slammed.

"Well look what the pole cat drug in," a familiar voice boomed behind her.

Chapter 14   Faux Pas

Jeff didn't leave his office the rest of the afternoon. Anyone who walked by and tapped on his door got the "not now" glare. He let all calls go to his voice mail and felt like hanging out a sign on the knob that read "If the building is burning, knock. Otherwise go away." But he felt that way every day lately. Maybe that should be my new motto. Except that disturbances came with the promotion. Welcome to middle management.

He didn't have any concept of the time, only that he had to finish the bid proposal before he left for the day. And, stop his mind from wandering so he could. Jeff flipped through page after page, trying to interpret what the architect wanted. No wonder this landed on his desk. It was a mess. None of the younger guys could have made heads or tails of it.

The next time he noticed the clock on the bottom right corner of his computer screen, it glowed 6:12 PM. The proposal was finished, his eyes ached, and the florist was now closed.

Julie B Cosgrove

Arms grabbed Christina from behind and pirouetted her around the room in a bear hug. Setting her back down as lightly as he had picked her up, Bud stood there grinning back at her. He'd maybe added fifteen pounds to his middle since she last saw him, and his high forehead had gotten a little higher, but other than that he looked the same—insanely handsome with sparkling blue eyes and dark tussled hair.

"Hey there, Bud." Christina huffed, as she caught her breath. She flicked away her bangs with her left hand, her wedding ring hand. He took a few steps back.

"Paw told me you were up here over at the cabin. I was sorry to hear about your Mom. She passed within a year or so of your Dad, right?"

"Yes. Last summer" The response was flat. Enough emotion for one day. She placed the last plate down on the table.

"They were mighty fine folk. Hear from Carrie and Carl?" He pulled out one of the dining room chairs for her.

"Yes," Christina she sat down. Out of nowhere a mason jar of iced tea appeared.

He decided to sit across from her instead of next to her. That was a good sign.

"I'll have a beer, Maw. Go on." The last remark was directed towards Christina. Their eyes locked.

Focused

"Well," Christina blinked and continued. "Carl married a socialite from L.A., but they are living in Austin. He's a lawyer."

"Figures. Runs in your Winslow blood." Bud replied in a matter of fact tone. He referred to her grandfather and great uncle. He casually spun the Lazy Susan like a Hip Hop deejay, never taking his eyes off of her.

"True. Dad's too." She tried not to keep her eyes on him. She traced the small, frayed hole in the vinyl table cloth with her finger, then knitted her brow to regain her train of thought.

"Anyway. They had a daughter. I think you might have met her. They came here a lot when Melanie was younger. She's grown and married. Has twins. Expecting again in December."

"Did she marry a lawyer?"

"No, a philosophy teacher at U.T. Well, he is now. They were both students then."

"Must make some interesting' conversation over the dinner table." He looked and winked as his mother set a beer down along with a bowl of mashed potatoes. The real kind, not instant.

"Let me help you with that." He rose, took a swig and bowed slightly to Christina.

" 'Scuse me." His Texas drawl and manners were showing. City life hadn't changed him all that much. In a way, she was glad.

Christina didn't know whether to follow or not. Mrs. Owens never did like to be crowded in her kitchen. Or, maybe she didn't want her secret recipes revealed. Being the younger woman in the mix, but not quite a guest, she decided to meet Bud at the door

101

jamb so he could hand her the steaming dishes. He gave her a serving bowl of green beans cradled in two pot holders. Their hands brushed slightly. Neither reacted . . . noticeably.

After everyone was seated and the blessing said, Bud continued as he passed the rolls. "And Carrie?"

"Hmm?" Christina halted, fork in her mouth. She covered her chewing with a gingham napkin and swallowed.

Bud's eyes twinkled, as they always did when he caught her off guard —one of his favorite pastimes when they were younger. Like the first time he had kissed her . . . Oh, never mind.

"Carrie, yes." She looked around the table at each pair of eyes. "She and Robert are living in Richardson."

"La, de, da," came the response from her old nemesis turned beau . . . once.

"Yeah. She married a banker. Excuse me, a financier." She emphasized the correction of the gaffe in jest. "They have three grown kids now, two girls and a boy. No grandkids yet."

"Like y'all." Bud paused from swirling gravy into his potatoes. Seeing her quizzical expression, he clarified by pointing with his fork, "Two girls and a boy. You, Carrie and Carl."

"Right." Why does he always have the knack to flabbergast her? Maybe it was those steel blue eyes or that boyish grin that somehow, on his grown-man face, made him even more handsome.

"And you?" she countered.

Focused

He stopped dishing out green beans, serving spoon dripping. He looked blank. *Touché.*

"Bud and Alice had three," Mrs. Owens replied passing more brisket to her guest. "Jamie, Jonathan and Judy."

"Alice thought it was cute to name them all the same letter. I thought it was confusing." He set the bowl of green beans down.

"Where are they now?" Christina innocently asked.

An uncomfortable silence hovered, thickening above the table.

"Uh, pass the butter please, Maw." Mr. Owens said.

To recover from the unintentional faux pas, Christina turned to her hostess. "You always did make the best mashed potatoes and gravy."

"Wait until ya taste the Mustang Grape pie." Her proud husband winked. Just like his son. That ol' Owens charm oozed over the table and dripped down the sides.

They ate in silence for a while and then shared their adventures of the flood.

"The rain was pouring down so hard, I..." Christina stopped as Mr. Owens' Nextel sounded. A call from the Volunteer Fire Department crackled into the receiver.

"Bob, you there? Over."

Mr. Owens dashed from the table, picked it up and punched the button. "Yeah, Tom. Whatcha got? Over."

"Mrs. Perkins is stranded in the low water crossin' at Miller's Creek there by y'all. She's a' top her car with little Jenny. Got a towline on yer truck? Over."

"Shore 'nough. On my way. Over."

Mr. Owens didn't say another word. He grabbed his jacket off the hook and headed out the back door.

"I'm going with you, Paw."

Bud rose from the table. His slam of the screen followed closely after his father's.

The two women sat in silence. Neither knew whether to eat, clear the table or just leave it all there to grow cold and follow the men.

Chapter 15 Protocol

"What should we do?" Christina asked.

"Don't know." Mrs. Owens picked up the Nextel.

"Tom? Tom Wilson? You there?" She forgot the protocol of saying "over".

"Yes, Ma'am." Tom obviously wasn't a stickler. But then few people would cross Dorothy Owens.

"Bob and Bud are on their way. Ya need anythin'?"

"A couple a blankets might be nice. And a pot o' coffee if ya got some made."

Five minutes later Mrs. Owens dashed down the path with coffee and Styrofoam cups. Christina tried to keep up. She shuffled along behind in her flip-flops as she hugged two blankets to her chest, sugar packets and a spoon in a Baggie dangled between her fingers. Almost sunset, shadows lengthened over the path in stretched distortions of the tree branches, the world washed in a muted yellow blush. They saw Bob's

105

red pickup as it sputtered mud and gravel. Its tires whined in an effort to grab traction. Same creek, same sound. Déjà vu.

Bob Owens was behind the wheel. Bud and Tom were mid-thigh deep in murky water pushing the rear bumper of Mrs. Perkins' Buick. She stood on the bank several feet away, holding her miniature poodle and the hand of a small wide-eyed girl, no doubt her grandchild. She looked close to five years old. Both shivered in the eighty degrees dusk, obviously not from cold.

Mrs. Owens began to pour coffee. Christina wrapped a blanket around Mrs. Perkins' shoulders, then picked up the little girl and rocked her as she mumbled soothing, honey-dripped tones of reassurance in her ear."Look, sweetie. They are getting your car out. Everything's gonna be just fine."

"I bet you two'd like some pie. Just baked it today. Come on up to the house." Mrs. Owens motioned up the road.

The little girl nodded, two fingers firmly planted in her mouth.

Mrs. Perkins sighed, "That'd be nice of ya. Don't see as there's much I can do here."

The four females started strolling back along the path. Christina carried Jenny, wrapped in a blanket, on her hip. The child's abandoned sandals dangled in her other hand. The whine of the tires sounded behind them, then a whoop from Bud. Progress obviously was being made.

Mr. Owens whistled. The women turned in unison, then realized by his hand gestures it was meant for Tom and Bud. He leaned out of the cab, elbow

106

bent, eyes cocked into his rearview mirror. The Buick edged forward out of the watery grip. Tom wiped his brow as Bud continued to push. The taught muscles in his biceps glistened with sweat in the amber glow.

"It just came up so fast. I thought the water was going down." Mrs. Perkins' voice shook a little. She cuddled her dog next to her heart, wrapping it in some of the blanket.

"Them creeks are tricky. Get run off from the river and up they go." Mrs. Owens shook her head. "Happened to me three o' four years back."

"It's not your fault, Miz Perkins." Christina's offering of tea and sympathy landed flat. Mrs. Perkins probably didn't remember her. Maybe she mistook her for Bud's ex.

The ever hospitable Mrs. Owens came to the rescue. "Do you remember Christina? One of the ol' River Rats. Her grandfather was Mr. Spencer, the lawyer from San Antonio who helped out your uncle."

Immediate acceptance dawned on the woman's face as they reached the gate. "Nice to see ya again. Ya all grown up, ain't cha? Dorothy, I can smell the pie from here."

Jenny wriggled down off Christina's hip and headed in. The screen slapped behind her.

"That child's mother taught her no manners. Sorry." Mrs. Perkins waddled her head.

"She's an angel, Vivian. Looks like her daddy." Mrs. Owens held the screen open for her guest. She could placate a mountain lion if necessary. Christina let her elders pass per protocol. There was a pecking order in the Hill Country.

Thirty minutes later the three muddy men arrived. The older women doled out towels and firm instructions to leave their boots on the stoop. The two dogs snoozed together on the hearth, Mrs. Perkins' cuddled into the ribs of Rex. Christina looked up from reading a story to Jenny, who had purple smudges around her mouth. On the table sat three coffee cups and plates in front of a half-consumed pie.

"We left ya some. Lessin' you want me to heat up what's left of supper." Mrs. Owens said to the men.

"I'd be plum stupid to turn down a piece of yer pie, Dorothy." Tom took off his cap and scratched his head.

"We got your car up. Water's all inside. Your mats are soaked. Better leave it to air out," Bud reported to Mrs. Perkins. "Wouldn't try starting the engine just yet."

"Well, Joe can come git me when the creek goes down. He's playin' poker at Bubba's."

"Oh yeah. It is Poker night. You can use the Nextel to call him, Vivian," Bob Owens offered. "Phone's still crackly from the wet lines."

Bud gazed at Christina with the child on her lap. A faraway look lingered in his eyes. He crouched down, sitting on his sock heels. "Is there someone you need to call?" he quietly addressed his old friend, a hint of "I hope not" in his voice.

"Oh, yes. But my cell wouldn't work."

Bud momentarily cast his eyes to the ground. "The Nextel does. You know he wouldn't mind." He nodded toward his father talking to the other women.

"I'll keep it short. Show me how to use it? Jeff has one but I never…"

108

Focused

Little Jenny squirmed in her lap and, as she rubbed her eyes with her knuckles, whined "But you haven't finished the story."

"They lived happily ever after," Christina said as she lifted the child off her lap.

"AAhhh. They always do," Jenny pouted.

Bud took Christina's hand to help her up. "Not always," he stated under his breath.

Chapter 16   Once Upon A time

Christina gave Bud a stern look, released her hand from his then went to ask Mr. Owens if she could use the Nextel after Mrs. Perkins. When it was her turn, Bud showed her how to use it, standing a little too close. His warm breath smelled of beer and brisket, surprisingly comforting and homey. The masculine sweat aroma from his shirt mingled with starch and clothesline smells. Christina edged away from him to gain composure and took the phone outside onto the porch to make her call. The year's first fireflies hovered above the grass as she breathed deep to ease the surge in her pheromones.

Three rings. Four…

"Hello?" came the familiar voice, a little too gruff. A cold tingle splashed her chest. She cleared her throat. What was she going to say?

"Jeff, it's me. Hi." *Okay, you can do this. Keep it brief.*

"Hi? Where are you? Working late? I thought everyone was back again." His voice sounded tentative. They hadn't exactly left this morning on amicable terms. It was this morning wasn't it? To Christina it could have been a decade ago, maybe three. In her peripheral vision she caught Bud's shadow moving in the wedged golden glow of the kitchen light through the screen. Katydids began to shrill in the trees over the roof.

"No. I took a day off. Jeff, look I can't go into it all now. I'm on Mr. Owens' Nextel and I have to keep it brief."

"Okay … Mr. Owens?"

"Yeah. Our old neighbors up here. On the river. Remember? I had to come up to the cabin. There was a flood. I'm kinda stranded. Probably until tomorrow. My cell doesn't work right now. Can you call and leave a message for me at work?" Why did I call in sick?

"I guess. Sure." His voice was vague. "Owens." He repeated to jog his memory. "Didn't they have a son named Bud? You two were close in high school. Is he still there?"

She steadied her voice. "Yes. Look, just tell them there was an emergency and I had to go out of town. This time it was my turn."

"Sure. Okay." Pause."You alright?"

"Yeah." The screen's spring screeched a long groan then whopped closed. She saw Bud out of the corner of her eye.

"Hey, Chris, you're staying here tonight, right?"

She said a little louder into the Nextel, "I miss you, hon. Love ya. Bye."

"Wait, Chrisitin…" Jeff's words halted in space when she clicked off.

"Stay?" she asked.

Focused

Bud eased his six-foot frame over to the rail and leaned on it, looking out at the purple hills fading into blurs with the last light of the day. "Maw and Paw were asking. It's okay."

"I don't know."

He looked out into the yard. "Look. They have plenty of room. I'm staying in the bunkhouse by the barn. They converted it into a guest house years ago so when we came to visit…" The rest of his words became lost in his thoughts.

Christina looked at an old friend, an injured one. She touched his forearm. "That's sweet. But I'll be fine down the hill. I might come for coffee in the morning."

He kept looking straight ahead. "It was forever ago, wasn't it?"

"Yes. We made better friends than sweethearts."

Bud kicked the post with his boot."I really screwed that up, didn't I?" He swallowed the memories back down. The steel blue eyes clouded.

"No. Life did. We just weren't meant for each other, Bud. Not that way."

He kicked the post again, harder, and turned from her. "Yeah, well Alice wasn't either." He stomped down the steps, head down with both hands shoved deep into his jean pockets.

She watched a once proud and sometimes obnoxiously loud guy slump off like a wounded animal. She remembered the whistle he used to make to let her know he was at the riverfront. She'd dash out the door, down the path and cannonball in beside him. He'd been there to hold her heart from falling to pieces when her first love broke it off with her. She cried on Bud's shoulder and he got her stinking' drunk for the first time in her life. It helped numb the pain and they laughed until she puked. Then he snuck her into the cabin under her parent's radar and tucked her into her bed. It took her years to get over that guy. She barely dated all through college.

Bud never brought it up again. He was well named. He was her bud. She hurt for him. She saw through the macho big guy image. She rubbed the lens of her new glasses with her T- shirt and turned to go back inside. *No, he let me see through it.*

She handed the Nextel back to its owner with a smile. "Here's your phone, sir. Thanks."

"Everythin' okey-dokey at the home fires?"

"Yes, thanks." She did a half turn. "Mrs. Owens, can I help you with the dish... oh, you did them."

"Do 'em every night. Don't fret yerself. You stayin' the night?"

"No. I'll be fine down there. But I'd love a hot shower. Water heater's off. The river's not quite fit for bathing."

They all laughed. Everyone knew you didn't go in the water until it turned back to green. That was rule number one. "Even without the flooding, it'd be too cold for my bones. Only time it's half way decent is mid-August," Mr. Owens chuckled. "Go on girlie. You have the first slot."

Christina nodded. "After that, do you want me to take y'all home, Mrs. Perkins? I can walk down and get my car..."

114

Focused

"Oh, Heavens no, dear. Sweet of you to go an' offer. My Joe's coming for me and Jenny here. I think I just might hear him now."

"Goodnight, then. Jenny, next time we'll finish that story, okay?" Christina turned to the child who sat on the floor, petting the dogs.

"I've heard it before. She eats the apple and the dwarfs take care of her 'til her prince comes and kisses her." The five year old synopsized with a shrug.

"Lucky girl," Christina said and cupped her hand under Jenny's chin. "I hope your prince comes someday, too."

"Did yours?"

Christina felt all eyes on her. She swallowed and whispered, "Yes. He did." *Though sometimes he can be an ogre.* She walked down the hall to take her shower. *But, then, I'm no princess at times, either.*

It was a tub enclosure, thank goodness. No tight space. Towels hung on the bars with a hand towel and washcloth folded on the sink counter. An extra house robe draped neatly over the toilet seat. Mrs. Owens had been there alright, in anticipation of housing a stranded guest, though whether that was her or Mrs. Perkins and Jenny, Christina could not be sure. She figured using a capful of shampoo was allowed, but not thirty gallons of hot steaming water. She resisted the urge to linger under its stream.

After her shower, she wiped the tub, just as she'd been taught. Next, she laid out another towel and wash cloth and smoothed the steam from the bathrobe, ready for the next user. Closing the door a touch to let the steam escape, she padded barefoot on hardwood floors back into the living room. Mr. Owens was snoozing on the couch, his dog at his feet. The Perkin's pooch had vacated its post. Jenny and Mrs. Perkins were nowhere in sight. Mrs. Owens peeked around the corner and motioned her to come into the kitchen.

"They're gone. He left the game to come git 'em."

A gurgle, snort, grunt, then soft snores resonated from the couch.

She nodded towards the snores. "Does that just about every night. When I start turning out the lights, he comes to bed."

"Jeff goes to sleep in his recliner. Until I turn the TV off."

The elder shook her head as she wiped her hands on her terry cloth apron. "Must be the male gene. You happy with him?"

Christina felt the barb stab her heart — she never saw it coming.

Chapter 17   Return the Favor

Christina remained silent, not meeting Mrs. Owens's eyes. How could she answer that question? Yes, no, I don't know anymore? Had this woman seen through her so clearly?

"Come, set a spell." Mrs. Owens poured herself a cup of coffee and motioned to her guest to do the same.

Christina poured herself ones as well. Obediently, she came and sat down across the table, waiting for the next barb to sling in her direction. A pair of worn, blue-veined hands patted hers, hands that had doled out grub and advice at this table for decades. "I knew yer parents a long time. Your Maw was a good woman underneath all that high falutin' act. Yer Dad? He was a fine man. He loved her and ya'll very much."

"I know. I miss him terribly. It still hurts."

Julie B Cosgrove

Mrs. Owens spun the Lazy Susan so the sugar bowl landed in front of Christina's cup. "I know, dear."

"Mom was wise. I know that now." She scooped two spoonfuls into the aromatic caffeine and gently clinked the spoon in the cup. Mrs. Owens handed her the creamer in a small white ceramic cow. Christina nodded and grabbed the tail-shaped handle, watching the Half and Half spew from his mouth. Small fractures in the glaze, like spider veins, marked it's age.

The woman laid her hand on Christina's arm. "Go on."

"Even though she stressed way too much why we kids should be mindful of how we appeared to others, unlike a lot of her friends she was . . .well, genuine. She could see through those people down into their souls. Maybe that's why she always warned us to be careful of the way we behaved around them. She knew how deeply their silver-edged tongues could slash."

"Humph. Never quite heard it like that, but yes, I must say she did."

"She tried her best to raise us right." Christina tilted her head, stirred her coffee some more then laid the spoon down. "Mrs. Owens. Can I ask you something? Just between us?" There was an aura about that room. Maybe it was the table with its Lazy Susan, the cup of steaming coffee, or the shower that opened up not only her pores but her soul. But she felt the bond between them—woman to woman, wife to wife.

Focused

"Sure. Ya know I've always treated ya as one of my own. But ain't it about time you called me Dorothy and him o'er yonder, Bob?"

Christina smiled. "Alright then, . . .Dorothy. Have you always loved Mr. Owens, uh, Bob?"

As if in response, a snort came from the couch as the dozing man repositioned.

The older woman rocked back in her chair. A distant smile crossed her lips making the younger woman realize the conversation had come full circle back to the first question. Christina bit the side of her lip. Maybe I should have bitten my tongue. After an eternity of silence, while Christina fidgeted with the spoon, Dorothy finally cleared her throat and took a sip from her own cup. She set it down with purpose and looked Christina square in the eye.

"Yes. And no. Deep down, always. There's been days, though. . .even a few years."

The honesty made Christina jolt. "Really?"

"Of course, child. I remember one thing the preacher man told me the night of our wedding rehearsal. He said, 'Dorothy, Bob. There are going to be days when the vows you take tomorrow will mean more than the person you said them to. But it will pass.' And it always did. I'd be fit to be tied and ready to toss him out on his ear. Then the good Lord would have that man do somethin' nice and I'd back down and my heart would melt. 'Course it works both ways."

Christina nodded and sipped her coffee. The two women were quiet for a while, each in their own thoughts, but sharing the same.

After a few moments, Christina asked, "What happened with Bud and Alice?"

"I don't rightly know all of it. Bud's so hush-mouthed. Male pride, I guess. I noticed the past few times they were up here with the kids, they seemed to be puttin' an awful lotta space between them. Heard them havin' a few knock-down-drag-outs, too. Last Christmas when they came they didn't argue. I knew then it was over."

Christina stared, marveled by this simple old countrywoman's wisdom.

"Done up and moved to St. Louis. Jamie and Jon followed her. Both have jobs and Jon's in some tech school. Alice waived child support on the youngest since she dang near makes three times as much as Bud. Maybe that was part of it."

"Bud is kinda old fashioned about that stuff, I guess." Christina replied.

"Bud's old fashioned about too much stuff," his mother laughed. "But I know he's old fashioned enough to think he made a vow and he shoulda kept it."

"Did she leave him?"

"That's what I understand." The older woman shook her head. "They've done made it all too easy nowadays. You know she's got another fish on the line? Sheesh. In my day, divorce branded a woman."

Christina watched as Dorothy went to the sink to rinse out her cup. "Deep down don't you think it still does? In the heart, I mean," Christina asked. "I think it would hurt a great deal no matter who left who. Even if they thought they were better off that way." Her words made her realize it was something she could never do—hurt Jeff that much, or herself.

"Bud shore acts that a way."

"You think he would talk to me?"

"I think the ear of an old friend tried and true is exactly the medicine he needs."

Christina pushed her chair back. She saw the woman at the sink turn at the screech of the chair legs across the floor and watch as she pulled open the metal kitchen cabinet. There it sat on the bottom shelf, as always. She pulled out the fifth of Southern Bourbon.

"Excuse me," she said to her hostess as she snatched two mason jars out of the drainer.

Dorothy raised an eyebrow.

"Just returning an overdue favor." Christina nodded and stepped out onto the porch. Through the open kitchen window she heard the Hill Country woman pray, "God, bless 'em. And keep their hangovers to a minimum. I'm almost out of aspirin."

Focused

Chapter 18 Three Fingers

Jeff dropped the take-out bags in the trash after he hung up from his wife. He stared at the trashcan which now held two of his meals that day, his appetite lost. The grocery store flowers looked puny compared to the ones he'd forgotten to pick up from the florist. He chunked them in the trash too. So much for trying to do her a favor.

Just as well. He peered out the kitchen sink window. For the life of him he couldn't figure out why his wife was up there. What emergency? He pondered whether he should call Carl. He was the executor of her parents' estates now. But Jeff decided against it. It might bring on too many questions. Questions he didn't have answers to and wasn't sure he wanted to know.

Jeff yawned and rubbed the cramps out of his neck. He felt a little out of sorts and achy. He decided he was just tired, so he turned out the lights, picked up the little black and white cat, and headed down the hall. Nothing on TV anyway. He didn't feel up to reading the paper. A nice long hot shower. That would do the trick.

Fat Cat stopped eating the kibbles in his bowl and trotted along behind them, tail straight.

"Come on." His master turned and waited for the cat to catch up with him. "Since she's stranded in the Hill Country with God knows who, you get her side of the bed."

His mind halted and rewound to the conversation. Owens. The name and the voice in the background of the phone call echoed. "Are you staying here tonight, Chris?" That's what he'd said. Was this jaunt really an emergency? Or planned? Had she been that ticked off?

A proprietary prickle raised the hairs on his forearm, just for a second, then he sloughed it off. No way. Maybe she went there to face finally her sorrow over her parent's deaths and the flood just happened. Of course it did. And Bud Owens just happened to be there, too. Maybe he and his wife were visiting. After all, he'd been married now for years, right?

The hot water handle screeched, released a sputter, then another. The pipes squealed in a high pitch that tugged his eardrums before the flow increased to a good force. It was time to re-plumb. They'd been stalling it off for years, knowing it would put them back in debt. George and Barbara next door had rerouted theirs last fall and it ended up costing in the thousands. He'd been hoping to get Christina away for her fiftieth birthday, or their twenty-fifth. Maybe a cruise. "A cruise cures the blues." That's what the sign said in the travel agency window next to the bistro.

Focused

Well, she was blue alright. Maybe so was he. Something had to change.

If the company landed that bid, perhaps he'd get a hefty yearend bonus. Then they could do both, cruise and new pipes. Could he stand the tense moods until then? He had to admit the atmosphere tonight in her absence felt fresher, lighter. Kinda nice, actually. Maybe her jaunt up there would be the catalyst to finally get Mount Vesuvius to erupt and he not have to be in the path of the flowing lava. Then they'd be good to go for a while. That is, until it all started building up again. How do you stop a volcano?

As the steamy shower poured over him, he remembered the forbidden Cubans tucked away in the back of his sock drawer. A special treat to end a bone crushing day. With a few fingers of that Scotch they got for Christmas from one of the fledglings at work who had drawn his name, the evening could be redeemed. If he sat outside on the back patio with his indulgences, she'd never know.

* * *

Christina stepped carefully over the path, barely illuminated by the light in the kitchen behind her and the yellow porch light ahead. The wind rustled through the oak leaves, dripping the last of the raindrops on her head as she walked. She smelled the dampness hovering in the air and noticed a small halo around the porch light, despite her new glare-free tints. Her skin felt moist with the heavy dew. She stopped to listen for sounds of life in the guesthouse. All she heard were the crickets and a bullfrog down near the creek. Somewhere over the hills a Chuck-will's- widow called. The leaves dripped onto the path, making a flat sound in the moist dirt. Then came a cough. She noticed a figure moved on the front porch just out of the light's reach.

"Thought I saw your car still here." The familiar male voice said.

"Couldn't leave without truly telling an old friend hello before I said goodbye."

"Everyone else does."

She stopped a few feet in front of him. His eyes caught the reflection of the bottle and glasses.

"What the heck?"

"That's what your Mom said. Told her it was about time I returned an old favor."

Bud chuckled. "Well whatcha waiting fer, girlie? Unscrew that cap an' pour." He mocked his dad's voice and plopped down on the stairs.

She joined him. Her rear felt immediately damp. Oh well.

She poured three fingers worth in each glass and handed him one. They sat in silence as Bud drank the first few sips. Christina left hers alone. She didn't know whether to let him speak first or not. Please, dear Lord, guide me in this.

She set her drink down. He downed his. He reached for the bottle and sniffed. "Paw's getting smoother hooch these days."

"As I remember, you doused me with Boones Farm."

"Strawberry something, right? Damn, that sweet stuff was nasty." He caught his cussing and apologized.

Focused

"It was potent enough for me." Christina defended the occasion and ignored his slip.

"It was your first drunk?"

"It was my only drunk."

"You're kidding? Really? I'll be. Not even in college? The night afore your wedding?"

"Nope. Not my thing. See what you did. Cured me after the first bout."

"Your welcome." Bud replied with a mimed tip of an imaginary Stetson.

A raccoon rummaged through the wet leaves, chattering to itself. Christina sighed. *Been there recently my furry friend. I've been talking to myself way too often lately.*

"Does Jeff know?"

"Huh?" Her thoughts returned to the present conversation. "About the Boones Farm? Ah, yes, I told him." Christina was surprised Bud remembered his name. The two couples had only met a few times in passing at the rodeo dance over the years. Even then, the tension seemed way too present. Maybe she mentioned his name earlier? "Jeff knows all about us, uh, you. . .our growing up."

Bud sighed and took another swig. He turned to her, the steel blues flashed with sharpness. "I never stopped loving you, you know."

"Bud. Stop it. You hardheaded bull." Christina stood and put her hands on her hips. "I love you too. . .just not that way. More than that way."

Bud rose and walked over to the edge of the little porch. He leaned against the post, sloshing his drink in the jar. "I know. Now. I just didn't then. Alice was a rebound." He chugged another gulp.

"Bud. . . I, I had no idea."

127

"Doesn't matter. We both knew it. I was her rebound, too. Truth is, when I married her, she was four months along with Jamie."

"I never knew." Christina didn't know what to say. She sat down, rocked back on her rear and clasped her knees. Something told her she'd be a while. His tongue was loosening.

"Yeah. I didn't either at first. I mean that Jaime wasn't mine. I married her anyway. We eloped. Drove all night and half a day to Vegas. But there it is. Dirty laundry out in the open." He shuffled a boot in the drying caliche mud. "Honestly? We tried to make a go of it. Felt a second baby that we knew was ours might do the trick. Then Judy just kinda happened one night after we had a rip-roaring fight." He plopped back down on the stoop.

"Oh." Christina felt that was a stupid response. But what other one was there?

"You two just had one?"

"Yes. I had to have an emergency hysterectomy after Josh. He's our one and only."

"Bright kid, I hear tell. Like his dad," he winked. "And his mom." The soft blue came back into his eyes, though somewhat cloudy. For a moment they sat in silence. The leaves misted them with rain droplets as a breeze rustled through the trees.

"You want to go see if the river's down?" He suddenly suggested.

"You aren't thinking of a swim?"

"Hell, uh, sorry, heck no. You know it's not good to swim until the water turns green again. Besides we'd freeze our. . .hmm, tails off. All I need is to send you back into Jeff's arms with blasted pneumonia."

128

Focused

That did it. Christina started to cry. She felt like a horse's patoot. She felt him move towards her, then stop. She wiped her eyes with the back of her hand and whispered, "I'm Okay."

Bud bent to pour more Bourbon in her jar. She covered the rim with her other hand.

"Please, I really don't drink. I don't want a repeat. It's supposed to be your turn." She sniffed.

"What's this all about, Chris?" He was the only one who could ever get away with calling her that. What started out as a tease because she was such a tomboy turned into an endearment over the years as they grew up.

"Something. I don't know. Lately my world's been a little out of whack, that's all. But I came over here so you could cry on my shoulder." Her voice was raspy with emotion.

"Turned the tables on you, huh?" The blue eyes danced again. Then the light behind them faded. "Talk to me about it."

She told him about her escape. About her non-fight with Jeff. He sat quietly and listened.

The katydids began to sing in the rain cooled night. Christina swirled a mud puddle around with a stick. "You know, many people said we were raised too differently. That it would never work out."

Bud repositioned to face her head on. His blue eyes peered into her soul, probing but not intruding. "You were never like your mother, Chris."

She smiled up at him. "I am more than you think. Early in our marriage, Jeff gave into my social entertaining gene." She laughed at his eye rolls. "It's true I have one. We'd invite couples over to barbeque

129

in the backyard or play a game of gin rummy. It was never successful. By the time the couple arrived, we were well beyond feeling hospitable. I'd be in a panic rattling questions. Do you think the beans simmered down too much? Should I heat more rolls? Is the centerpiece too much in the way?"

Christina shrugged. "Poor Jeff. I still recall him saying 'Calm down, Christina. It's just Betty and Jim, not the Queen.' " She gave the royal flip of the hand back and forth.

Bud laughed and took a swig.

"Still, the sarcasm in his voice stabbed me. I remember one time he crossed his arms folded over his chest and locked his knees in a military stance." She sat up straight and imitated him. "He said, 'I'm surprised you didn't dash down to San Antonio to borrow your mother's sterling and crystal.' "

"Ouch. I've had a few of those fights myself. Said crap just to get in a stab. Trouble is, she always pulled the knife out and slung it right back at me. Then I'd do the same until one of us stomped out."

Christina shook her head. "Not us. He'd grouse, I'd cower. I know it's inbred in me to play hostess, so I found another outlet. I volunteered to be the one to organize, decorate, and more often than not, host events held at church or at Josh's school. They usually ended the same way. Jeff fuming, me wondering why I even tried." Her voice shook.

Bud remained quiet and let her settle her emotions. He pushed the drink towards her. She shook her head. "I'm okay."

"You still into all that Bible stuff like you were in high school?" He cocked his head, looking at her T shirt to check for the little gold cross, the one she'd worn since she was thirteen.

In a subconscious response, Christina reached for it then held it in her hand, running it back and forth on the chain. "If you mean do I pray and study His Word. Well, yes." She dropped the cross, took off her glasses, then dabbed her eyes with the neck of her T shirt and stared at him through residual tears. Even fuzzy and slightly out of focus, his handsome face shone through. "Why do you ask?"

"I could never figure that out about you. Everyone else who claimed they were Christians seemed too pushy. Shoving it down your throat. Repent or else. We tried it for a while after Jamie was born. Tried out three different churches in two years. Couldn't keep up with all the rules. Then we just slowly quit trying." He scooted closer to her.

"But you. You have always been real. Maw and Paw, too, but they are old school. It was a part of their generation. Not ours. Still you always lived it."

"Bud, I haven't been so great about doing that lately. That's why I drove up here, I think. I always felt His presence here on the Guadalupe. I think I needed to feel that closeness again. I've been pushing everyone away. God. Jeff. Even my friends. I just didn't want anyone to get so close they'd hurt me. I never ever want to hurt like I did when Dad died. Then when Mom followed him later. . ." She stopped before the tears erupted again. She'd done enough of that to last her a month of Sundays.

"They loved each other too much to be without each other for long I guess." Bud thought out loud.

"Bud. That's deep!" One look on his face and Christina knew her voice implied too much of a surprised reaction.

"Didn't think I had it in me, Chris?" He laughed and rubbed her on the back. The way he used to, a century ago. She didn't mind. His touch was warm.

"Do me a favor." His hand stopped in the middle of her back. His voice became low and serious. "You two keep working' it out. You keep close to your God. You're my only hope that there's something permanent and good out there for our generation. Don't think I didn't notice how Jeff still looked at you last time we caught up with y'all at the rodeo."

Christina was again surprised. Must be my night for them. "How?"

"Chris. The man's always been gaga over you. I could tell the first time you brought him up here all those years ago. The last time at Steppin' Out, what, five or six years ago? He still had that look. I could've belted him."

There was a moment of silence. Then Christina spoke. "What are you going to do now?"

Now it was Bud's turn to look startled. "To Jeff?"

She felt the heat rise in her cheeks. "I mean, with your life. Your mother told me the circumstances. You know, Alice moving away with the kids." Christina felt a twinge of guilt. Had she betrayed a confidence?

Bud leaned back a bit. "That kitchen table. Mom's place to open hearts and conversations. She told you over a cup of coffee, right?"

Focused

"Right."

"Yeah. Well, I just sold the house in Houston. Didn't want to live there anymore. My job wasn't all that great anyway." Then he paused. "You and Jeff haven't, uh . . .?"

Christina waved both hands in front of her. "No. No, nothing like that. It's just not having Josh around has taken some getting used to. Plus, Jeff's new promotion has him working extra hours. We just seem to be . . ."

"Ships passing in the night? Sounds lonely." The warm hand moved to rub her shoulder blades. It had been a long time since anyone had done that.

"Why don't you come and visit?"

The words were out of her mouth before she could stop them.

Chapter 19   Mud and Eggs

"You sure?" Bud stared at her. He gently pressed his hand into her back. "Stay with you?"

"Josh's old room is vacant. You'd even have your own bath." Christina back stepped in order to make her invitation more clear. "One of Jeff 's old school chums stayed in there for a week while in town for a convention. Then a couple from our town stayed for a while after they had a fire until their insurance found them housing. We like guests. You don't mind cats, do you?"

"Would you make me go to church?"

"Probably. Jeff would." She replied with a shrug.

The hand dropped from her back and shook hers. "It's a deal. I've been thinking about checking out the Austin job market anyway."

Later that night, Bud helped her open the shutters, turn on the power and prime the pump. The rain-cooled breeze felt rather brisk, but the dampness in her city clothes had not quite dissipated. He watched as, out of habit, she shook them for scorpions. In the Hill Country you always shook out clothes, mops, and brooms. Rule number two.

"Good, you haven't forgotten."

"Like riding a bike." She left them to hang on the hooks outside, traditionally designated for bathing suits. The yellow aura from the bug light, unhindered by a shade, silhouetted the curves of her cheekbones, and other curves under the T-shirt. The woman had done a good job of keeping her figure. Then, as if her God sent a warning from Heaven, Bud caught the flash of her wedding ring. As she turned towards him, the slogan on her chest became visible. Don't Mess with Texas. Right.

He noticed she caught him looking at her. "Oohh." Bud drawled and smiled. "I, uh, wasn't going to comment on your choice of attire."

"Courtesy of long ago visitors who left the premises without all of their things. The flip-flops, too." She stuck out a muddy foot and let out a soprano pitched "tah dah" that just might attract a hyena, if there were any such thing in the Hill Country. It resounded up the hill and bounced back flat against the bluff. That made Bud laugh.

"What was that poem your Mom recited?" Bud was eying her foot dripping with goop at the end of a calf a Playboy Bunny would still grit her teeth over. 'Only a rose knows. . .'"

Focused

". . .how good mud feels between the toes." Christina finished the verse. She slopped the flip-flops off one at a time, then rubbed her feet on the river rock porch as she grasped the doorjamb in a balance that reminded him of a ballerina's move at the bar. Bud looked around the premise in a protective way. He wondered if he should turn his back, then couldn't figure out why. Maybe he should get her a wet washcloth. Or not.

"You sure you're gonna be okay, Chris?"

"I'm home. I'll be fine." She raised her head from her task and grinned the way that always melted his nerve without even trying.

"Goodnight then." He paused, just briefly, and then turned to walk down the path that led back through the woods to his property, and put a safer distance between them.

Later that night Christina lay on the cot, looking out over the bluff. The almost full moon cast a soft bluish glow over a hushed earth. The river had stopped roaring, but she could still hear the rush of the current as it tried to dump enough downstream to get back into its banks. Maybe by morning, she yawned. The swishing hum became a white noise, almost shushing the other night sounds of crickets and frogs.

What the riverfront would look like after the water receded? Would there be any grass left or would it have all washed away in the undercurrent swirls? How many times had her family painstakingly wheel-barrowed squares of sod, then one by one squished them down into the mud like Italian grape press

137

dancers? Only a rose knows. . . Christina smirked at the memory of her high society mother in short-shorts with grass bits and dirt splatters on her calves. Just like her daughter today.

How good mud feels…but it hadn't in a long time. They had neglected this place too long. Remorse hung over her shoulders in the form of a shadowy shawl like her grandfather's specter. She and her siblings had dropped the baton in the relay race against time's endeavor to decay what was not cared for and buried in years of fallen leaves. This place was too precious, too uniquely blessed, to decompose from neglect. The obligation rose in her as a form of duty to God and Country. She started a mental to do list along with cobweb demolition and dust busting. She hoped Carl and Carrie's clan could be persuaded, Jeff and Josh as well. Maybe a family reunion. All together, once again. A weekend of laughter, food, and work. The Fourth of July would work. Rodeo, fireworks, rakes and shovels, and of course, hamburgers and hot dogs.

Outside she heard the distinct shuffling of leaves. Not anyone raking them. Footsteps of an armadillo. These animals fared better than their human invaders. They knew the river. It rose, it went down. They rolled with nature's punches. They patiently waited and didn't let it upset their routine lives. She could learn a lesson from them.

She'd invested too much in making her life, her marriage, and her world status quo. Stability was as much a part of her as her own blood vessels. When life's erratic storms came, she became impatient—no, more like frustrated. Angry. Hurt. They upset her

Focused

controlled, orderly 3existence. She was swirling in one of those storms now, as the river had literally been today. She saw that now. It too would pass. That didn't mean she wanted to fly the coop, even if she had done just that on a whim today. Not permanently, anyway. Like the riverfront, she could replant square by square and restore her routine. It might be slightly different, but in many ways, it would be the same.

Sometimes your vows will mean more than the one you said them to.

That preacher had been a sage. She thought it should be printed on every marriage certificate. Maybe if it had been inscribed on Bud and Alice's. . .but, then again, maybe not.

Christina drifted into the silvery blue shadows cast by the moon and dreamt of squishing marriage licenses with her toes, while Dorothy bent to hand them to her after stamping them with the saying. The armadillos and raccoons pushed the wheelbarrow as her grandfather supervised. She kept stomping, talking on a cell phone at the same time, assuring Jeff she was almost finished. Carl and Carrie had sent their regrets with lame excuses. Jenny was coming down the path from the bluff in a Snow White outfit, bringing a tray of Mustang Grape pie. Bud, oozing his charm, carried Mrs. Perkin's dog in one hand, and a fifth of Bourbon in the other, which happened to be the same color as the dog.

Six hours later she was jolted out of the dream by a whistle. Like a bell to Pavlov's dogs, she jumped up and pulled on her clothes before fully awake.

Dampness only remained around the pockets and the waistband of her skirt. Her blouse felt cool, but dry. Thank God there were no scorpions.

A knock followed on the door. She peered out the window while pulling a brush through her pillow-hair. There he stood with a thermos and a tray draped with red gingham. "Room Service."

Christina opened the door. "What, no single stem rose in a crystal vase?"

"It broke. Can't trust the kitchen staff."

She opened the screen and backed out of the way as he crossed the threshold. She ran her hands through her hair. She wondered if she had any makeup left on her eyes. Doubtful. Thank goodness for glasses. A laugh spurted out.

"What?" he set the tray on the dining table.

"Nothing. Sorry. A stupid thought. Not about you."

"Whatever." His tone flattened.

"It's a long story. Yesterday, I left my old glasses up here so I had to stop off on the highway and get new ones."

"Huh? But you're here?"

"Yeah, well, it's like this. When it started raining I remembered I had left the awning up. So... oh, never mind." She waved her hands to erase the whole conversation. "It's just that I noticed I had the old pair on."

"Well, if you ask me. They look like the ones you had on last night."

"See? That's the thing. I got almost the same frames so Jeff. . .never mind." *Didn't I just say that? Am I that nervous?* "I'll show you."

Focused

She went to switch her glasses so she could see better, and took a deep series of breaths. When she returned, she swung the old ones in her hand then shrugged. "Now, I've got two pair."

"Uh-huh." Those steel blue eyes danced circles around her. No wonder she always liked Paul Newman movies.

Bud took off the gingham to reveal scrambled eggs and creamed sausage gravy over biscuits.

Christina sat down and grabbed the fork. "Looks wonderful."

"Have you ever known Maw's cooking not to be?"

"No," she said with a mouth full of eggs.

She watched as he unscrewed the cup from the thermos and poured her coffee, then went to look for another mug. Christina took a deep sip. It was already creamed and sugared. *Bless that woman. Note to self. Send her roses.*

Bud returned, mug in hand. He turned a chair around and straddled it, wiping out the mug with his T-shirt.

She tried to ignore that gesture and kept eating.

"When are you leaving?" He eyed her as he poured his coffee.

"Soon, if the river's down. I'd like to get home, change and put in some work at the office."

"Still with the same accounting firm?"

"Yep. And it's darn near tax time. A real pain. I shouldn't have taken off."

"Yeah, you should've. You already look better than you did last night."

"Bud, I don't think I have a stitch of makeup left." Her voice held disbelief.

"Don't need it. Though for the life of me I don't know why you cut your hair so dang short. I always liked it long ..."

"Next subject. You really want to come for a visit? You're looking for a job?"

" Maybe. Like I said, I just couldn't stay in Houston. Her friends were my friends. Been helping out doing odd jobs up here. Summer's coming. Lots of rich folk will need work done to their vacation bungalows before they come up for vacation."

"Especially now." She pointed her fork towards the river.

He nodded and sipped his coffee, trying not to cringe from the sugary, creamy taste. She remembered now. He always drank his black.

She wanted to tell him she knew a friend in Allensville who needed help in his landscaping business, but she decided not to Band-Aid the situation, which was her normal tendency. Let the man keep some dignity.

"I'll bring this back when I leave." She pointed her fork at the plate.

"No need. I planned on a sitting here 'til you're through." His eyes smirked through his Texas drawl.

Oh, just great. Christina smiled back.

"Gotcha Chris." The blue eyes gleamed. He rose and headed for the door. "Don't bother rinsing those dishes. Maw never did trust your water pump." With a slam of the screen door he was gone.

She sat back in the chair and breathed.

Chapter 20 Routine

Waking up to two foursomes of paws on his backside, Jeff realized he was alone. It felt odd seeing the unrumpled pillow next to him, as if the right half of his body had been severed even though he could still use it. Amazing what twenty plus years of living with someone can do to you.

With a deep sigh, he threw back the covers and announced breakfast would be served momentarily in the kitchen. The patting of paws and two straight tails swished past him to lead the way.

Jeff waited impatiently for the aromatic brown liquid to drip into the carafe as the coffee pot gurgled its morning song. Christina always set the timer so it was hot and freshly brewed by the time he awakened. He had forgotten to do that. Oh, well. What were a few minutes? He poured food in the cats' bowls and gave them fresh water. Christina could handle the cat box when she got home. Not up his alley. No way.

Julie B Cosgrove

Jeff went down the hall to shower and dress. He figured he would just pick up something at a drive-through on the way to work. Dirtying a skillet and eating alone didn't appeal to him. Actually, not much did this morning. He felt achy all over. Maybe he missed her more than he thought. Maybe it was the Scotch and cigar. Nah, it was because he hadn't slept well. All night long the figures from that bid had swum around in his head along with something else less tangible. Something he couldn't quite put his finger on. *I wonder how she slept?*

There were a few times in their married life they'd been apart overnight. A couple of business trips for him, the time she went and stayed with her sister after she had surgery, and then with her mom for a week after her dad passed. And, every year the women of the church went on a weekend retreat together. She encouraged him to sign up for the men's retreat but it never met with his schedule, or so was always his excuse for not going. Somehow pow-wowing over a campfire singing Kumbaya with a bunch of guys didn't sound like something he would look forward to doing. Yet he admitted he enjoyed the Scout campouts as a kid, and went on a few with Josh's troop during his scouting years. Still, there seemed to be a difference.

See, he told himself as he contortioned his foamed face in an effort to rid it of the daily stubbles, there have been lots of times she has been away, or you have. No big deal. She'll be home tonight. But as he dried his chin and neck, the thought didn't bring any comfort. An empty pit hung in his stomach, connected to his heart, despite the fact that was anatomically impossible.

144

Focused

Maybe he had been taking his wife for granted. Twenty-four years with the same woman could do that to a man. Day in and day out, routine flowed smoothly week after week, month after month, then on into years. Christina had seen to that. She was always so organized. Everything all neat and tidy. He never had to worry if his socks matched. They were always folded in pairs. His shirts were pressed, his food hot, his house clean. And his child? Well, at times Josh had been a handful in high school, but nothing major. He prided himself on being the good father, friend and disciplinarian. Now he wondered if she hadn't been the underlying cause of why their son turned out okay.

When Josh was a baby Christina underwent an emergency hysterectomy. Sure, her mother came to help out when she was in the hospital and for a few more days when she got home. Back then they cut you open tip to stern. Not like now with all the laser stuff they did. Marge had only been out from work two weeks. Or was it three?

After Christina's mother left, he figured he could handle things. Wrong. At the end of six hours, he plopped on her bed in total exhaustion and asked, "How do you do it all?"

His wife pulled herself up on the pillows and grinned through the pain. Her words still rang in his head as if it was yesterday. "Jeff, you haven't done the dishes, or the laundry, or dusted, or cleaned the toilets. You have only been watching after Josh. Thank goodness Mom left us several meals in the freezer."

The next year she went back to work and put Josh into day care. Jeff vowed he would never take his wife for granted again, so he tried to help with the housework here and there. And, he had to admit, for several years he'd done his fair share. Even kept up the lawn and house repairs to boot. Then Josh became old enough to do chores and he slacked off.

Yet she never missed a beat. She still made all of the Christmas presents by hand two years in a row when they were in an economic slump. Started them over the summer and worked on them in the evenings after work while he watched TV.

The guilt began to seep in as Jeff tightened his belt and went down the hall to check on the snail-paced coffee pot. He thought of all his wife did day in and day out over the years. She cooked, cleaned, led Josh's Cub Scout meetings, volunteered at the church. No wonder all those times she just felt too tired to be romantic. . .Now he understood. He felt like the biggest horse's patoot ever made.

He'd gone back on that vow made many years prior when his son was a crawling ball of energy, hadn't he? Not all at once. Just eased into it, like into a steaming hot tub, slow and smooth, a dawdling decline into slothfulness. Now, he even paid the Stemson's boy down the street to do the yard work. With Josh out of the house, Jeff figured it would become a lot easier for her. Maybe not. She still had him to clean up after. He washed his coffee cup and put it in the drainer. Then, in a light bulb moment, he headed back down the hall to the master bedroom.

Jeff hung the bath towel on the rod instead of leaving it in a clump on the bathroom floor as he normally did. He rinsed the residual shaving foam and hair stubs from the sink. He even made the bed. One glance at the bedside clock revealed all that effort had only taken a few minutes. He could do this, no sweat. Who knew?

It was time he stepped up to the plate and took on more responsibility. Starting today, things would be different. Yes, sir. And he'd tell her how much he appreciated all she did the moment she got home. Maybe he'd hire a maid to come in once a week. That could be her 50th birthday present, along with flowers and dinner someplace swanky, of course. After all, it was about six weeks away. The cruise? They'd take it for their twenty-fifth anniversary the next fall. Screw the pipes.

Yeah, that would be the ticket. Jeff felt a surge of husbandly goodness. In fact, if he hadn't felt so darn lousy and achy, he might have kicked his heels and whistled. 'Bout time I got on board with this 50/50 thing called marriage again. Make that 75/25. He confessed it to himself and the Almighty. Maybe this year he would sign up for the men's retreat. That would be the way to show her he was sincerely trying.

Chapter 21   The Road Home

An hour later Christina was on the road. She'd drop off the dishes and have another cup of coffee with Mrs. O... Dorothy. That meant a pit stop would be in order in an hour or so, but it was the least she could do. She scribbled her address, cell and house phone numbers on the back of one of her business cards, and also her email address in case Bud had hooked up a computer in the guest house. She placed it on the tray in her car, locked the cabin and headed up the road to the Owens.

She tapped on the kitchen door. Mrs. Owens sat darning a sock. The radio played a Willie Nelson classic, "Blue Eyes Crying in the Rain". How apropos.

"Come in," she motioned. "You just missed Bud and Bob. They're are off helping a neighbor cut up a tree that had tumbled over their road during the storm."

Christina heaved a sigh of relief. God does take care of the details. She'd wondered what else they'd have to say to each other and feared the goodbye scene. It would be like the porridge in the Three Bears storybook—too hot or too cold, never just right. She slid through the screened door and set the tray on the kitchen counter.

"Breakfast was delicious. Thank you so much. Just what the doctor ordered."

The woman nodded and set down her sewing. "Cup o' coffee?"

"Sure." Christina grabbed a cup from the shelf. Much to her delight, the conversation stayed casual. She showed Dorothy her latest picture of Josh. Dorothy smiled, then fetched a picture frame off the cupboard shelf. The photo showed Bud, Alice and their kids sitting on the porch along with his older brother Bill with his brood, too. Christina figured the photo to be two or three years old. As she got up to leave, she snapped her fingers. She grabbed the card form the tray and handed it to Dorothy.

"What's this? You two decided to stay in touch, huh?"

"Bud mentioned he might come visit us since Jeff hadn't been here with me and it's been a while since they've seen each other." *Get the hint. I am married. Nothing happened. Nothing will.*

"I'll give this to him when he comes back." Dorothy shoved the card in her housecoat pocket.

Christina hugged her new old friend good-bye.

"Ya take care, now. Drive safe. And let us see more of ya this summer, Okay?" Dorothy's voice cracked with emotion. She got a Kleenex out of her other pocket. "Dang spring pollen."

"Yeah." Christina responded. "That storm must've shook it all loose."

Focused

Her tires popped as she headed down their gravel drive onto the road that led back to the highway, and home. She left the old glasses at the cabin. Somehow that seemed fitting. Maybe someday she'd get them and take them to a charity. But now, they were safely tucked between the surfer shorts and Don't Mess with Texas T-shirt. She once again wore her now dry business casuals, minus the hosiery. They were her city clothes. That seemed fitting as well. Pun intended.

Looking back over the past twenty-four hours or so, Christina knew she'd done the right thing escaping to the Hill Country. She felt God's hand in the entire adventure. As she drove down the highway, she became contrite and asked God's forgiveness. She shouldn't get irked over the petty little things Jeff did. God knows she had her quirky habits, too. Maybe she needed to see the big things instead, like remembering more often why had she married him.

Because he's honest and gentlemanly. . .and ethical, and worked hard. . .she parroted what she had told her mother close to a quarter of a century ago. A quarter of a century. Twenty-five years in June since that conversation over the sudsy dishes, and then, their silver anniversary coming up in November. That made her feel ancient.

Brushing away the thought, she started to think of other good characteristics Jeff possessed. He didn't go bar hopping or women gazing. He went to church. He had even agreed to take on Father Rick's latest challenge. Christina's brain rewound the tape of that particular sermon last month.

Julie B Cosgrove

"Dear people. This Lent I challenge each of you to do what I ask you to do every Sunday right before the General Confession. 'Draw near with faith.' How? Three ways. Pray out loud together as a family at least once a day. Yes, the dinner table counts. But I warn you, once you get into this, your dinner might get cold."

Giggles filtered through the pews. Jeff actually grabbed the stubby pencil out of the well in the pew along with a Prayer Request card.

"What are you doing?" she whispered.

He flipped over the card to the blank side. "Sshhh. Writing this down."

That day over lunch at the local diner he held out his hand, took hers and said Grace. It was a beginning. For several nights after that, even though they sat in the den to eat and used TV trays, he pushed the mute button then came over to the couch to sit with her. They said Grace and sometimes a short prayer for a sick friend or hurting co-worker. Then he'd move to the recliner, tray and all. Instead of being upset he picked up and moved to his sanctuary of the recliner, why hadn't I just been thankful he was making an effort and had actually hit the mute button?

She tapped her nails on the steering wheel. Bud was so easy to talk to. Jeff used to be as well. Maybe she'd become the one to clam up. Lately she'd had these inward tirades which she never let out in the open. She hadn't been letting any of the good thoughts out either. Regret crept into her tear ducts. She blinked it away and changed the subject in her mind.

152

Focused

What had Father Rick's second challenge been? Oh yes. To be expectant. To believe God did all things for the good. To be like a child at Christmas anticipating the presents. . . Or was it presence? She smiled. One of her favorite hymns was "Surely the Presence of the Lord is in This Place". They often sung it at St. Martin's during Eucharist. She started to hum the tune, then stopped.

Oh. Now I see. I drove three hours to find you on a rock stoop, God. But You've been by me all along, haven't You? Your presence is anywhere I need it to be.

Just then, a car pulled in front of her into her lane so another could whiz by them to the left, going well over the limit. It had a bumper sticker, rather faded, but still readable.

"If you think God is not in your life - Guess who moved?"

She had to pull over. That was too surreal. She dialed Jeff's work number.

"Jeff Willis." His words sounded strained.

"Hi. It's me. I'm on the road. I had breakfast first. Mrs. Owens made eggs, sausage gravy and biscuits. We had a nice talk. Anyway, I'm headed home." She took a breath and swallowed.

"Right."

His tone of voice had not improved. She hardly could blame him. Still, there was something else in his voice she couldn't quite put a finger on.

"Jeff? You sound... strange."

"I'm okay. Just got a heck of a headache. Sinus. Was there anything else you wanted to say?" He sniffed and swallowed hard, followed by a shallow cough.

She caught the harried tone. He was too busy. Trying not to let it sting her, she said "Not over the cell. Later when I see you, Okay? Hold on."

A high-pitched grind grew increasingly louder and then a whoosh rattled her car. "Dang that eighteen-wheeler was loud. He nearly pushed me off the road, he went by so fast."

"I heard it."

"Look, I just called to let you know I was on my way back. I'll explain later once I've sorted it all out."

There was no response. Only silence and the whir of the traffic whipping by her other ear like a hive of irritated bees. "Jeff?" For a moment she thought she'd lost the signal.

"I'm here." His voice softened. "I always will be, hon."

Christina remembered the third point to the sermon. Forbearance."I know. I do love you Jeff. And I'm sorry I've been such a ...you know."

"Yeah. I know. Maybe I have, too." She heard the creak of his desk chair as he repositioned his body. His throat cleared. "I've sorted some stuff out, too, while you were away. We'll discuss it all tonight. Got a bid proposal in thirty minutes."

"Good luck. Bye, hon."

His business tone of voice returned. "Drive safe. Oh, and call your son. Bye."

She sighed and clicked off her phone. Short, sweet, to the point, non-emotional, don't waste my time. That's my Jeff.

Chapter 22   Off the Hook

Christina got back in her lane and up to speed with the other travelers experiencing Texas at seventy miles per hour. She flicked on the satellite radio again. Suddenly she heard an old song she hadn't listened to in at least ten years, "My Father's Eyes" by Amy Grant. It told of how the singer wanted to see the world through God's eyes, not her own.

"Okay, Lord. I think I got it," she said out loud to the upholstered inside of her car's top.

She accepted the holy remedy for her outlook. With her new glasses she had better sight. With her Hill Country revelation she had better insight.

She could now see people a little more the way God sees them, as people worth cherishing. Faulty, stumbling sinners, just like her, but all with a potential in them if you knew where to look — inside their hearts. Everyone sought a purpose to life and a loving God who cared and made sense of it all. It's easy to see Him in a stranger. But in a person you see day in and day out and know where all their moles are . . . well, that was harder. And yourself? Well, that was the hardest of all.

She didn't want Pollyanna-like, rose-colored lenses anymore to mask her world, as if all was hunky dory and status quo. She needed her Father's eyes to see clearly the world as it is, yet filtered by love for the potential it held and forgiveness for the shortcomings. And, that meant altering the way she saw Jeff, and Josh, Bud, her friends. . .and herself.

To God, and to herself, she made a vow. No more worrying what everyone else saw. No more goldfish bowl mentality. From now one, she'd be too busy doing what she was supposed to, going about God's business. There would be no time to worry about what others saw in her. Maybe, they'd just see Him.

Her pep talk broke when she noticed flashing lights inching closer in her rearview mirror. Wasn't for her. She had the cruise control on. Christina switched lanes so the state trooper's vehicle could safely pass. She said a quick prayer, hoping wherever he was headed and for whatever reason, it wasn't too bad. Maybe he was after that eighteen wheeler which dashed by so fast. Maybe she should veg out a while and stop thinking so much. She noticed the little needle edging towards the "E". Maybe, Christina, it would be a good idea to stop up ahead, use the facilities, gas up and get a Diet Coke.

She pulled into a roadside station. Though its sign was chipped and faded, no hose ding-dinged when a car ran over it. Whatever happened to the real stations where servicemen dashed out rags in hand ready to be of service? Wasn't that why they were

156

called Service Stations? Or were they called just Gas Stations now? Texans did hang on to old terms.

She giggled at the sign above the door. Gas N' Git. Underneath it sprawled a poster announcing chilidogs for only a dollar twenty-nine. From the anticipated gastric distress she'd get if she devoured one of them, the convenience store's name seemed appropriate. The pun transported her thoughts back to one of the few real vacations her family had taken. It was to New York and Washington D.C. Christina was thirteen at the time.

"I just can't believe all these people," her mother had said, jostled by the crowds all heading their own direction with speedy determination. "How rude. Excuse me. Please." She had to speak at each one that went by. That was the Texan thing to do. The looks she received in reply resembled the expressions of criminals on the wanted posters in the Post Office.

"Anyone would be nuts to live here with millions of other folks." Carrie grumbled. She hadn't liked going on this trip. She was missing the pool party of the century at Becky's house.

Her father stopped in his tracks and began to laugh. He pointed at the coffee shop across the street on the corner called Chock Full of Nuts.

"Yep, even they think they are." The Texan tourists looked at the line to get in the coffee shop wind around the corner. The coffee shop was chockfull alright. Not used to big Eastern city hustle and bustle, surrounds and sounds, and swarms of shoulder to shoulder people, the frazzled family burst into laughter, causing even more alienating looks.

Julie B Cosgrove

Now that coffee was sold in bags at her local grocery store in the gourmet section. Well, it was really only one half of one aisle—hardly a section as the sign above it claimed. Another example of small town trying to imitate big city. But, the memory gave her an idea. Maybe she and Jeff should get away for a vacation for their twenty-fifth. A real one. They had never traveled, unless it was to visit a distant relative, go to a wedding or a funeral.

After getting her car's tank refueled, and hers emptied, she sat on the hood of her car in the parking lot sipping on a cold Diet Coke. She still had plenty of time and she suddenly felt tired. Drained was more like it. She bopped herself in the head, thinking of the pun, considering she had just noticed a piece of toilet tissue stuck on her left heel. Punning was contagious. Once your mind started, it was hard to stop. Her father had been a master of it.

What had she been thinking about? New York? Nuts? Vacation? She wandered to the picnic area on the side of the station. Suddenly like slides from an old projector, her family, her life and her friends appeared lit in front of her mind, one after another. Christina saw the good in them, the reasons they were special. She sipped her drink and watched the traffic whiz by her too fast to notice the peaceful smile on her face.

The trees in the field surrounding the picnic area began to sway as a welcomed breeze blew through them. She could see every leaf gleaming in the sun, the breeze making them sparkle as if they were glittered. Gosh, these new glasses make everything so much clearer. Oh, well, can't sit here all day. She sighed,

158

walked to her car and clicked the keyless entry button. Putting the rest of her drink in the holder, she buckled up, checked the rearview mirror, and then started the ignition. Then the voice of her husband played again in her head. "Call your son."

The dash said 11:17 a.m. He'd be awake. But, does he have class? She racked her brain for his schedule. What was today, anyway? She plugged her cell into the car jack, flipped it open and punched J. His cell number gleamed back at her. She punched the send button.

" 'Lo?" A groggy grumble answered.

"Josh. Hi, it's Mom." *Sound cheery, all's okay.*

"Where are you?" He yawned and made a stretching noise.

"On 290, heading back from the cabin."

"The cabin!" The male tone raised two octaves. "Mom, there was a flood."

"Yeah, hon. I know. I was there. But, I'm fine. The place looks really bad, though. I think next summer we all should…"

"I called you. Twice." Anger and hurt mingled in his response.

Yep, he's awake now. "You can't get good reception up there, especially when it's stormy. Sorry."

"Yeah, well next time, let me know when you go off on a whim. I was worried sick."

The disciplinary tone of his voice amused her. "Josh?" She laughed. "Did you just hear yourself?"

"Yeah. Weird, huh. I sound like you." An embarrassed snort. Then his throat cleared. Now he sounded like his dad. Same sinuses. Same mannerisms.

Julie B Cosgrove

"Being an adult means worrying about those you love."

She heard him groan and stretch. His bed springs did the same.

"Does this begin a lecture?" His voice sounded impatient.

"Not at all, if you won't give me one. Deal?"

"Deal."

She smiled into her cell phone now warm against her cheek. Matched her mood. "Love ya. Guess we both need to get to work, huh?"

"Yeah, guess so. Glad you called. Bye Mom. Talk soon."

Her boy, all grown up, clicked off.

Pulling out of the station, Christina continued on her trek back to her reality. About 50 miles down the road, she slowed when she saw the taillights ahead. Back to the traffic was more like it. Welcome home to humanity.

Christina exited off the highway and turned onto the less congested feeder lane, a trick she had learned long ago in her daily commutes. A bit of exhilaration always inched unto her shoulders as she threw them back and watched her fellow citizens crammed in like sheep on the highway beside her. For once, being different and not following the crowd was a good thing. She vowed to do it more often, not just on the highway. She remembered Robert Frost's poem she'd memorized in sixth grade, *The Road Less Traveled*. "... I took the one less traveled by. And that has made all the difference."

Focused

She really should make an appearance at work. But in wrinkled day-old clothes? Maybe she should just blow the rest of the day. But Christina knew better. Instead, she should stop off at the German bakery a few exits further and get Kolaches for everyone. Her mouth watered at the thought of the soft dough rolls with fruit jam centers.

Why was she even thinking about food after Dorothy's humongous breakfast? The clock on her dash now said 12:15. *Oh. Maybe that's why.*

Kolaches it would be, and apologies all around. The people she worked with were great people. No one backstabbed or gossiped. Mr. Caruthers respected each of them and the part they played in his steadily growing company. Most of them had worked there at least ten years, except Casey and Shermika who were each hired to help handle the load increase over the past few years.

And maybe I'll buy some specialty tea or coffee, too. She admitted to herself the gesture would be mostly out of gratitude, but a little out of guilt for playing hooky and leaving them in the lurch so close to April 15th.

But, the Old Christina tried to rationalize, that's why they had a Personal Time Off policy, so an employee could take off when they needed to. Yesterday morning, she justified, she needed to take off or she might have blown a fuse. The flood had been out of her control. No one could blame her for that.

Then, the Christina with a newly focused attitude kicked in. She called Sandy from her cell phone. "Listen, I apologize if I've been short with you or anyone else at work lately."

Sandy said, "Don't even think a thing like that," adding, "The way we all have to work, and keep a house and a family, it's a miracle we are not all in the loony bin."

"I guess so. Is it nuts there?" Chock full of nuts, she thought with a grin.

"Nah, we're good."

"I know that." She punned, again. They were used to it at the office.

Sandy laughed. "Here's Angela."

"Hey, are you okay? Jeff called and left a message," her friend and coworker's voice boomed.

"He did? Good. I asked him, too. An old friend was in trouble and needed me up near our summer place. It started pouring and then the flood came. I was stranded." *Well, it's mostly true.*

"Are you on the road? There's a lot of background noise," Angela's voice boomed again.

"Yeah. I'm on my way into work," Christina raised her voice as well. "Thing is I'm in crumpled clothes and no hose."

Angela laughed. "Then you've got to come in. No one will believe it if I tell them you aren't wearing hose."

"Or have any makeup on?"

"Oh. That would be too much a drastic change. Everyone would keel over from shock. Call me when you are pulling in. I'll meet you in the Ladies and you can borrow some."   After a few more minutes of discussing trivial events in the office, they clicked off.

Focused

Next door to the Czech Bakery was a small boutique. It had a cute blouse in the window. She hesitated. Nah. The cat was already out of the bag. Besides, she'd spent enough on her new glasses. Arriving crumpled it would be.

A little after 2p.m., she texted Angela's cell as she pulled into the parking lot behind her office complex. True to her word, Angela waited in the Ladies' Room with her bag of makeup and a curling iron.

"Good God. Look what the cat drug in."

Christina cringed. Maybe she needed a total make-over. That's the second time in twenty-four hours someone said that to her.

Chapter 23 Kolaches and Cheeseburgers

"Well, I was helping stranded grandmothers get pulled out of creeks. What did you expect?" Christina looked in the mirror. She really needed to get her hair cut. Maybe a whole new style to go with the new glasses. *Right, the ones nobody's suppose to notice?*

"Really? Wow, I want to hear all about it." Angela leaned her back against the sink and crossed her legs.

"Maybe someday. Not now. I'm bone tired. I've been wet then dry too many times in the last two days. Uh, thanks for the goody bag of makeup." She flicked on the curling iron.

"You know I always keep them in my desk."

"I had heard rumors…"

They both laughed. Their voices bounced off the tile walls and echoed into the stalls.

"Sshhh. We'll have the whole office in here. Oh look." Angela opened the first stall door and took something off the hook. "It's a blouse I just got back from the cleaners. It may be a little big, but…"

Julie B Cosgrove

"Bless you. You are an angel. I owe you."

"Just hand over what's in that marvelous smelling bag." She picked it up and sniffed.

"It's a peace offering. Save some for the others, okay? By the way, how's Marcos? Has he gone back to day care? Is his throat still sore?" The two chattered as Christina preened.

Being gone a day was a poor idea. It had all hit the fan and landed on her desk. Along with a dozen peppermint carnations nestled in fern and baby's breath and a sealed florist's card.

She sensed all eyes on her as she ripped it open and read the message. The note simply said, "No matter what's going on, I love you. Jeff."

She stuffed the card in her pocket. "It's just from Jeff. He knew I had to leave town on family stuff."

"So, no huge fight and make-up attempt, then?" Angela asked for the rest. "That was our guess. Thought you'd left in a huff. Things have been building between you two."

Christina waved the idea away. "No, nothing like that."

Well, almost not like that. Christina thought she'd done a pretty good job covering up her home troubles. But then again, they were all far too close after working together so many years to hide much from each other. She supposed she'd let snippets slip out over hen sessions during lunch a few times.

In spite of their closeness, only one of her coworkers noticed her new glasses. Sandy, on the way back from the break room, a Kolache in her hand,

166

winked a thank you at Christina, then stopped. She did a double take and began to walk backwards. Pausing at the front of Christina's desk, she locked her elbows, leaned forward and said, "Okay, I give up. Something is different. It's not your hair is it? No. New makeup?"

Christina could hear Angela snicker over the new makeup guess. She smiled and patiently waited for her friend to figure it out.

Sandy stepped back, snapped her fingers and crowed, "I've got it!"

That sent the other women and even her boss dashing over to her desk. Christina felt like hiding under her mouse pad.

"Glasses! When did you get new glasses?" she shrieked.

All at once the murmuring and the "Oh, they are so nice" comments started.

Her boss smirked, "Did I overpay you by mistake?" He then turned to go back into his office with another piece of her peace offering in his hand. Everyone laughed. Christina turned crimson.

"So, does this mean no more head bobbing in front of the computer?" Angela demonstrated for effect.

"And, no more peering over the glasses like a school marm, either, I suppose?" Sandy quipped, not to be outdone.

Christina dragged the vase in front of her and crouched behind the peppermint blossoms. "Come on y'all. Was it that bad?"

In unison, came the "Yes!"—even from the boss's office, along with, "Recess is over, ladies."

Julie B Cosgrove

They slowly filtered back to their workstations. But off and on through the rest of the day, the compliments continued. Relief poured over her when the hands of the clock hit five. She turned off her computer, locked her desk and grabbed her purse. She never liked being the center of attention. In the goldfish bowl of life, she always sought to hide behind the seaweed or the bubbly windmill.

Being an accounting clerk, Christina wasted no time figuring out how to compensate for the charge that would appear on her VISA. She would take her lunch for a month or two and tell everyone she needed to save money. Maybe they'd figure she had to shell out to the IRS.

Then she caught herself. No, she wasn't going to worry what the others thought, or what Jeff did either. She needed new glasses. Period. Over a year ago he had said it was her choice. It wasn't a matter of deserving them or not, but needing them. She'd squeeze it into the budget somehow, with God's help, who had given her the talent of accounting anyway.

Forty minutes later, Christina was on the road again, as a Willie Nelson tune stated. This time, it was back to Allensville. She flicked on her headlights as the pomegranate sun off her left started to set in wispy fingers of pink and gold clouds above the hills beyond the skyline. She decided to stop off at Bubba's Burger Barn and order Jeff's favorite type of cheeseburger, and two chocolate sundaes with nuts.

Maybe then he wouldn't ask too many questions she didn't yet know how to answer. This Hill Country jaunt and its eye-opener was her secret, her

168

insight, a shiny trinket just for her. She wanted to cherish it a little longer before she shared it with him—and mull it over in her heart more. Besides, she owed him for the flowers.

Old habits die hard. Would he begin to notice a change in her? Did he ever notice anything about her? She told herself to stop that talk. No more. Her inner mind waggled its finger at her. Otherwise called The Counselor, The Holy Spirit, and her eternal guide. She had silenced Him for too long in favor of her own self pity and pride. Two sides of the coin. Both focused on herself, not Him. Something she would endeavor to stop doing.

Still, I wonder if Jeff will notice my new glasses.

So often the "blight flight" of urbanites leads to encroachment on the small towns and ranches, eventually engulfing them in the name of progress. What was once an open field surrenders its existence to strip malls and treeless subdivisions. The boundaries between the sprawling metropolis hustle-bustle and small town familiarity become blurred.

It was in one of those dichotomous areas that Jeff and Christina decided to make their home. They owned a half acre lot in a neighborhood sandwiched between the town of Allensville and yet to be annexed county land, fifteen miles from the capitol city. The best of both worlds. Unlike her mother to her father, Christina chose the small town life over the big city, thus relieving Jeff of the social burden of proving himself worthy enough to have "landed a society chick". Besides, they could never afford the "goldfish bowl" social life in the old money neighborhoods. In the past, she feared that fact might have labeled her, and him, as a failure, though she preferred the term rebel.

Now the substitute goldfish bowl she had created in her world of suburbia was shattered as well. A freedom swept over her as she headed down the hill to the small lights beginning to flicker in homes and hearths of the valley that nestled her town.

Pulling into her driveway, she noticed the front porch light on as well as the carriage lamps at the front of the recessed garage. But, no lights were on inside, except the one over the kitchen sink, a universal signal of no one awake or at home. The shock flushed the back of her neck. Where was he? He was always home, except on Boy Scout council night. And that's not tonight, right? She idled the car in the driveway as she flipped open and punched the app for her calendar. No, it's next Tuesday. Hmmm. Where is he?

She shook off the mounting gloom of abandonment, refusing to entertain that thought a nanosecond longer. She punched the opener and pulled her car in . . . next to his? As Christina opened the kitchen door and set down her purse, she saw a note on the counter in Jeff's hen scratch, still as undecipherable as the Navaho submissions in WWII, even after twenty -five years of trying to read it. It told her he came home early from work feeling lousy and went to bed early. She guessed that was what the note said. Something close to it anyway.

That was one of the differences between her and Jeff. When he felt sick, he slept it off. She never could sleep when she was hurting or had a cold. She always envied him that talent.

Focused

Well, at least she'd the rest of the evening to herself for a change. Then she felt bitchy for thinking it. Old habits do die hard, right?

She put the sundaes in the freezer and put her Mandarin chicken salad in the fridge for lunch the next day. She shoved the Paul Newman face on the salad dressing pouch in there as well. *No more piercing blue eyes today, please.* Tonight, she'd rather chomp into the bacon cheeseburger and fries she had ordered for her husband whose waist never expanded. She prayed hers wouldn't, then asked for forgiveness for her gluttony.

Fat Cat trotted over to rub against her legs, twisted back and forth in a lopsided figure eight, and looked up with woeful eyes. He always missed her and felt abandoned when she was out of the house, whether it was ten minutes or ten days—at least he purposely made her feel that way. She picked him up and nuzzled into his fur, then passed through the kitchen into the den. She flicked on the lamp to better navigate through the den and down the hall to the first bedroom, now their office. She caught up on her e-mails as she chomped on her dinner. After the tenth one, her eyes drooped. Not even the cute one with the deer licking a kitten and the one with the latest Maxine jokes couldn't even keep her attention.

"A bubble bath. A hot steaming bubble bath. That's what I need." She informed her feline dinner guest.

She ran the tub in the hall bath, filling it with billowy suds. Christina eased down into the luxury, leaned her head against the blow-up bath pillow, closed her eyes and drifted into comfort. The chill of the past thirty hours finally oozed out of her pores. She soaked until her fingers pruned. Then she crawled into bed, all warmed, relaxed and reeking of the lemongrass bubble bath Jeff gave her for Christmas.

The lump next to her grumbled into its pillow. "Hi. You back?"

"Yeah. You sick?"

"I caught that cold going around the office. I took some nighttime cold medicine." He slurred, then yawned. There was a tug on the covers as he rolled over and settled back down into his nest of sheets.

She leaned over and brushed a lock of grayish hair out of his eyes. "Sleep tight. Hope ya feel better tomorrow."

"Mmhmm." Was the response followed by a snuffle and a snore.

Welcome home, she thought. Missed you, too. She suddenly missed the warmth of the Owens' home. And their company. One in particular.

Chapter 24 Hindsight

In her women's Bible study the next Tuesday, they read in Psalms about David. He asked the Lord to seek out the motives in his heart and correct them. The study leader asked if any of the ladies felt their motives or thoughts needed correcting.

Timidly, Christina half-raised her hand with every ounce of inner strength. I've known these ladies for over fifteen years. Why can't I feel safe enough to tell the truth? Why can't I just admit my life's not Christian perfect, especially as of late.

A yearning for commonality nudged her forward. Maybe, just maybe, someone else here felt the same way."My thoughts sometimes turn into…well," she closed her eyes and gulped, "into these, these, oh, I don't know." She rushed to get the words out before it became too embarrassing. "Into internal tirades I never thought I could be capable of thinking, and would never, ever, let out into the open."

She swallowed her emotions down like reflux acid. Come to think of it, she experienced indigestion lately. Her eyes darted around the circle of women with Bibles balanced on laps, pleading for acknowledgement but not holding out a chance of finding it. "Do any of you…?"

"Welcome to the road of turning middle aged. It gets bumpy from here, dear." Olive sang-sung. Murmured chuckles sounded and heads bobbed in response.

"Honey," Mildred said with a wave of her hand as if she'd swatted away a pesky mosquito, "that's totally normal. It's just hormones. Right, girls?" She nodded around the room for affirmation. Several others acknowledged back with nods, a short laugh, or a sympathetic peer over reading glasses. "God understands. He made us that way."

"My mother just went through all of that last year," Janice volunteered. "I thought she was going to drive us all nuts."

Several stifled cackles and Bible page shuffles filled the room. Janice crimsoned. "Sorry. I didn't mean you are driving us nuts, Christina. I just meant that, yes, it is normal. I guess." Janice stopped and slumped in her chair, staring at an imaginary spot on the rug.

Mary Ellen, sitting next to her, reached over and squeezed her hand. "No harm done, dear."

Christina felt relieved. Her friends didn't believe that she'd turned into a heathen ogre. With a sigh she said, "Sorry for interrupting the study. Go on."

The women smiled and continued with the next verse.

Focused

When the study was over, Christina scooted into the driver's side of her car and noticed the clock on the dash said 9:23. She sped home and dashed in the door and dropped her stuff on the bar between the kitchen and the den. Jeff watched a Star Trek rerun on TV through the evening paper held up to his face, a feat only men knew how to do.

"Sorry I'm late. Were you worried?"

"Why would I worry? I know hen sessions can drag on and on. You carry the cell phone I got you. Josh did program in your ICE, right?"

"My what? Ice?"

"I-C-E. In case of emergency numbers. The ones highlighted in red."

She hated his condescending tone of voice. She had a fleeting, impish inspiration of deleting his cell phone number from the list. Then she chided herself for the thought. She wasn't sure she knew how, anyway. Instead, she apologized to Jeff for the past few days for her harried state of mind.

"The day after I got back to work Angela's grandson had to have a tonsillectomy. He can't go back to daycare for a few more days. She'll be out for a week."

"Why?" Jeff snapped the newspaper and peered over at her. As usual he was holding court from the recliner.

"Her daughter's already used all of her sick leave on his frequent sore throats. Then this afternoon, Mary's aunt passed away and she dashed out of town."

"So that leaves who to handle both the account payables and receivables for the rest of the week? Let me guess. You, right?"

Julie B Cosgrove

"Well, Angela did print and send out the statements. But that's left me to handle all the phone calls of customers who just got their bill in the mail and of course have oodles of questions."

"Of course. You take on too much at that place."

"It's a small office, Jeff. We depend on each other. Mr. Caruthers does, too. He did give me a hefty bonus last Christmas." she shrugged off the added stress. "Besides, I can't fault Angela. She tried to help out instead of leaving us in the lurch." Christina parroted what she told the receptionist Sandy earlier that day. "Sandy's solution was to make a recording on Angela's voice mail."

"But you couldn't do that could you?" Jeff responded.

Worry and hurt stabbed her as she misinterpreted his comment. But she didn't ask for clarification. She just assumed . . . Instead, she picked up a magazine and blinked away the tears. *Welcome back to normal. Why would I think it would change?*

Two nights later, when she still couldn't sleep, she lay in bed thinking of what the women and Jeff said. Maybe Jeff was just upset because he worried about her working so hard.

In fact, Jeff became very understanding. The last thing Christina wanted when she got home was to talk on the phone. Jeff surprised her by playing personal secretary and screening the usual "Hi, how are you, did you hear about" phone calls from friends and family.

Focused

Hmmm. So he's not all that bad after all, right? Maybe he did understand. I know deep down he is just as hard working so, maybe he's tried to identify with me.

Twenty-twenty hindsight now made her see she might have assumed wrong—about a lot of things. Perhaps there'd be fewer restless nights. *How hard it is to slough off these old feelings, Lord. Please help me do so.*

Fat Cat sensed she was awake. He hopped onto the bedside table and swished his tail back and forth. Her new glasses flipped onto her pillow. She had to laugh. *Got the message, God. Thank you.*

On Sunday, it was Christina's turn to clean up after the pot luck lunch at church.

"Can you possibly hurry it up?" Jeff muttered in her ear as he leaned on the fold-out table in the church's parish hall. "The game's on in twenty minutes."

"Move. I got to wipe it down." She didn't look up, but waved the cloth at him. "Go on. I'll meet you in the parking lot."

He could have taped the darn show. She wiped the table a little harder. He knew the potluck was today. She heard him stomp away and the door shut just a bit too strong.

"The game's gonna be a landslide and he'll be in a foul mood anyway," she predicted under her breath.

Harriet happened to be walking by folding a table cloth under her chin. "You say something?"

"Huh. No. Mumbling to myself." She looked up. Evidently her expression caught her friend's attention. "Jeff's anxious to get home to the game."

"Can't see why," Harriet shrugged. "They never have a good basketball team. To be in the final 16 is a fluke. All the broadcasters said so. Men, huh?"

Christina sighed and looked outside. Through the narrow windows she saw Jeff pacing, jiggling his keys and the change in his side pants pocket.

Boy, how I hate that. "I better get, Harriet. See ya Tuesday for Bible study?"

"Okay, dear. Thanks again. You always work so hard to make these a success."

"Pfft. No more than you do." Christina felt her face crimson.

"And that casserole was yummy. I need that recipe." Harriet dug in her purse for a pen, the pew bulletin on the table in front of her, poised and ready.

"The recipe was in last month's *Stylish Southern Home*. It's not original. I'll email it, okay?" she called as she closed the door.

She hurried to the truck. He started the engine.

"Are you mad?" she asked as she slid into her seat and shut her own car door.

"No, I just want get home." He twisted around behind as he backed out of the parking space.

"Did you like the casserole?"

"Sure. It went down okay." He tapped his fingers on the steering wheel as he watched for a break in the stream of cars. He pointed to the street. "Dang. See, this is what happens when you stay behind. Now the Methodists and the Baptists have let out. Look at the traffic."

Focused

Christina turned to watch the cars zip by her side-view mirror. She kept silent the rest of the way home, as usual, wishing to avoid any conflict. She wondered why it never occurred to either her or Jeff to just come in separate vehicles. Perhaps because everyone viewed them as a couple, two halves making a whole. Out of habit, perhaps they did as well. They went together and left together. Always had.

Did the people in their congregation admire them for sticking it out so long when so many others of their generation divorced and went their separate ways? Christina wondered how many couples who'd been married as long as she and Jeff still really liked each other.

She took off her glasses and rubbed her eyes. Why did I expect it all to change after my escape? We haven't even talked about it.

She longed for a friendly shoulder rub and those wonderful steel blue eyes who'd listen to her troubles.

Chapter 27   Tea and Sympathy

That evening, Christina sat on the steps of the back porch listening to the night creatures begin to stir and make their sounds—crickets, an owl, the toads down by the pond at the end of their street. She heard a little questioning mew and felt the familiar soft pressure of Fat Cat rubbing across her back.

"Momma's boy. He can't bear to be without you." Her husband chided as he pulled the slider screen open and brought her a glass of iced tea.

"I don't mind," she replied as she picked up the purring cat and nuzzled his fur. "Is the game over?"

"Yeah, before it began."

"Sorry." She looked at her husband whose pallor no longer resembled a mime's. "You seem a lot better, hon."

"I feel better." He plopped down next to her with a creak of his left knee. "Now what about you? You've been different since you went to the cabin. I want to know why. Can we talk about it now?"

Julie B Cosgrove

"I guess. . ." Her voice cracked, imitating his kneecap, and she took off her glasses to rub her eyes. His questions caught her by surprise and she felt a pang of guilt that she could have entertained the thought he was too shallow and self-involved to notice a change in her attitude. It made her feel like she was the one being shallow. And here she'd vowed to see things differently. Yep, it's true. Old habits die hard. Old thoughts patterns, too.

She felt her husband's warm weight shift beside her, then his hand on her knee. The look on his face proved Jeff didn't know how to judge her mood. *Can't blame the guy. Even to me it keeps flipping back and forth.* She sniffled down the clump her heart lodged in her throat. "I guess it has all just been building."

"Yeah, it has," he replied and squeezed her knee. He started ticking off the stressful events over the past few years on his fingers—her dad's death, then her mom's, settling both of their estates with her siblings. "That was a real headache. Being an only child, I had no idea how siblings could bruise each other's feelings so much." He shifted his hand to her shoulders and rubbed the tension from them.

"Hmm. How did you know I needed that?"

He stopped for a moment, then continued both with the rub-down and the litany. "Then Josh moved out, started college and the nest emptied. Add to that training two new people at work, your sister's surgery, tax time, housing another couple for two months until their lame insurance agent admitted their fire was not the work of arson … Have I left anything out, like, maybe a shift in hormone levels?"

She felt her cheeks flame.

182

Focused

"I was wondering when Mount Vesuvius was going to spew." Jeff dropped his hand.

"Okay. You're right." His kindness stabbed her in the heart. Had her escapade been a revelation for him as well? Was this real or forced? It had been so long since she had experienced any tenderness from him. How could they begin to be a couple, again? Her questions swirled in a waterspout of doubt, trust, chastisement and pardon.

After a few moments of silence, Jeff cleared his throat. "Honey, is that all it is? I mean, something's been going on over the last few months...maybe longer. It's like this cloud hovering over our house."

She cast her eyes to the wooden planks on the deck. A Cub Scout troop had practiced their knots in her stomach for several minutes. One of the knots now moved into her throat. She tried hard to swallow it back down and breathe slowly.

He turned to face her and lifted her chin with his hands cupped on either side. "I can never replace your dad. I know you miss him, but you have me. He gave you to me close to twenty-five years ago. Dang, I feel like I need to walk on egg shells in my own..."

His words blasted open the flood gates that rivaled any in the Hill Country. Shaking sobs burst forth from her body.

Jeff put his hand on her shoulder, then pulled away, perplexed as to what to do. Finally he drew her into his chest and let her burble all over it.

It was a good fifteen minutes and four Kleenex later before Christina felt she could speak. She shook off her angst and gave him a weak nod. *I have to gain control. He deserves an explanation.*

Julie B Cosgrove

Jeff sat quietly and listened as his wife babbled on about her Hill Country revelation. He stared at the bottom step, often nodding as she spoke. He hoped not looking directly at her would make it easier, like sitting behind a confessional screen. She told him all about her secret excursion to the cabin, her insight and her glasses, how she'd felt so angry inside and how everything seemed clouded in negative and hurtful thoughts. Next, she apologized that he kept getting the short end of the whipping stick she'd been using on the world, and herself.

"I thought maybe it was your dad's death and maybe a middle-aged female hormone thing. But, it's so much more, isn't it, Babe." He finally said.

She grinned. "You men. That's your excuse for everything, isn't it?"

He shrugged.

She playfully slapped his thigh, then chided him, her hands on her hip. "Jeff."

Another shrug, with a small smirk.

She brushed his back with the palm of her hand. "Seriously, I'm sorry, hon. My emotions, up until my jaunt to the Hill Country, kept bouncing off the walls inside of me no matter how hard I tried to stifle them. Now I realize I've stifled all my emotions out of fear if one broke from the chain of pearls, the rest would burst off and roll helter-skelter, good or bad. "

"Mostly in my direction?" He shrunk back in mocked fear.

That made her laugh. He couldn't hack seriousness for too long of a stretch. Comic relief was his defense, one she at first took offense to, but later

184

understood. In fact, she developed the habit over the years, seasoned with her father's punning gene. It often eased tension between them.

"Want more tea?" He stood and put space between them to give his wife time to compose herself.

When he came back with full glasses, her tear ducts were empty, her nose blown and her hands steadier. "There's more Jeff," she whispered apologetically.

"Go for it," he muttered from his tilted glass. The ice clunked together and settled. So did her thoughts.

"Okay. Do you ever remember me telling you how I always felt the Hill Country was God's country. Literally?"

"Sure. Wait, you mean like Mount Sinai or something? That's a little Old Testament, isn't it?"

"Well, yes, maybe. I mean I just always felt I could talk to Him up there. Maybe its being in the middle of nature. I don't know."

"Hon, I think that's a pretty common reaction. That's why they have retreats in the sticks." His eyes gleamed. She rolled her eyes and took a gulp of the cool amber caffeine.

Then she spoke of her newly found closeness to God and her sense of guilt for drifting from Him over the years, turning Scripture into platitudes alongside her mother's life-quilt of sayings.

Christina could tell by his look that he knew this was important stuff to her. Instead of the normal glazed over effect when she began a "God talk", Jeff kept his eyes glued to hers. He appeared to be really listening to her words and occasionally nodded.

Julie B Cosgrove

When she finally caught her breath and quit talking Jeff rose from the deck, then whispered, "Stay put. I'll be right back."

Puzzled, Christina watched Jeff go into the house. Maybe too much iced tea? *Did I babble on that long, poor man?*

She heard him open the pantry. He brought out the bottle of Bordeaux one of the neighbors had given them for Christmas, which she kept meaning to throw out or give away. In his fingers dangled the wedding toasting goblets she'd kept in the china hutch along with her grandmother's tea cups and silver spoons. Her heart melted. *He's really trying.*

He sat back down, put the bottle between his knees and began to wiggle the cork loose with his thumbs. "I guess this has aged enough," he quipped as he poured them both a glass.

She watched, rather perplexed. "But…we rarely drink except possibly a toast on New Year's and maybe on our anniversary. If we even remember to do so." *And this is the second time in a week a man's offered me a drink. Well, I did offer one to Bud first.* Her attention returned to Jeff's voice.

"… and anyway, If I recall right, in the Bible Paul told Timothy a little wine in moderation was a good thing, you know." He handed her a glass then clinked it against his. He winked, tilted his it back and took a deep swallow.

Surprised he remembered that in Paul's 2nd Letter to Timothy, she raised her glass and took a sip. She tried her level best not to winch as the dry sourness slid to meet her tonsils. *Definitely not Boone's Farm. Perhaps that was a good thing.*

Focused

"It's not all you, Babe," her husband admitted. "I've been a royal pain in the tush. Even the guys at work have said something." The look in his eye bordered on that of a puppy sitting near a puddle on the rug.

"Well, I…"

"No. I admit it." He raised his hand in surrender. "I have. I've been so caught up in the pressures of this new promotion, trying to grow the company for the boss, proving I was worthy. He started his Elmer Fudd imitation, "Wowking all sort of houuws, most weekends. I've been gwousing about it to myself - poor wittle me."

He stopped and looked at her straight on. He pounded his chest. "Martyred employee. Worthy of praise. AND an ulcer."

She gave him a sympathetic look.

He shook his head. "I'm not letting your sympathy wiggle me off the hook. It's my turn at this confession game. I'm rolling the dice again and moving two more spaces. "

"Okay, your move then." She raised her goblet again and gestured him to continue. "I realized you work all the time—days, nights, weekends. You keep the house clean, the accounting firm straight, my life all moving along, clearing out all the bumps along the road, covering the pot holes."

Christina gave him a quizzical look. "You do?"

Jeff crossed his heart with his finger. "Honest. I have been taking you for granted. You always keep things running smoothly and I just stay out of your way. It never occurred to me you might need help, much less a day off."

Julie B Cosgrove

"Who are you and what have you done with my husband?" she jibed.

"I'm trying to be serious, hon." Jeff pouted, but there was no hurt in his voice. He grinned slightly into his wine glass. The reflection of ruby liquid splashed on his cheeks.

"It's about time we spent a little of this promotion money. I want to get you a maid. I'm too old and decrepit to vacuum."

Christina felt her eyes pool again, but the tears had already been cried. She silently thanked God for this change, in her, in her husband, in their relationship. She hoped it would last awhile and not be a fleeting moment.

She shoved him in the shoulder. "You're just feeling guilty you've gotten Pete Stenson to take care of the yard."

"Yep." He wiggled his eyebrows then swallowed down the rest of his wine.

Then it hit her. A maid?

Chapter 28   Remember When?

Over the next few hours, the two sat with arms intertwined, curled up on the back porch steps, talking and sipping. It was one of the most intimate times in their married life. He admitted he'd been worried about her moodiness but hadn't realized he'd been moody too. Maybe they'd just been feeding off one another's negativity instead of the love God had given them for each other. "I guess it's easy to hurt the ones closest to you. And be hurt by them," Jeff said.

"You are way too understanding." Christina felt the guilt weighing her shoulders again. "Did you take a sympathy pill or something? Is this going to wear off?"

"Maybe, doubt it. Anyway, I'm not very observant," He replied and pushed her glasses up her nose a bit with his finger. "I'm sorry I didn't notice them before."

"Well, that was the point in getting the frames that matched so close to the old ones." She tapped her temple.

"You smart woman, you." His eyes glistened, the way they used to when he looked at her. Maybe the way Bud described Jeff at the rodeo. It put a lump like a lardy dumpling in her throat. She couldn't quite swallow all completely in one gulp.

Bud. Could she explain to Jeff her feelings for him, the ones which had laid dormant for decades, the ones she was never sure about from the beginning? Was that too much honesty? She had yet to sort them all out for herself.

"You know I felt guilty keeping it from you. I don't know why I did." Christina stared off into the backyard, arms wrapped around her waist. She didn't mean the glasses necessarily, but she knew he'd take it that way.

"Did you think I would get mad at you for spending money?"

From the corner of her eye, she noticed the muscle in his jaw twitch. She offered no response. He blinked and stared at the ash tree in the yard that held her focus.

After a moment his eyes returned to her. "When have I ever chided you for that? You have always kept this family's finances in good order. Better than I could have ever done."

She couldn't remember the last time he had complimented her on something. She looked into his face and saw his eyes were damp. She touched his sleeve as he continued.

"Christina, I always admired you for that. Do you have any idea how proud of you I feel when I listen to other guys at work complaining about their wives shopping sprees?"

190

Focused

"How would I?" She immediately knew it came out too harsh.

"I just assumed you knew." The little boy pout emerged, innocently denying he'd whacked the huge baseball-size hole into the window of her self-esteem time after time.

Seeing the hurt in his face, she shifted gears. "I don't know why I took off like that."

"And were so reluctant to talk about it?" Jeff finished the thought. His eyes narrowed.

"Maybe it was just all part of the excursion. It was all so special, so uncharacteristic. Kinda like playing hooky, you know? Like something too hush-hush to share, so you want to keep it just to yourself. Does that make sense?"

"I guess." Jeff shrugged. Maybe it's a girl thing. Like a secret diary."

"Yes," she replied. "It's kinda like that."

Suddenly he laughed. "Headline: Little Miss I've-got-to please-everybody actually does something kinda bad." He followed his words in the air with his finger.

"Jeff." She snapped in a scolding tone reminiscent of her mother's. Then laughed at it in spite of herself. He had her pegged alright. She told him about the goldfish bowl.

"So, it's smashed? Are we flopping on the rocks without water now?" he asked, then quickly added, " Don't get me wrong. I'm not alluding our marriage might be on the rocks. I just. I . . ." he didn't know what else to say.

She smiled. "I don't know. Maybe we are just swimming away free."

She saw relief appear in his eyes.

"That sounds good. I like free." He winked back at her.

A few moments passed between them as they sipped the wine and watched the fireflies hover above the lawn. Several houses over a dog barked. They heard a screen door slam and children's voices. In the distance came the repetitive whistle of the coal train heading to San Antonio."Remember that train trestle near the park that caught on fire back in what? '59?" Jeff asked, reaching for a shared memory they had talked about on their first date.

"How about the school tours to Rainbow Bakery?" she replied.

For the next few minutes they played do you remember when? Just like when they were dating. It brought back fond memories. Once again. Then she returned the conversation to the present. She grinned and stared into her wine glass, watching the deep red glow swirl around.

"Now, Jeff. About this maid idea of yours. How's about a cruise instead?"

She enjoyed the "how does that woman know" look on his face. She'd seen the brochure in his brief case.

Chapter 29 Leaky Faucet

When she came home for work, half of her husband's body was under the kitchen sink. Most of her cleansers and scrubbers were sprawled across the floor like bowling pins after a strike. Not that she ever had too many of those in her life, even on computer games.

"What are you doing?"

An echoed mumble emitted from the cabinet. A hand, reminding her of the one on the Adaams family groped around on the floor. She interpreted it as meaning he needed the flashlight. She scooted it closer to his fingers with her shoe. Something resembling a thank you sounded from underneath the sink.

Christina leaned against the counter, waiting as the grunts and repositioning finally accomplished whatever he was doing. He inched out, red faced, on his back and looked at her, his glasses catawampus on his face. "Leaky faucet. Couldn't take the drip. Gotcha a new one. It has a built in vegetable sprayer." He scrambled onto his feet and slid the nozzle out of the goose necked base. "And a magnet. Pull it out, it automatically whips back. See?"

Her mouth formed an "O". Up on her toes she exclaimed, "Barbara next door has one of those!"

"I know." The pompous reply. "George told me. But when he bought his, it wasn't on sale. This was." He leaned against the sink and laughed. "From the look on your face, why did I bother with flowers? I should have sent you pipes."

"Funny, my dear man. Plumbing fixtures would have looked great on my desk." The look on his face made her realize she had never thanked him for the carnations. "Oh. I'm sorry. You were sick, and had taken that cold medicine. You were barely conscious, and, then . . ." She stopped. Excuses, excuses. "They were nice. My favorites. And they still look fresh." The gratitude came too late and rather wilted, like they had actually become. Jeff shrugged it off. She couldn't.

He peered over his glasses at her as she bit her lip. She knew he saw her expression. She never had a poker face. Always the gentleman, he changed the subject. "Barbara and George also re-plumbed. We should think about that."

"Really?"

"After we pay for the cruise, of course." He grinned and walked off. Christina watched the grungy wet foot prints traipse across her kitchen floor and sighed. Tomorrow she was going to order a sign that read "horse's patoot" and hang it around her neck. She got the paper towels and wiped away the remnant images of his size 11's. Down on her hands and knees. Penance.

Focused

That next Saturday morning as the couple passed the sections of the paper back and forth over breakfast, Christina commented, "You know, it's funny, but now that I see better with these glasses, I am starting to see my life differently, too."

Jeff squirmed to face her across the bistro-styled table and gently touched her cheek as he pushed back her hair. "So," he quietly asked, "Are you happy with what you see, now?"

She leaned back. "If you mean us, oh Jeff, of course…" she said a little too hastily. *But do I? I still feel this new closeness is more of a fantasy.*

He held up his hand, accepting her response. "Then, are you happy with your work and living here in this small town? I mean, you were raised as a city girl with operas and concerts and balls and stuff like that."

"And hated it." She stuck out her tongue, a defiance she never dared to show as a child wearing stiff petticoats and scratchy lace.

He chuckled. "Still, I know we moved out here for Josh's sake, so he'd have a more wholesome life and better schooling."

"True, we did. And I don't regret it, Jeff. Even with the commutes every day. I live thirty minutes from Austin. If I wanted to go to the ballet, we'd go." His face turned a slight hue of green, so she added, "I meant we as in me with one of the girls from church, of course."

His color returned to normal. "I know. I'm just saying. There's nothing written in stone saying we should stay here. Do you need a change of scenery?"

Christina wondered if she should feel his forehead. "Jeff, Allensville has been my home for over twenty years. My life is here. My friends. My church is down the road. We have wonderful neighbors. Heck, even The Fresh Basket, my favorite grocer is here. And Bonnie's Bakery." She smacked her lips. "Why would I want to move?"

Jeff folded the paper in quarters and set it aside. "Well, are you looking for a new avenue to explore? Have you been bored?"

Christina looked down at her clasped hands. *He's grabbing for any straw. He doesn't begin to grasp what been going on inside me, despite my heartfelt outpourings.*

Thinking of all the years of being a working mom, all those last minutes projects, soccer games, Boy Scouts, keeping a house clean, her family fed and dressed, her activities at church … well she could hardly say it had all been boring. But, was she bored now that the whirlwind of raising a son was gone? Sure, there was void in the vortex Josh left behind along with the box containing his teddy bear. Did she miss the swirling of life all around her?

"I don't think 'bored' would describe it," she thought out loud. "I don't know how to explain it. It's more like is my life bored with me? It's kinda like expectancy. Now that I have this newfound knowledge, what am I to do with it? Do I take on something, let go of other things? Besides you, of course." She patted his hand. He grabbed it and squeezed back.

"Bob's wife went through this a few years ago, he said. Kids grown and she wondered what she wanted to be next. Is that it?"

Focused

"You've talked this over with the guys at work?" The thought disturbed her. Their home secrets revealed. She pushed away the goldfish bowl mentality which surfaced. That's silly. I talk to the girls at the office, why would he not do the same? "Sorry. Of course you do. You've been that worried?"

"Perplexed would be a better word. I feel like there's something you're still not telling me."

I know. Christina looked out the window at the bright yellow butterfly flitting from leaf to leaf. She pointed. "See that butterfly? I refuse to imitate it, fluttering willy–nilly from one half done project to the next in a futile attempt to void-fill my time. If God wants me to take on something, He'll let me know. I mean, I am just not sure of my motivation up to this point."

Jeff shook his head. "Huh?"

She became more animated. "Has it all been so I would look good in everyone else's eyes, or be liked by everyone, or did I do it to please God because I thought that was what He expected? I'm not sure any of those motives are pure. They just focus on me."

She picked up her coffee cup, went to the sink to rinse it, then hopped up to sit on the kitchen counter, unconsciously putting distance between them. "I guess I need to spend more time by myself and think this through. Maybe it's the realization I am about to hit the half century mark. Maybe God is calling me to do something and preparing me for it, sort of like what Father Rick said last Sunday in his sermon. Remember? When Peter walked out of the boat and on the water to meet Jesus?"

She saw a glaze forming over his eyes. No, she wasn't going to go into a Bible study mode and intellectualize it away. "I guess I didn't know how to tell you I wanted to be left alone to work it all out and not hurt your feelings."

"Hon," Jeff took a deep breath, let it out and stood to make eye contact. "You forget I get up a good hour before you do. That's my reflection time. And when I am out piddling around in the workshop, that's my time, too… to think things out." His voice had an impatient edge.

"And you had been spending more and more time out there. Even in the winter." She hopped down and put her arms around his bathrobed middle."I suspected girlie magazines or drugs."

He put up his hands in mock surrender. "Anyway, what I am trying to say is if you need time to yourself, do it." Jeff added, "Why don't we turn Josh's old bedroom into your sitting room? We could put in some built-in bookshelves where you can have your Bible study stuff, your books and all of those knick-knacks that are so special to you."

"That you can't stand to have cluttering the tables all over the house?"

"It's not that. But you have stuff he made in Cub Scouts displayed as if they were precious crystal."

They both felt an old argument surfacing. He returned to the original thought. "Look, you could put the winged back chair in there, the one you used to love to curl up in but never do anymore? We could turn the trundle bed around against the wall and make it one of those daybeds they show on those home decorating shows. Or we could give it to the firehouse for burned out families and buy a sleeper sofa. It can be your personal sanctuary."

Focused

"I suppose." Her feelings were still back on the knick-knacks barb. She tried to push her thoughts forward to the current topic.

"Paint it the color you like. It will be your new project. Besides, it's a lot bigger than the bathroom." Jeff eyed her, letting that comment hang as he picked his coffee cup, placed it in the sink and walked towards the den.

Christina knew her blush rivaled the color of the roses on the wall calendar in front of her. She'd always found the bathroom the one place in the house where she could shut the door and not be disturbed. It had been her crying space, her place of prayer and contemplation, and quite a few nobody-understands-me pity parties. She thought only she knew of its secret purpose. After all of these years of marriage, why should it surprise her that he knew why she ran the water in the tub so long?

"I really like mauve," she volleyed, raising her voice a little as he walked away. "And I would like to put Josh's old teddy bear and his school years pictures in there. And our photo albums." She heard what sounded like "sure, whatever" float back though the open doorway.

Christina stood, stretched her back and sighed. She walked towards the direction of her husband's voice. He stared out the slider, watching Precious chase a bug in the backyard, whether real or imaginary remained unclear. She slid her arms around his waist and leaned into his warm back.

"I don't know, Jeff. I'm sorry I have acted so aloof." She let go and stood in the middle of the den rug. She waved the thought away. "I guess it all boils down to this. I am just not sure my life has made any difference to anyone, especially if I have been focused on me and how I came across to everyone else instead. And isn't that what we are put on the earth for? To make a difference?"

Instinctively, unaware of the significance, she took off her glasses and began to wipe the smudges off so she could see out of them better. Then she turned to go back into the kitchen.

But Jeff caught the symbolism. He'd just had his own little revelation. He realized what might get her out of this roller coaster slump she kept riding. It also might be the way he could thank her for all the years she had been there for him and everyone else.

Maybe then she'd stop saying he never told her how much he loved or appreciated her. To save her and their marriage, he now knew what to do... or so he hoped. It wasn't a cruise a year or so down the road or even a maid, though he'd still make sure both happened. He wasn't sure he could fix it all, but for her, he'd try. If she were a leaky faucet it would be easier. He knew how to fix stuff like that.

Chapter 30   Maid to Order

Jeff wouldn't let go of the maid issue. She wasn't exactly sure why. Maybe for him it was an appeasement, his way of doing penance for all those years of not helping her out, especially the last few. Whatever it was, she couldn't figure out why she felt so against it.

"Tell me why I feel this way, Betty?" She asked her guild partner while they ironed the fair linen cloth for the altar.

It seemed every time it was their week to serve, the acolytes were extra messy dripping sooty wax droplets all over the place. Either that, or maybe neither Marge nor Virginia, the ladies that had duty the week before, could see them. They were getting up into their seventies now.

"You tell me. Is it because you don't feel you need one?"

"Yes. Well, I mean I have always been perfectly capable of cleaning my own house."

"Of course you have. Jeff isn't saying you do a bad job."

"I'm not so sure."

Betty looked over her readers at her friend. "Come off it Christina. Everyone knows you could eat off your floors. If the Queen ever came to Allensville, you would be nominated hands down to have the reception at your house."

The Queen. Was she that transparent? "Okay. I guess not. But why all of a sudden?"

"God gave him a revelation we all wish our husbands would have?" Mary Ellen shrugged and went back to filling the candle wells with liquid wax.

Christina grinned and shook her head. She tugged on the linen to straighten it. "Betty, you have a service come in right?"

"Yes, but only after months and months of whining." Betty laughed. "Thomas never suggested it."

The two stopped and each grabbed an end of the cloth to spread it back evenly. Then stepping back they measured to make sure the embroidered cross was centered so the fair linen hung evenly down the sides.

"Virginia's aunt made this you know. Must have been over thirty-two years ago now. Made it for her wedding as a gift."

Mary Ellen came in carrying the chalice and cruets of wine and water on a tray. "Mother told me it was in thanksgiving that Virginia finally hooked a guy."

Christina grinned. "Beautiful work. And it has lasted so well."

Betty gingerly smoothed out a corner. "Mary Ellen? Come see how we do this."

Focused

The younger bobbed blonde head nodded Okay. She was the newest guild member on the team, still learning the ropes. She wiped her hands and came over to the two experienced women.

"You should line up the candles next to the little embroidered crosses like this." Betty demonstrated as Mary Ellen watched in reverent silence. Betty returned to their conversation.

"Anyway, I think you should try it out. I have the number to the service I use in my purse. I'll give it to you before we leave." She crossed her hands over her ample bosom as if to say conversation ended.

"Thanks. I appreciate it." Christina replied. But she wasn't sure she did.

* * *

After mulling it over, Christina bounced it off of her son the next day. He had the day off, a rarity on a Sunday for a college student who worked in an electronics store at the mall. So, of course he came over to do his laundry after they were home from church. When she asked him how he rated the day off, he just shrugged and said, "I have seniority now, I guess. Been working there almost two years."

His mother smiled, proud her son made assistant sales manager of the department. One of three, but it still remained a feather in his cap."So, you think I should get a maid, too, huh?"

"Why not, Mom? You deserve it. I'm not around to help out. Dad's too busy. You've been busting your bones all your life. Now you two can afford a luxury here and there. I think it's great." He held a towel under his chin, folding it the same way she always did.

"But it's my house and I like things…"

"Yes, Mom. We know. 'Just so.' So tell her what you want her to do. Lay down the rules, you know? Give her strict boundaries. They're professionals. They're used to that sort of stuff."

Christina handed him another towel and folded the washcloths. "Betty says they are bonded. And none of them are illegal. She made sure of that."

"Even better." He son replied.

"I just don't know."

"Mom," Josh sighed as he put the folded laundry in his basket. "Promise me and Dad you won't run around cleaning the house before the maid comes, Okay?"

"You know me too well." his mother confessed, tossing a washcloth in his direction.

The next day she took her cell phone into the restroom and called the Maid Your Day Agency. She nearly gawked at the price of having a maid come on a weekly basis. She should make so much an hour!

"So, what about once every two weeks? How much is that?"

When the woman told her she became more astounded. "That's more than double, how come?"

"Because your house gets twice as dirty, at least." The rote but pleasant voice assured Christina many other people ask the same thing.

She took a gulp and grabbed a pen. "Alright. I'll run it by my husband and call you tomorrow. What was your name?"

Focused

"Elli, but if I'm not here Juanita can help you, too."

That night she told Jeff the price as soon as he came in the door. He set down his briefcase and without looking at her said. "Do it."

"But Jeff..." she started to object but his raised hand shot her objection down in mid air.

"Hey, Betty says they are good. And reliable. That says a lot. You trust her and you have seen her house. They do a great job, right?"

There was no more argument left in her. She couldn't put a handle onto why she still had objections. But she would comply. Everyone else thought it was great. Maybe she'd warm up to it too, given time.

* * *

For several days, Christina poured over the Internet and decorating magazines searching for just the right color scheme. She searched the fabric stores on her lunch breaks to find the perfect fabric with Angela dutifully in tow.

"You're being way too obsessive about this, you know." Angela said on their fourth trip.

"No, I just know what I want and I'm just not seeing it. All of the fabrics are too bold, or too busy. I want something soothing...and classic."

"In pastels."

Christina nodded as she thumbed through bolts. "Yes, mauve, taupe, muted greens, baby blues...that sort of thing."

"And you want pattern, like flowers." Angela flipped through some swatches.

"Yes, but not too Laura Ashley. It needs to be a guest room, too. Maybe two fabric patterns? A geometric and a floral? Perhaps a solid?"

Angela flopped down the last thick binder of samples."Girl, you know the patterns here better than the sales clerk. If it's not here, it's not here."

"I know. Let's go back to work." Christina said, her balloon of happiness thoroughly popped.

Jeff had her look through designs of bookshelves as well. Should they have cabinets underneath? How about drawers? She became overwhelmed as she tried to picture each style and the various ways to display her books and treasures on the shelves. She combed the discount stores choosing little accessories for the room. She taped the decorating shows the Cable TV guide stated were about guest bedrooms and studies.

As she watched a few and took notes, Jeff hammered away at the bookcases in the garage and tried to stay out of her hair. After all, he had stuff to mull over, too. Plans had to be made.

His wife peered into the man cave, also known as the garage when tools were not crowding out any space for parking the cars. Back and forth footprints in fine sawdust covered the floor. "You holding a square dance contest in here?"

Jeff peered through the safety glasses. "Ha, ha, woman o' mine."

"Maybe we should postpone the maid until the study is finished."

Focused

Jeff took the carpenter pencil from behind his ear and marked another measurement. "Nice try, hon, but, no."

Christina gave him a deflated nod and slumped back into the kitchen, into women's territory. Humph. And he worried about me wanting a project? He's the one who needs one. His mood's elevated once surrounded by wood shavings and nails.

Christina told everyone at work she had an appointment on Thursday morning and would be in about ten.

Angela, of course, asked, "Why? You sick?"

Christina confessed about the maid thing.

"That is so cool, girl. You deserve it. Heck, we all do."

Christina shot a glance around the office and put a finger to her lip. "Don't tell everyone about this, Okay?"

Angela knitted her brow. "Why? Afraid they'll be jealous?" She waved the thought way.

"So? Let them."

Christina thought for a moment. No more worrying what others think. "Maybe I do deserve it. It would make my weekends a lot easier. I'll have time to volunteer more, or maybe just relax and read a book."

Angela tapped her temple.

Christian returned to her desk. The more she thought about it, the more she realized what really bugged her. Her mother always had a maid and never worked a day in her life. Well, that wasn't fair to say, really. Her mother had been involved in many non-profit and civic groups. She had done a great deal for

207

the community and her husband's law career. Still, it was her old defiance against the social thing to do which once again reared its ugly little head. Old habits, old patterns, old way of seeing things.

After a few minutes, she looked towards Angela."I am helping someone do their job right? I don't balk at the guy wanting to carry out my groceries or the dry cleaners clerk, right?"

"Right?" Angela said with a perplexed look on her face. She leaned across her desk calendar. "Christina, do what you need to do to convince yourself. It's a gift your husband wants to give you. How you guilted him into it, I don't know." She tapped her pencil. "But you rock, Lady. You rock."

"Maybe I ought to run away from home more often." Christina smirked.

Angela sat up erect. "I knew it."

Chapter 31   Shades of Mauve

The next weekend Jeff took Christina to look at paint colors and crown molding styles for her sanctuary. Then they browsed once more for fabrics she could sew into curtains and throw pillows for the daybed. Nothing suited her.

They drove to the third store. Christina rubbed her temple. "There really isn't any rush in this, Jeff." She had an exasperated look on her face.

"It's as if you want all of this finished for your birthday."

"I never put that stipulation on…"

Jeff took his right hand off the wheel and patted her knee. "I did."

She laughed, put his hand back onto the gearshift. "Okay. But I don't want to hear you complaining to our friends now about what a slave driver I am and how I don't understand all the pressures you have."

He flinched at the truth her words. "Ouch - bull's eye, right on target." He looked to turn left. "Have you crawled into my thoughts? Is this new God thing making you that insightful?"

"No, I've just known you forever."

Jeff laughed. "And I've known you. That doesn't mean I can figure you out."

In jest, she stuck out her tongue.

They walked in silence hand-in-hand into the air conditioned store. Suddenly she stopped in her tracks. There is lay. The perfect pattern. Flowers in soft pastels of mauve, beige, muted jade, printed on top of soft baby blue stripes. She swore she heard angelic choruses and a ray of Heavenly light shining down.

She dashed over to the display. Sheets and throw pillows coordinated in pastel striped shams perched tastefully on the bed. Exactly what she had pictured in her mind.

"This is it!" She hugged her husband and gathered up a package of shams, three of unfitted twin sheets, one fitted bottom sheet and four pillow cases.

"Isn't that a lot of sheets, hon? We do have some at home, right?"

"But these aren't going to all be sheets. You'll see." She winked at her very perplexed husband.

* * *

Avery was a jewel. Younger than Christina, but recently widowed with two small kids, she obviously needed the job. According to the agency, her husband had been killed in a drive-by shooting. Christina didn't

210

ask for more details. It was none of her business. The maid had a tattoo on the back of her neck, but many women did nowadays. Besides, it was a simple, small rose. Nothing Goth or gross.

From the moment they shook hands Christina knew the woman was sent by God. As they walked through the house, she noticed every little thing and complimented Christina on her taste. She knew where to use bleach and where not to. Even the cats didn't run and hide from her.

"We had kitties when I was little." Avery talked to them softly and scratched them behind the ears, just like a pro. "Can't have them now, though. Little Josh's allergic."

Christina put her hand over her heart. "Is that your son's name? Mine is named Josh as well."

"Straight from the Bible. It means 'God is salvation', you know."

Then Christina noticed the small silver cross around her new maid's neck. She smiled. "Yes, I know."

Before she left for work, Avery turned to her and said, "It will be fine Mrs. W. I will treat your house as my own and I always pray over every room that peace will dwell there."

Astonished at the maid's bold witness, Christina replied. "Avery, I was hesitant about doing this. I guess you could tell. But I know God is in on this. I know we will become great friends. Bye, now."

Avery nodded with a sweet grin. "I know we will. I have your work number right here." She patted her pocket. "If I have any questions, I'll call first."

Julie B Cosgrove

Christina closed the door to the garage, leaned against it and smiled. *Thanks, Lord.*

The next Saturday Josh came over to help measure and cut the pieces for the bookcase. Christina, always excited at the chance to be with her grown son, knew the bribe of homemade blueberry waffles would get him there early.

She poured the batter into the waffle iron. Her son leaned in to watch. "Josh, are you sure you're Okay about doing this? I mean it was your room."

"Come on, Mom," He closed the lid for her. "Sure. Think of all you did getting my apartment set up. Of course I don't want it to remain 'my room'." He wiggled his fingers gesturing the quotation marks. "I think it's a great idea."

"Really?"

"Yeah, really." He hugged her from behind as he watched the light on the waffle iron dim, signaling the first batch was cooked. "This is yours and Dad's house. I don't live here now. You guys do what you want. By the way, the place looks super. You found a great maid, huh?"

That stung her, she didn't know why. "What? It didn't before?" she quipped to hide her emotions.

"Mom. Come on." Her son sighed. With another squeeze, he went to find his dad to tell him breakfast was on.

As if the aroma of Canadian bacon and waffles wouldn't do it. Christina put the first batch in the microwave and poured the next set.

Though relieved, the motherly gene in her saddened at the permanency of it all. Her chick had

212

Focused

truly flown the coop and only fluttered in occasionally with a full basket of dirty laundry or an empty stomach and wallet. She had to admit, she loved those times. Though she liked the peace and quiet, the house was just not the same without Josh around. Change is good and maybe not so good all at the same time. But there's one sure-fired certainty. Life's all about change. Nature rings true. Stagnancy stinks.

After brunch, Christina leaned into the door jam of the garage, her left leg crossed over her right, drying her hands from washing the dishes. As she watched the two men in her life with their heads down working closely together, a warm glow slid up her face. In her mind's eye, Josh was ten again and the project was his scout troop's Derby Day. It had taken the two guys every spare minute for three weeks to get that racing track just right. But Jeff insisted Josh make his own car, fudging only to show him the right way to use the tools. Josh won first place. He earned his badge and the respect of his Cub troop.

She went back to finish her sewing, stopping every once in a while when she heard the familiar male camaraderie of laughter. Some sons and dads never got along. She felt blessed that hers did. Several hours later, after some huffing and puffing and a few poorly chosen expletives, the bookcases were in place and painted creamy white. Calling it a long, hard but fairly successful day, the three decided to spend the next Saturday morning painting the room the perfect shade of mauve.

"I'll come over early, Mom. You don't need to bribe me again with waffles." Josh confided, "I don't have to go to work until 4 pm on Saturdays."

"Okay. How about cinnamon rolls from Bonnie's?"

"Deal!" Two male voices sounded in unison.

Her heart swelled with pride over her two men. Were these warm feelings colored by her new insight and the way she strived to view her world now? Christina wasn't sure, but she felt happier than she had in a long, long time. Work didn't get to her as much now. Even the way she felt about the endless crawl to the office and back home in rush hour traffic improved. That, in itself classified as a miracle.

She knew strife would come. It always did. She convinced herself that she was not being pessimistic, it was realistic. But for now, she basked in the blessings bestowed and hoped she had the strength not to backslide into that old fishbowl again once trouble knocked at her door, as it surely would. That was life. She felt, with this new outlook, she could face it head on, see it for what it really was without pity party emotions, and ask for God's help to deal with it.

That next weekend, the three stood together, bits of mauve paint splattered on their clothes, staring at the walls. All three were pleased with their accomplishment.

"Sure 'nough. That salesman was right. It did darken into the right color." Jeff's voice sounded relieved as he slipped an arm around his wife.

The crown molding, pre-manufactured in creamy white, went up in a few hours. Walls complete,

Focused

Christina scanned the room. "We did good." She smiled and patted her husband turned co-worker's backside.

"Mom, Dad. Please." Their son groaned at their display of affection as he gathered the drop cloths.

"What?" Jeff shrugged.

Josh rolled his eyes.

The doorbell rang. The grown son strolled down the hall. "I'll get it while you two come back down from the love nest."

"You look cute with mauve on your cheek." Jeff cooed to his wife a little too loud so his son could hear.

"And you look debonair with it streaked in your hair." She stood on her tiptoes and tousled his blackish-gray locks.

Jeff twisted around and drew her to him. "You're a poet and don't know it. Think Josh can handle the neighbor or salesman at the door?" he asked in a husky whisper.

Christina blushed. "Well, it's almost 3 o'clock. Josh should be leaving soon and we do need a shower."

Suddenly a familiar voice boomed down the hall. "Hi y'all. I'm here. Hey Chris, which room is mine?"

Chapter 32 Reservations

Jeff looked blankly at his wife. Christina slapped her forehead. "Bud!"

"Bud?" he gestured with his thumb. "Hill Country Bud?"

"I did tell him he could come stay with us while he job hunted. But I thought he'd call first." Her expression held one of a child caught with a week's worth of dirty laundry shoved under the bed. "Actually, it was a spur of the moment thing. I never really thought he'd take me up on it."

"The guest room, now your sanctuary, is hardly ready, hon."

"Oh, the paint is almost dry. It won't take too long to put it back together. Bud can help move the furniture in." Her hurried words covered up her lapse of judgment, now revealed.

"Okay ..." Jeff's sentence trailed off as he started down the hall, dragged by the hand.

Christina played hostess."This is my old friend from the Hill Country. Bud, meet Josh, and you remember Jeff."

Jeff stepped up to the plate. "Welcome to our home, Bud." He looked him square in the eye, territorial testosterone dripping. The unstated sentence

217

that gleamed in his eyes stated this is my home, my son, and by the way, my wife. From the set of his jaw, Christina saw Bud acknowledged the fact.

"I was her beau once, or tried to be, Son." Bud addressed Josh but still square-eyed with Jeff. "Best man won. Water under, ya know." He brushed his hand in the air as if to erase the thought.

"Huh?" Josh looked confused.

"He's referring to the old proverb that something is better forgotten like water which has already flowed under the bridge." Jeff displayed his fatherly prowess.

Christina became slightly nauseous at this overt show of maleness. "But, we've been friends forever. It's great to see you again. How long can you stay?"

Jeff shot her a look. Translated - when will he be leaving? She shot a look back to him to behave.

"Heard about the divorce, man. Sorry. . ." that you couldn't hold onto your wife. I plan to hold on to mine so watch it, was left unsaid. Christina read his mind. Bud probably did, too. It might as well have been stamped on her husband's puffed out chest.

Josh leaned against the back of the wing-backed chair to be moved into his mother's retreat. His expression had yet to change. His eyes moved back in forth watching the verbal tennis match between his elders.

Bud's expression did change though. Christina surmised he couldn't help but feel the younger Willis' stare penetrating his back. She could almost hear the guttural growls. Male boundaries.

Focused

"Hey, you didn't move back in or anything did ya, Son? I can get a motel..." Bud half turned to look at Josh out of the corner of his eye.

The protective bear-child snarled, just a bit. "Uh. No. I'm just here to help get Mom's room..."

Christina moved over to her son and put her arm on his back. "What he means is, we are sort of renovating the guest room now, Bud. We've been painting it." She pulled her T-shirt out in front of her. There were several blotches of mauve on it. "Like it?"

"Looks good to me." Bud replied.

Jeff coughed. His look revealed he wasn't sure Bud exactly referred to the paint on the front of his wife's shirt. Josh looked away. Christina smoothed her T-shirt back unaware it only emphasized the situation.

Josh brushed his foot back and forth on the carpet. An awkward moment lingered in the living room.

Christina broke the silence. "Well. Wanta help move the furniture back in?"She looked at Bud. "That is if you want a bed." She tried a little laugh but it stuck half way in her throat where no matter what she said next would also lodge.

"Hey. Where's my city manners. I shoulda called. If this is a bad time. . ." Bud looked down and ran his hand through his hair. When the three didn't respond, he looked up and clapped his sides. "No problem. Sure. Let's move furniture."

"You sure?" Jeff volunteered. "We can do it." He made an encompassing gesture with his hand to gather in his family. It resembled circling the covered wagons in an Old Western against an attack. "You've had a long drive."

Julie B Cosgrove

Christina rolled her eyes. The situation was not improving. "Bud. Welcome. Let's all have something cold to drink first. Jeff do we have any beer? Bud likes beer. Or do you want Sun Tea? A Coke?" She started walking towards the den and the kitchen.

The three men obediently followed like ducklings in a row.

Jeff went to the breakfast bar that separated the den from the kitchen and took orders. Christina handed him glasses: two with ice for tea, one without ice and a Diet coke for her, and an empty one along with a can of beer for Bud. She grabbed a bowl and filled it with chips, then reached in the drawer of the fridge for the onion dip. She squeezed a little lime juice in it to freshen the taste. The three men's stomachs gravitated to the bowl.

Within minutes the conversation was light and lively dripping with playful one-ups-man-ship. "Well if you think that is funny, let me tell you…"

Christina slipped a plate of chocolate chip cookies onto the bar. Three male hands grabbed, not missing a beat in the discussion over who might be in the NBA finals. Bonding occurred. Swords were sheathed.

"Perhaps, we should get the room in order? It's after 3:00 and Josh needs to get to work," the female of the group hinted. There was a unison of grunts, shuffled feet down the hall, and acknowledgement of who really was the authority under this roof.

It took less than half an hour to put the room back together enough to accommodate Bud. As Christina handed her husband and son the curtains on the rod, they each raised an end and in unison clipped it in place. The blue background for the cream, soft green and mauve flowers pleased her as she fluffed them.

"That's really pretty, Chris." Bud stood with his hands on his hips nodding. "Now the paint color makes sense. You always had a good eye."

"They're sheets." Jeff announced. He climbed down and proudly, perhaps possessively, put his arm around his wife. "And…" he motioned with his head, "Those throws are the pillow cases she cut down. Used the trim to make the tiebacks, right, hon?"

Christina smiled at him as she looped the tiebacks onto the hooks. "But those are store bought," she clarified to the pair of striped shams in the wing chair. As if Bud cared.

"You two sure you don't mind me hanging my hat here for a few days?"

"Least we can do for a guy who spent the last hour moving furniture." Jeff released his wife and winked. "Let's get your stuff, then another beer."

Yep, above all else, Texas hospitality ruled. They don't call it the Friendly State for nothing. The name "Tejas" meant friendly in the tongue the original inhabitants who lived there centuries before Santa Anna or Stephen F. Austin ever stepped foot on the land. Maybe it was in the water.

As the two men went to Bud's truck to get his things, Josh asked, "Mom? What's going on?"

"Nothing, Sweetie." His mother replied as she handed him a sheet corner to tuck in. "Bud's been through a bad divorce and a rough time. He's an old, old friend and he needs a break."

"Yeah. I know. But, exactly when did you invite him?"

Christina's hands stopped tucking in the sheet. Did she need to tell her son everything about her hooky romp to the Hill Country? No, she didn't. She felt sure her son held secrets. Well, so can I.

"A while back when I heard about it from his parents. When I went up there in March, remember? The Hill Country grapevine must have got the message to him. I just didn't specify a time and I guess he felt it was an open invitation, which it was...but..."

"Yeah. He could've called."

"Well, Bud's always been a bit impulsive. Hand me the pillow case, please." Christina mumbled with a pillow tucked under her chin.

"How come I never remember meeting him?"

"You were younger. He moved away with his wife to Houston for a while. And of course, we got busy with life as well. You don't see a lot of your high school buddies very much anymore, right? Same thing."

He looked at her with a "Huh?"

Before he could respond further, she added. "Have a nice day at work."

That night, she watched as her husband and her old beau chatted and poked the sizzling ribs on the barbeque. While she set the patio table with mats and flatware, Christina observed both of their shoulders were relaxed and their laughter easy. She finally took a deep breath. Maybe this will be alright after all.

Bud seemed to follow along without missing a beat as they joined hands and Jeff offered Grace. He grabbed his napkin and with a snap, put it in his lap. "Jeff? So what time's church?"

Focused

Jeff held the bowl of potato salad in mid-air. "Uh, we usually go to Bible study first. That starts at 9 a.m.. Service is at 10:30. I can give you directions…"

"That's real nice. But can I go with y'all at nine? I could use a bit of Bible study." He winked at Christina.

She smoothed the napkin into her lap.

Chapter 33 Strangely Blessed

The next morning, Christina and Jeff's nostrils awoke to the aroma of fresh brewed coffee and sizzling bacon. Christina threw back her covers and yawned the grogginess out of her system. Then, seeing the lump next to her move, she remembered that there was a third person in the house. The memory of the past twenty-four hours replayed in her mind as she orientated herself awake.

It had been after midnight when she left the two chatting about who would be the best candidate for State Senator in the upcoming primaries. The clock on the bed stand now read 7:45.

"Up, Jeff. We better hustle if we are going to eat and still make it to church on time."

A mumble answered back as the covers moved to reveal disheveled hair sticking on her husband's forehead.

Julie B Cosgrove

The two tied the sashes of their robes then stumbled down the hall. A bright, sunny "Good morning, folks" greeted them.

There stood their houseguest, showered, dressed in tie and coat, with Jeff's BBQ apron wrapped around him. With one hand he sipped coffee, with the other one, he slung hash.

"Breakfast's up."

The robed couple shuffled to the breakfast table.

"Glad to have you with us," Jeff said as he sniffed the bacon and eggs being plopped on a plate in front of him. "Coffee sure smells good."

Christina chose to ignore the condition of her kitchen and, instead, shoved a piece of bacon in her mouth.

When the blue-eyed, dark-haired wonder entered the adult's Bible study meeting room, several heads turned. Mary Ellen dropped her Bible on the floor. Bud's eyes kept falling on her as Jeff and Christina introduced him around.

Christina had never seen Bud so polite and, well, quiet. Though he didn't say a word and twice needed help to find the passage in the extra Bible she lent him, Bud appeared to be genuinely attentive to the conversation and the study leader's comments. In the service, she caught his eye wondering two rows up and over as May Ellen sang, sharing her hymnal with Harriet.

The same old tingle surged up her arm to her heart when they brushed hands as she helped him find

226

Focused

his place in the prayer book. She felt the warmth creep into her cheeks and tried to halt its progress with a small cough. *What is this? Surely not jealousy. I have Jeff. Honest as the day is long, non-boozing, non-cussing Jeff.*

She swallowed down the awkwardness she felt and concentrated on the list of the sick in the parish they prayed over at the moment. "…Mary, Todd, Janie and child, Buffy, Maria and child, Nancy, Barbara's parents named Nell and Charlie…" The reader announced each slowly and clearly. "And for those serving our country here and in danger abroad: Steve, Carrie, Bob, Pete, Madison, Jason, Billy, and Betsy. And finally, for those for whom no one else ever prays, Amen."

When it came time to pass the Peace, she hugged Jeff and Josh to her right then extended her hand to shake Bud's. He winked as he clasped her hand in his, then in a split second turned to the couple behind them and exchanged the Peace with them. Christina saw Mary Ellen try to navigate over to them. Instead, Christina made a beeline to meet her first, stepping over Bud and hugging her way as she went. She felt Bud's eyes on her back as she and Mary Ellen exchanged the Peace. Is Bud's stare for me or Mary Ellen? As she pulled away, she saw her friend shyly look around her, smile and wiggle her fingers in a tiny wave. She turned to see Bud smile and nod in her direction. After church, she noticed the two huddled in conversation at the Coffee Hour.

Jeff noticed them as well. "Seems like a whiff of romance in the air."

"Yeah. Well, Mary Ellen's divorce just became official a few weeks ago. She's still very raw." Christina's voice had a little too much of an edge.

"Okay?" Her husband's pondering tone hit her like a slap in the face. "You don't have to be snippy about it."

"I'm sorry, hon," Christina made a weak smile. She was being snippy, like a jealous female and Jeff picked up on it. She backpedaled to cover her tracks. "I guess I'm just tired. And I think I found some muscles I hadn't been using a lot before yesterday."

Jeff put a hand on the small of his back and sighed. "I hear ya."

Christina placed her hand over his and gave him a sympathetic look. *Whew. Dodged that bullet.*

"Okay. Look, they're both your friends. I know you don't want them to get hurt. I'll talk with Bud, you talk with Mary Ellen. Deal?" Jeff offered.

"Umm. Not yet. Let's see where this leads. They are both adults. Bruised, hearts on their sleeves and lonely, but adults. I've done my parenting."

"Sure you have." Jeff threw back his head and laughed, which made a lot of heads turn, including the just-meeting couple.

Bud gave Christina a look she could not quite interpret. Harriet whispered a little too loudly, "Jeff, I need to talk to you about that function we are having soon." Her voice ended in a higher note.

Christina shot him a quizzical look.

Jeff replied, "Sure. Be right back, babe. They need some advice on ..."

"...constructing a stage for the end of school shindig." Harriet caught her faux pas and quickly

228

Focused

finished his sentence. She ushered him away, chattering non-stop. Bud got Mary Ellen another cup of punch. Christina stood in the middle of the parish hall perplexed and suddenly, a bit lonely.

Later that afternoon, Josh came over. He, Bud and Jeff settled in to watch the Texas Rangers on TV. Not really interested in baseball if her son or his friends weren't playing, Christina decided to drag out the teddy bear box, as she called the carton full of her son's childhood memorabilia. She sat on the floor of office and unwrapped each tidbit as if it was made of the finest spun glass.

There was the construction paper Christmas snowflake Josh once cut out, jagged-edged and torn from using baby scissors with the rounded ends. Scrawls of purple and red littered the center, crayon marks hastily added with a tongue tip hanging out the side of his mouth, no doubt. She could see him sitting there cross-legged on the floor beside her. Where had the years gone?

She picked up the tassel from his graduation cap. It seemed like last year he walked across that stage, and now he was a sophomore in college with an apartment of his own and a job with potential advancement. Josh had grown up, a bit more as of late.

She peered into the den to observe him interacting with Bud and his dad. Three grown men on the couch in male-bonded camaraderie over a team not exactly winning. Christina couldn't help but get a warm, fuzzy feeling. All the stages of her life—her

229

Julie B Cosgrove

carefree teens, her married life and motherhood —sat
blended together on her couch.
　　She felt strangely blessed.

Chapter 34   Fair Maid

Avery came at 7:30 in the morning on Thursdays so she could get a bright and early start. She cleaned another house that day, so she wanted to be off by the time the bus dropped off her son at 3:30. Her daughter was in daycare all day. Christina liked her coming so early. By then, Jeff usually headed out the door for work. He'd politely acknowledge Avery's presence, thank her for the job she did, and dash off to his job. Christina didn't have to be at work until 9:00, so it gave them time to sit over a cup of coffee, chat and go over what needed to be done.

They also prayed together and shared lists of people who needed prayer. Avery went to the mega non-denominational church where so many of the younger generation were drawn these days. It was something Christina could not understand. Sure the music rocked the house. She loved contemporary and gospel music, too and often wished they would loosen up and have more of it where she worshipped. But she wouldn't give up the intimacy of St. Martin's, the sense of family she always felt there. Maybe that feeling existed in the mega churches, but she doubted it. After they prayed and poured their coffee, Christina informed Avery of the latest twist in the household.

"I need to tell you we have a guest."

"I wondered whose truck that was I saw at the curb," the astute young woman said.

"His name is Bud. He is an old high school friend going through a rough time."

"Then he's... your age?" the maid asked as she stirred her coffee.

"Avery Joseph. Are you looking?" Christina asked, a little astonished and a little glad. It meant her friend was healing.

She smirked but wouldn't look up from her coffee cup. "I saw his head in the bedroom window. He's pretty good looking, isn't he?"

Just then the familiar stride of boots came down the hall.

"Morning... uh? Ladies?" Bud asked, seeing the two sitting where usually one sat. He came up and extended his hand to the younger. The Owen charm began to dance in his eyes.

" Howdy. Name's Bud. And the pleasure's all mine. And you are..."

"Avery," the younger woman replied with a slight blush in her cheeks.

"Did I mention we had a maid?" His hostess responded. And perhaps I should stay and chaperone?

Bud answered no, but never took his eyes off Avery.

"Coffee?" Christina kept her tone upbeat. "So, how'd your date with Mary Ellen go?" She saw his hand drop to his side as she poured him a cup. Avery looked away.

"We're, uh, not really, you know, dating. Just went to the movies together. In fact, we met two others in the Singles Again support group from your church. It was a group thing, really." The man tripped over every sentence but never lost the twinkle in his eye.

Christina couldn't help but notice Avery hung on every syllable. His explanations obviously were not geared to his hostess.

"Time we both got to work, right Avery?" She smiled at her maid then turned to Bud. "Will you be here tonight for dinner or are you all going to the movies again?"

Avery scooted the chair back and went into the utility room for the broom. Bud's eyes narrowed. He had a "what's going on" look on his face.

Christina ignored it. "Gotta run."

Why did she feel so catty? Her actions stupefied her. *Who cares if Avery or Mary Ellen or any single woman under the age of ninety-five took a shine to Bud. Not my problem.*

As she drove to work, she tried to analyze the uneasiness. He brought out the high school in her again as if her feelings were stuck in a time warp of past memories and reactions. He made her feel young and stupid again, as if they were still floating in the river, he is his cut-offs, she in her psychedelic colored bikini, bobbing in the water to the beat of the Doors' latest hit as it blared from the transistor radio on shore.

Maybe the hurt from that summer night in high school still loomed. Bud betrayed a lifelong friendship

233

in one hormonal-surged gesture planted on her lips when she'd cried on his shoulder over the breakup with her first beau. Caught off guard by the mood and the Boones Farm wine he'd poured into her, she melted into it, half wishing he was the cure for her broken heart. Feeling his touch, she hoped Mr. Right existed after all, all these years right under her nose. Then the alarm inside her head blared when his hand slipped under her blouse. In response, her stomach returned what had previously been in her glass, all over the seat of his truck. Those were the days—better never repeated.

Could it be she still didn't trust the guy? Was she just being protective? And of whom? Christina wished she could bounce this off Jeff. No way. Honesty was one thing. Stupidity another.

She wanted her dad more than anything. Stopping at the intersection, she fought the urge to turn to the west again. Instead, duty called. She had to earn her pay like a grown-up. No more sixteen-year-old emotions. Buck it up.

Besides, that rocker still sat empty up at the cabin. She guessed it always would.

* * *

Jeff, however, wasn't sure the world was as rosy as it seemed at home. He sensed an underlying chemistry between his wife and her old River Rat friend. Trouble brewed under the surface. He just couldn't put a finger on it. Perhaps they just shared a childhood bond? Perhaps more after their recent meeting during the flood. Women still fell for

234

Focused

that knight in shining armor stuff. Could his wife be immune just because she had a gold band on her finger?

Then again, Christina did tell me she began every morning now with prayer. Perhaps that's the reason she seemed more put together and cheerful? Jeff tapped the dashboard with his hand as he waited for the line of cars ahead of him to inch another few turns of the tires before jerking to a halt, again. Craning his neck, he could see the pulsating blue and red flashes ahead. Must be a really good wreck.

Flipping his cell open, he punched in the speed dial for the office and let the answering machine know he was stuck on the highway, still about fifteen miles out. Marjorie lived south so she wouldn't be stuck in this muck. She'd get the message then tell Bob and the apprentices.

Jeff settled back into his thoughts, and wiggled his already sticky back away from the car seat to air it a bit. He couldn't deny something about his wife had changed. Something happened in the flood up in the Hill Country that altered her outlook. It had to be more than new glasses, though he knew the old pair had long been a thorn in her flesh. He should be grateful she appeared more cheery and relaxed. The atmosphere in their home had improved since she came back. Even more so since that late night porch talk. Now, she seemed downright happy. Could it be her new focus on God? Maybe it's because she has Avery around who is, by the way, doing an excellent job. That thought made Jeff nod and smile, which perplexed the grouchy driver next to him honking his horn in frustration. Jeff lifted two fingers off the steering wheel in a short wave then looked ahead again. Maybe he had fixed something after all. Then again . . .

Jeff couldn't get rid of the nagging suspicion the reason for his wife's change in mood stemmed from Bud being back in her life. He had been up there when the flood hit. Then he shows up out of the blue at their front door. What was that about?

Jeff gripped the steering wheel tighter. He'd never had any reason to doubt his wife's fidelity and love up until now. To force the nagging thought back to the rear of his brain, he flipped on the Talk Radio channel and half listened to the political chatter that bantered through the speakers. But the uneasiness kept resurfacing the way Christina's recipe for chili cheese meatloaf often did.

After mulling it over for a few days, Jeff couldn't stand it eating at him anymore. One night, he came into the bedroom and sat on the bed as his wife brushed her hair. He noticed she hummed.

He blurted out, "What's with you and Bud?"

Christina stopped with the brush halfway in her hair. "Excuse me?"

He noticed her face as she peered into the mirror at his backward image. Her skin looked paler than it had been a second ago. I've got her.

"If I didn't know better, I'd say you were a touch jealous of Mary Ellen, or is it Avery? I caught him talking to her. Is he dating them both?" Jeff said. He sat on the bed, hands on his knees and leaned in closer to her.

Focused

"Oh, for goodness sakes!" She slammed her brush down and walked into the bathroom. She slammed the door, too.

Jeff might have let it go some other time, but not tonight. Not after that reaction. He got up, walked over and pushed the bathroom door open, whacking her in the rear. He smirked at the fittingness of the action.

"Well...?" This time it was his turn to stare at her backward image in the medicine cabinet mirror. She turned with daggers in her eyes and stuck the toothbrush in her mouth. Then she pulled the door closed.

Jeff felt the flush in his cheeks and the muscles ripple in his back. He threw the bedspread back, grabbed a pillow and the afghan throw off the bench then headed down the hall to the couch in the den.

* * *

Christina tried to spit out her anger with the toothpaste, but it didn't work. She rinsed out her toothbrush and opened the door. She noticed the tousled bedspread, then the missing afghan and pillow. She hissed under her breath and headed down the hall to the den.

There on the couch lay a lump under the throw in the shape of her husband. He was curled in a fetal position, his face squished into the sofa back. Christina sat down, nudging her hip into his back.

"Jeff, for Heaven's sake." Her exasperated voice quivered with emotions she couldn't begin to sort through and didn't really care to either. "What are you doing out here?"

The lump shifted and replied. "I've had it, Christina. I want to know exactly what went on between you two in that flood you haven't told me. Don't tell me 'Nothing'."

"Why not? It's true."

"That's not the way it looks from my side."

"Oh? And how does it look, Jeff? What on earth have I done to hint that anything went on?" She wanted to hit him with the throw pillow he'd tossed aside onto the floor. Where did this idea of his come from and why? She couldn't, for the life of her, figure it out.

The lump shifted some more and sat up, unwrapping the throw which had been around him. "Oh, you've been real good at not hinting. Bud, however, hasn't. I see the way he looks at you."

"Jeff…" Christina got up and sat on the coffee table. She ran her hands through her hair and stared at the floor. She knew whatever she said next would be the fuel to flare this smoldering inferno. She thought of heading back down the hall and avoiding it all. The way she used to. Just swallow it down. Tell him you love him and you are sorry if you did anything to worry him. Tell him he's the best man you could ever ask for. Walk away. He'll calm down. Status quo will resume.

No. Not now, she told herself. He was being absurd and secretive and she wasn't sure he was the best man. She sighed and looked her husband straight in the eye.

Trouble had come knocking after all and she refused to splash back into the goldfish bowl. She needed to get a real perspective on her husband's sudden outburst. She determined to meet it head on, and do it in love.

Here goes nothing. Talk through me this, Lord.

240

Chapter 35   Look in the Mirror

Christina couldn't keep the lump out of her throat. Her brain warned her not to let a sound out of her mouth just yet. Her eyes began to swim and she turned to look at the hutch with all the bits and pieces of hers and his story on it. Their toasting glasses. The candlesticks her aunt gave them as a wedding present. The picture of them sitting on the bench in the park at Josh's third birthday party, gathered over the cake miming how to blow out the candles. The china cardinal perched on a dogwood branch he had given her for her birthday when they couldn't afford for him to even give her a card. The silver framed picture of them on their twentieth anniversary surrounded by friends on a rented dinner boat. Jeff got seasick on an hour excursion around Lake Travis. How on earth would he handle a cruise?

She blinked and turned back to him. "I'm afraid whatever I say will be taken the wrong way," she whispered through the hoarseness. Secretly she prayed that she could do this. She could face conflict.

"Okay." came the response. He stood up and went into the kitchen.

At first her heart sunk. Why did he walk away? I thought we'd come so far. Why this, why now?

Then, Christina heard the water running and the clink of glass. His footsteps sounded on the rug again. He gently set a glass of water down beside her.

"Not exactly the way I clunked one down next to you the night before my escape. Maybe you've calmed down a bit? "

She looked up at his eyes peering over the glass of water tilted over his mouth. He wiped his lips with the back of his hand and put the glass down next to hers. His eyes were clouded in mystery. She couldn't read them.

"I'll try not to react." He sat down on the couch, clasped his hands together and leaned into her space, invading her comfort, and yet, providing it.

Christina blinked the stinging saltiness from her eyelashes. She rubbed them on her nightgown hem and sniffed. "I think he was hoping there would be something. Bud, I mean. But I never led him down any path, Jeff. Never."

"Why did you invite him here?" her husband's voice dropped a few decibels as he remembered the subject of their conversation lay sleeping a few doors down the hall.

"I don't know. Honestly," Christina softened her voice as well. "It just blurted out as if someone else was doing the talking. He just seemed so hurt over Alice. I was afraid if I reacted too quickly to comfort him, he'd take it the wrong way. Maybe I wanted him on my turf instead."

242

Focused

"Go on."

"Jeff, he helped me through a lot of stuff when I was in high school. The hurt when Mark broke up with me and took Martha to the prom instead. Losing my brother Carl when he moved to L.A. for those four years so Dawn could take care of her mother. Dad finally 'fessing up that his alcohol was out of control and admitting himself into that hospital in Dallas."

Jeff nodded. "If I had known you better then…"

"But you didn't. Bud did. And I was vulnerable. Every male in my life was deserting me or letting me down, except him. I sent the wrong message and he picked up on it."

"You mean back then."

Christina straightened up and her eyes narrowed. "Yes, back then." She stopped and swallowed some water, shoving the desire to slap him silly back down into her stomach. "It really hurt him, Jeff. For years he wouldn't talk to me. He'd walk away. That's why you never met him until the rodeo dance a few years ago."

"The man holds a grudge… or something… for a long time doesn't he?"

"You mean a flame?" She looked him in the eyes again. This was getting easier. The knots in her gut and lower back were slowly unwinding. She felt a mighty Hand by her side.

"I'd say a spark of it is still there, Christina. Not that I can blame him."

His response jolted her. Was he hinting that she was worth carrying a flame over after all these years? That he thought she was attractive or desirable? "You, you can't? Why?"

"For the love of Pete, woman, look in the mirror." His tone was exasperating, not compassionate. Then his eyes softened. "You're still easy on the eyes, hon. Don't you know that?"

"No. You never tell me. I didn't think I was to you anymore."

Jeff slid back into the sofa and rested his head against the wall. He examined the ceiling intensely. The look in his tense-jawed face revealed his thoughts. There it was again. The same thing shoved in his face. May as well engrave it on the forehead, "I never tell my wife."

Christina averted her eyes to a path of slivery moonlight splashing across the rug. Well, it was true. It was about time he knew how it affected her. Everyone wants to be told now and then that they look nice, or did something right, or whatever. Mustering her strength and new resolve not to cower or smooth things over, she willed her voice to reply, "Everyone needs compliments now and then. Even from Jeff Willis." It came out in a croaky whisper, but it came out.

Silence.

She heard the crickets chirping in the warm spring night air. Her husband's breathing was returning to normal, and perhaps his blood pressure. He folded his hands across his chest and sighed. "My fault." he simply stated after a moment. Then she saw his gaze return to her. "Is that why you drove up there? To find out if another man would tell you…"

Focused

"Jeff. No. I told you. I drove up there to talk to God. I needed to find out if I was still Okay in His eyes, no one else's."

She paused and looked away for a moment. "I guess that sounds stupid. But, trust me. I had no idea Bud was up there. I had not seen him in years. Never stayed in touch with the Owens at all. I didn't know where he was or that he was divorced or anything like that. Not till his dad drove down to check on me. After the flood."

Her eyes couldn't hold back the tears any more. She got up and sat beside her husband. She felt him shift his weight, wrap his arm around her and draw her close.

The next few minutes Jeff held her as her shoulders heaved back and forth in quiet sobs. Had she seen his eyes well up as well? He hated to hurt his wife, it was like stabbing himself. It tore at his gut. But they had decided to be more honest with each other. Tonight, both kept that promise. Nostrils had flared and tears had flowed, but truth prevailed. Maybe tomorrow they'd actually like each other again. They both needed a good night's sleep to even the situation.

"Let's continue this after he's left, Okay? He will leave someday, right?" Stretching, he stood up to grab his pillow. "It's late and I got a heck of a day tomorrow."

"You always do."

He shot her a look. She looked down and bit her lip. From her face he could tell she was sorry those words had come out of her mouth. He also knew she was still a bit ticked off. *Join the club.*

"Comes with the territory, I guess." He let it go for now. "Let's go to bed. I'm bushed."

"Then why did you bring it up in the first place?"

Jeff peered into her. He lifted a finger in warning, lest this turn into round two. "Not tonight." He padded down the hall, afghan dragging behind him.

He heard his wife's footsteps following the back of his robe down the hall into the master bedroom. Simultaneously, they crawled into bed. No more words were spoken. He air-pecked her cheek. Then rolled over and flopped his head on his pillow.

For the rest of the night she slept on her edge of the bed and he on his, neither wanting to touch the other. The cats took advantage of the situation and sprawled out in the middle.

Chapter 35 Planning Stages

In a few weeks, Father Rick's son, Gideon, graduated from high school. Christina noticed the graduation announcement on his desk in the church office while she looked for the stapler. She always volunteered to help the church secretary Jean print, fold and mail out the quarterly pledge statements. She glanced at the announcements in that week's pew bulletin but saw nothing about the end of school or graduation. Something didn't fit.

"Jean?" she asked as she busily folded statements. "Are we planning anything for graduation?"

"We always get them a Bible," Jean responded with an eyebrow raised. "Why?"

"Never mind. It's just that…" she stopped and decided to divert her thoughts away from Harriet and Jeff's conversation a few Sundays ago. "That…" she started over, "Gideon is graduating, right?"

Julie B Cosgrove

The boy had been in an accident six months prior when a drunk driver ran a red light and plowed into the driver's side of his car. His legs pinned, the EMS firemen used the Jaws of Life to get him out. Luckily, his date only suffered some scrapes from shattered glass and a few bruised ribs from her seat belt's grip.

Gideon underwent three surgeries on his legs and had only recently been able to walk without crutches. The honor student kept up with his courses through pure determination. With the same conviction, he vowed to parade across the stage at his graduation ceremony with his class, the effort supported on prayer lists for months in several churches throughout the area. Despite some objections, Father Rick had seen to it that the drunk driver was prayed for as well. He placed the man's name on their weekly parish prayer list right after the accident along with his son's.

Father Rick explained, "If God could forgive the crowds for crucifying His son, I should be able to forgive the man who maimed mine."

Though many admired him for it, he confided to the women's Tuesday Bible study group the gesture was purely for survival. Praying for the guy was the only way he kept his faith together through it all. Otherwise, his bitterness would have numbed him from experiencing God's presence.

"Yes he is graduating after all," Jean replied proudly. "Father Rick says Gideon has caught up and will receive his diploma with his class."

"Thanks Jean. I have to run. I'll call you later today." If Jean didn't know of a shindig, there wasn't one in the planning. Jean kept abreast of all the parish happenings. Christina decided to discuss that one with Jeff later. In the meantime, a little small voice told her to do something else. She decided, for once, to obey.

That afternoon, she quickly notified the rest of the women on the Parish Functions Committee and together they met at her house after work on Thursday to sneakily plan a reception in Gideon's honor. To her surprise, Jeff did not retreat to the garage, but stayed and offered his suggestions as well. No stage was mentioned.

"I think we should get a cake from Bonnie's Bakery, frosted in his school colors." Gladys offered as she rose to refill her coffee cup. Gladys could drink coffee right up until she went to bed. Christina often wondered if she kept a cup on her bedside table.

"Will one sheet be enough? How many does that feed?" Harriet pondered, as her hands mimed piece sizes and her lips counted.

Then it occurred to Christina."Wait a minute. Aren't there others graduating this year as well?" She quickly phoned Jean, who was still up at the church for the Vestry meeting. Putting her on the speakerphone, she relayed their question and Jean confirmed that four other students from two other schools were graduating as well.

"But why do you ask?" she inquired and sounded a little hurt. "You know I ordered the Bibles for them already. You asked me that a few days ago. We always give the graduates a Bible…"

"Oh, of course, Jean, of course." Christina yelled into the speakerphone to make sure the secretary heard every word. "No. We, uh… the Parish Functions

Committee is here meeting at my house, and well, we thought it might be nice to give Gideon a reception."

Harriet piped in, "You know. To honor his recovery and his where-for-all to graduate with his class. After all, the circumstances are unusual, Jean. We just didn't want the other graduates to feel slighted. That's all. What schools do they attend, do you know?"

Pacified, Jean rattled off the names and the schools they went to. "But you know", she added, "We've never had a reception before. Some of the parents of past graduates may get bent out of shape."

Dear Jean, always the diplomat and thinking of all the little angles. It came with the job and she did it well.

"I know." Christina responded a little disturbed. For once she determined not to let what everyone else might think deter her. "I'm one of those parents, remember? If they can't look past their noses to see Gideon is a special case, well pardon my French, but they can go to you know where."

"Here, here," chanted in the background and Betty patted her on the back.

"Good for you, Christina. Good for you. Those prayers are working, girl." Harriet echoed.

Christina squeezed her hand. By now, her Tuesday group was well aware of her refocused revelations . . . well, most of them.

Jean just chuckled. "Okay. Frankly I think it's a wonderful idea. I will do some damage control and call a few of the parents of the last two or three years' graduates to let them know that it is mainly for Gideon because of all he has been through, preacher's son or no. I'll also ask if they want to help out with the food. If that doesn't pacify them, who cares."

"I knew you would know the best way to handle it," Christina replied, pumping up her friend's ego. Jean defined the mortar that held all the little bricks in the Church together, figuratively and maybe, at times, literally. She didn't want her feathers ruffled at all.

As a ruse, Betty suggested that they have an "Invite Your Friend to Church" Sunday that day just like the Presbyterians did. "Jean, tell Father Rick we're having a small reception after Church for the guests."

Harriet spoke up again. "Jean, let them know in the Vestry meeting that the Functions Committee wants to do it that day because it's right before the schools let out."

"Yes, before summer starts and attendance drops, as it always does," Gladys said, adding in her two cents to the reason for doing it then.

"We better not remind them of that or they'll get off track discussing how we'll pay the summer utility bills," Jean laughed.

The trick worked. Jean called back to say she had put it on the agenda first, and that the Vestry unanimously agreed. In fact, they voted it should be done on a quarterly basis. The women hooted with laughter. Then, with thumbs up, they all congratulated Betty on her slyness before they all grabbed some more cookies and coffee. Refreshed, the committee continued to plan the event.

"There should be plates in each of the schools' colors as well as streamers," Linda suggested.

Christina added, "I know the Party WareHaus Outlet will have graduation themed napkins and centerpieces. Maybe they'll give us a discount."

"Or donate it all together. I heard they did that for the Baptists when the pastor's daughter married." Harriet always heard everything, though sometimes a little skewed.

"The third through fifth grade Sunday school class can make a banner that day and we could hang it up while communion is going on. The younger kids can decorate pennants. I'd have them pre-drawn and cut out in advance," said Susan, the head of the Christian Education program.

The next day during lunch, Christina put in an order for two quarter sheet cakes and one half sheet cake, each to be frosted with the three school colors and the names of the graduates from each school. The parents were notified by letter not to tell their students about the surprise. In the letter, Jean assured their son or daughter would get their Bibles in Church as well, per tradition. Most of all, they were not to let Father Rick nor Mary, his wife, find out about it since their son was graduating as well. And of course, the families were more than welcome to invite their relatives and close friends. It would be "Invite a Friend Sunday" as well. Bases covered.

The following morning, the youth leader Barry called and left a message on Christina's voice mail volunteering him and his wife, Belinda, to get the ice and the chips. She called back, only to get his answering machine.

Focused

"Tag you're it. Thanks. Would love for you to get the ice. As far as chips, can you get both tortilla and potato chips? Thanks. God Bless. Bye."

Thank God for a generous person like Barry. And all her other friends, big hearted, willing to pitch in. Several women were bringing finger sandwiches, fresh fruit and veggies, and plenty of dips to go with them. Betty volunteered to create her famous Lime Sherbet punch.

* * *

Christina spent two full evenings at home enhancing the store bought centerpieces with ivy and little diplomas tied with ribbons in the various schools colors. Jeff helped by cutting the ribbons in precise measured lengths. Bud stayed in his room, getting changed for a night on the town, no doubt with Mary Ellen. Christina tried to not let it get to her as she wove the ivy into the first of the twelve centerpieces. Jeff picked up a plastic bag. "What's this?"

"Oh, they had that on special. I couldn't resist. It's a banner with "Congratulations" on it, for over the beverages table," she proudly announced. "And look. I found some balloons in the colors of the schools."

"Good job, hon. But then, you always do." Jeff volunteered, as he tied the scrolled diplomas, and cut manageable lengths of floral wire for the ivy. She blushed at his rare compliment then wondered what had gotten in to him. He acted like a child two weeks before Santa came. Way too nice. Have our tearful conversations sunk into his brain? Or, is it something else?

253

He never mentioned his covert conversation with Harriet. It started to irk her so, as she placed the diploma decorations in the next center piece, she asked in a matter of fact tone,

"Any progress with the stage?"

Jeff stopped. "Huh? Oh that. The Sunday school teachers were thinking of a little end of school skit. But they are having a hard time getting it together. No stage." He deposited more ribbon at her feet.

Just then Bud came in the room. His aftershave arrived first. "See y'all later," he said as he adjusted his tie. He waltzed out whistling.

Jeff turned to Christina. "Bud in a tie twice in two weeks? That's an oxymoron. Mary Ellen again?"

"I guess. He didn't exactly ask my permission."

Jeff shrugged.

"Lord help them if either one of them gets hurt..." Christina's tone had a warning in it.

"Let's pray for them, okay?" He grabbed her hand and closed his eyes.

Christina was taken back at this sudden pious act. She felt the warmth through his squeeze, and God's presence, too. Maybe he had taken that sermon to pray more often together seriously. Could that be the catalyst for this change she noticed? Or is this all just . . . staged?

Jeff was glad the subject had drifted away from the stage. He didn't want her to have an inkling of what he was planning. He hated to lie. That really bugged him. Their marriage was supposed to be based on trust.

Focused

Still, he'd noticed an edge in Christina's voice about Bud's activities. It hinted of jealousy. Maybe the trust was not as solid as it had once been. One thing for sure. His Texas hospitality was wearing thin when it came to this old friend of his wife's. Could his marriage with Christina stay intact until his plans were firmed or should he spruce up his grandfather's dueling pistols?

Chapter 36   A Good Man

The master plan was to generically decorate the Parish Hall in between services, and then after the services started, hang the children's contributions, put out the centerpieces and bring out the cakes. That way, Father Rick wouldn't be the wiser. The school colors were primary colors anyway, pretty common colors for any occasion. A secret offering request had been sent out over the internet to parishioners who had e-mail addresses. More than five hundred dollars had been mailed in and confiscated by Jean who always sorted the mail. She converted it into gift cards to Value Mart to be put inside each Bible.

It all went off without a hitch and Father Rick, Mary and the other parents were blown away with gratitude. Gideon was appropriately embarrassed, but less so than if the limelight shown solely on him. The Bibles and the unexpected gift cards inside of them humbled the other graduates as well.

The senior warden, head of the church elders, came up to Christina. "Great idea. The congregation swelled by twenty-eight visitors today, twenty of who were relatives of the graduates."

" Many of them commented about how wonderful the sermon was and how warm the congregation seemed to be. Five even said they would be back to worship with us again," Jeff added with pride. He volunteered to usher that day and spoke to many on their way into the service and out.

"Score one for evangelism," Father Rick said as he passed by. Christina saw him wink.

"Does he know?" she asked the warden.

"Father knows best," he shrugged and walked away.

Christina rolled her eyes. That described what they were at St. Martin's. Family. What family could ever keep a secret?

All in all, only two ladies grumbled that their grandchildren never got gift cards or a reception when they graduated. But they were the types who were likely to find fault in the Second Coming if they were still alive when it happened. Christina didn't let it get to her. Or, at least she tried and fairly succeeded at the attempt. Peering through her new specs, she chose to be pleased with her and her friends' efforts and refused to let anyone rain on the parade.

Josh came, and he didn't appear bent out of shape. Especially since the cakes were from Bonnie's. He ate three slices. Christina envied him because it wouldn't put a pound on him. Just like his dad. He definitely hadn't inherited her metabolism.

Focused

"Mom, y'all ought to do this every year," he commented, pointing his fork to the last few bites of cake. "This was really nice. Ashley, Paul and Marla all said so." Josh referred to some of the juniors who would be graduating next year. Christina inwardly moaned. It seemed just yesterday she served them milk and cookies in Vacation Bible School.

"I second that motion." Jean came up behind him. "I think this should be an annual event, or the juniors will be really upset with us."

"Traditions get started easily in this Church, don't they?" Josh quipped.

"Oh, yeah," The two women said in union, then laughed.

Par for the course, Christina stayed along with a few faithful others to clean up after everyone had left. She was pleasantly surprised to see Jeff out of the corner of her eye folding the tables and helping to put the stackable chairs back on their carriers to be hauled off to the storeroom. Later as she swept, she noticed him gathering up the trash to walk to the dumpster behind the parking lot. Of course, so did Bud. The two passed back and forth as ships in the night, nodding slightly, beads of sweat forming on brows. Could it be a contest? For whose benefit? Hers or Mary Ellen's? Come to think of it. Where was Mary Ellen? Had she left?

"Jeff sure is being helpful today," Betty stated without malice or jealousy that her husband, Thomas, had left to watch the Rangers game on TV.

Christina knew that the two loved each other more than newlyweds, even after thirty-five years. She often marveled at and a little envied their closeness.

Betty once told her it was because they decided their marriage was worth the effort, plain and simple. And she admitted it had not always been that way.

"He sure is." Harriet winked as she came over to take the last of the punch cups away. "What's gotten into ol' Jeff anyway? Letting you get a maid. Acting all charming. Maybe I should have an old beau move in for a while and make Ralph jealous."

Christina laughed. Harriet was a widow. Ralph was her Boston terrier she mothered to death.

"And to think now he's planning….." Harriet stopped and bit her lip when Betty shushed her.

Christina didn't catch the blunder. Lost in her own thoughts, she nodded, wiping her brow. "I have married a good man," she simply said… and meant it.

* * *

Christina went to the Ladies' room. There stood Mary Ellen, huddled in tears.

"Oh, Mary Ellen. I thought you'd left. . . honey, what's wrong?" She rushed to her young friend's side.

Mary Ellen blew her nose then gulped. "Bud and I. We called it quits."

"When?" The cold splash hit Christina's spine and inched up into her tear ducts, for both of them.

"Just now. He was so sweet about it. Said he was still in transition and didn't want to get serious over anyone. 'The burns are too fresh,' that's what he said."

"Oh?" Christina replied. Too fresh? Or did he have two fresh eyes for her maid? And why did the green-eyed monster rear its ugly head in her? Was it

Focused

because he seemed to be ignoring her while noticing every other woman she knew? Christina took a cleansing breath. This wasn't about her, or Bud. Her friend was crying.

"And how do you feel?" Christina wrapped her arm around the woman's shoulder and drew her near to her side for comfort.

Mary Ellen let loose a wimpy laugh. "Does it sound strange to say, relieved?"

"No, not if that's how you feel. Tell me why."

The younger of the two turned and dabbed her eyes, leaning into the mirror to repair the runny mascara blotches. "He came on so strong. I was afraid I was rebounding. I mean the ink is still wet on the divorce papers." She stopped and spun around. "Have people talked?"

"Not within my earshot. But then of course they wouldn't. But I have felt stares. I figured they're talking about me letting him stay in my house under my husband's nose."

Mary Ellen bobbed her head up and down. "Perhaps we both have been targeted. Anyway, Bud got a little too close on our last date, if you get my drift. He scared me. Maybe I turned him off?"

Christina's skin crawled. It reminded her of what happened to her all those years ago in his truck. Time hadn't changed the man, it seemed. She hugged her friend. "God knows best. Give it time. If it is meant to be, you two will pick it up again."

She couldn't help but think of Avery. Was she the real reason Bud backed away? The feminine blood in her began to quietly boil into soft ball stage, just like in her mother's recipe for fudge. Maybe she should give him the benefit of the doubt. She had to admit she felt relieved he was no longer dating one of her friends, especially if he couldn't keep his hands to himself. Maybe Mary Ellen eventually would, too.

Christina left Mary Ellen to regain her composure, but in truth, she needed to regain hers. She wanted to whack Bud. Why? For hurting her friend? For being a cad? Or for looking another direction than her own? Whatever the reason, Christina knew she had to swallow it back down before Jeff came back from taking out the trash.

A slight chill hung over the house the next few days. The same chill that had been present since she asked about Mary Ellen in front of Avery. This time it was mutual.

One day Bud came into kitchen. He eyed Christina as he poured some coffee. "You off to work?" He had his back to her. The clink-clunk of the spoon in the mug sounded louder and faster than usual.

"Yes. In a while. Jeff just left."

"I know. Gotta moment?" He swaggered to the bistro table and flipped the chair around, straddling it. His hand motioned to the chair opposite him.

Christina felt immediately back in high school, this time in the principal's office. "Bud," she started, then stopped and sat down. *Here goes nothing.*

The steel blues penetrated her soul, cold and sharply focused. She continued. "I'm sorry. Who you see is your business. Not mine. I've acted like a duffus."

Focused

He shifted in the seat and flexed his back muscles. She could see them ripple through his T-shirt. It reminded her of James Dean. She told herself to stop it.

"Yeah. You have. I just want to know why?"

"I don't know, really."

He leaned into her space. "I don't believe that, Chris." The blue ice melted and softness emerged in his eyes.

"Bud, I should go."

She went to get up, but he grabbed her forearm. "Should I?"

Her veins steeled. "Should you what?" She stared a hole into his hand, willing it to release her. He finally obliged.

"Go." He sat back and crossed his arms over the chair. His eyes never left her face.

"If you think you should." *Stupid response. Why can't I say yes, get out of here, out of my life, my friend's life, my maid's life?*

"I made a huge blunder once in a truck. The one you puked in. Almost made the same one again during the flood. At least I thought that's the message you broadcasted. Yes, or no?"

"No. I mean yes. Bud, I love my husband," she stammered and looked away.

"He's a good man, Chris."

She whimpered, "I know." She plopped back in the chair, eyes welling. "We've had a rough time of it, lately. Dad passing, then Mom, Josh growing up…"

He reached for her hand. "I know. You told me. Not that I couldn't see it for myself. Seems I keep coming around to patch your broken heart. Too bad you can never patch mine."

"Bud, that's not fair."

"Life isn't, my girl." He rubbed her knuckles with his thumb. He inched his face towards hers, then stopped as if an invisible hand came between them. His thumb landed on her wedding band.

Christina took a breath. Bud stood up. "You better get to work."

She nodded.

"Right." He rubbed his hand through his hair and began to walk away. Then he turned back to her. His eyes gleamed with mischief. "By the way, is that Avery's number on the fridge door?"

She resisted the urge to throw the frying pan at his head. None of her business, that's what she'd said. She grabbed her purse and slung it over her shoulder. On the way to the garage she pointed to the pink paper stuck to the refrigerator with a magnet.

"Yes. The first is the agency's. The second is her cell."

It took every bit of control not to slam the door behind her.

Chapter 37 Aftershave and Lemongrass

Avery wished Christina had forewarned her that they had a guest in the house. Not that it really mattered. What was one more pair of sheets? She always cleaned the hall bath anyway even if it looked as if it had barely been used. Still, it unnerved her a bit. Never someone who liked surprises, the cleaning woman preferred her ducks in a row, tidy, neat, organized. That was why she got along so well with her employer. She knew her style and could keep up with it.

But having someone else in the house when she was used to her own pace, her own pattern disturbed the woman. What was she supposed to do? Tiptoe around him? Not clean his room? Avery chided herself. She was a professional. Personal items meant nothing to her anymore than a naked body meant something to a physician. Part of the trade. In her business, you saw a bit of everything. None of your bee's wax. Just keep cleaning. That's the job. Where has this mysterious disappearing guest gone off to anyway? As she scooted down the hall, she glimpsed through the living room blinds. Yep, his truck still sat at the curb.

She couldn't help watching for him as she floated in and out of the rooms, dusting, humming various tunes from the previous night's Bible meeting. Finally, she sensed him standing there at the entrance to the den. She saw his shadow and caught a whiff of his aftershave. The same whiff that had been on the sheets she had just taken off the guest bed and on the towels in the hamper, now swishing in the washer taking on the scent of Christina's detergent instead. She liked that aftershave. A woodsy and musky smell. Very male. Her husband had never worn cologne or aftershave. She tried not to acknowledge how much it heightened her senses.

"I know that tune," came a low drawl. "It's a hymn or something, right?" The shadow shifted as the sunshine through the slider highlighted his shape.

"Uh, huh. 'It is Well with My Soul'."

"Oh." The shadow moved towards the bookcase she cleaned. "You like it that much?"

"I...what?" She stopped, duster in mid air and turned to face what had been in her peripheral vision. He came into focus, smiling. Something caught in her chest. She chose to ignore it.

"You said it made your soul, something. Made it well?"

She couldn't help but laugh at his response, a squeaky snort. Not exactly feminine. Not the willowy tee-hee that accompanied fluttering eyelids. But then,

Focused

she had never been a flutterer. And why on earth would she start now?

Avery looked at Bud, afraid her reply would wound him. Instead he laughed, too. Another plus. The guy was sure enough of himself to snicker at his own blunder. But then again, it wasn't like she was tallying up his qualities. Hearing him made her laugh even harder. It was contagious.

After a moment or so, they both sat down on the sofa and took a breath. Avery wiped her eyes with the back of her apron. Her sides ached. Her laughter muscles were definitely out of shape. Been a while, a long while.

"You have a great laugh." Bud slipped his arm casually onto the back of the leather. It didn't strike her as a forward pass, more like an innocent interception, as if he included her in his huddle of fun.

Avery shoved aside the offhanded compliment, letting it fall softly to the floor to be vacuumed up later. "Sorry, I couldn't help it. Let me explain. 'It Is Well With My Soul' is the name of the hymn." She tried to keep her response in a matter-of-fact tone. "It's one of my favorites. Whatcha might call a golden oldie."

The laughing grin reduced to a thin line. "Oh. Gotcha." The egg began to show on his face.

Avery didn't know what to say next. The woodsy musk lingered before dissipating into the lemon oil on the duster she wrung through her hands. The two sat in silence. It began to feel a bit awkward.

Then, a slap on the rawhide couch jolted her. With that he got up, the whoosh barely audible as the cushion rose beneath her. The guest raised his hand to his forehead, tipping an invisible Stetson. "Let ya get back to your work, ma'am." With a slight bow he turned on his boot heels.

Avery's heart turned over. Off in the utility room, the washer's motor thunked as it shifted into the spin cycle. "I've got some time."

Did I really say that? Avery fiddled with the strips of paper cloth in the disposable duster. Blue, striped, blue. It reminded her of picking daisy petals when she was ten with a crush on Timmy who lived two blocks over. She set the thing in her lap.

The footsteps sounded back and the cushion shifted. "Good. Me, too. What shall we talk about?"

Avery willed the rising warmth to not make it to her cheeks, but she knew it had. Those deep twinkling blue eyes melted into her resolve, smooth, swiftly, barely leaving a mark. And she a widow with two children. What would he think of that? Sitting there so casually, so sure of his maleness. He knew he had an easy-going style. He also knew how to fine tune it to the beat of her heart. How dare he?

The familiar iron clad wall suddenly rose, daring him to knock it back down. Avery shifted to meet his baby blues square on."I could tell you about my kids?"

Bud's face didn't change expression. Maybe he knows, she thought. Perhaps Christina told him all about me, even though she didn't tell me all about him. She looked down at his tanned hands. A slight whitish ring of skin appeared on the left ring finger. Tell tale sign of divorce. Her heart bled for him.

"Great and I'll tell you about mine." He shifted his weight, pulled the wallet from his back jean pocket and repositioned a bit closer to her. He opened it, licked his finger and flipped through opaque plastic sleeves. "Mind you," he added, "they are a little out of date. My ex-wife isn't too great about sending me new ones."

Avery chuckled. "I guess I can't be guilty of that. I'm a widow."

"Oh, I'm sorry." Accord registered in his face. "I understand. A loss is a loss."

She smiled back. "Yes, I guess it is. Pain's the same."

Bud nodded and cleared his throat. "This is Jamie, Jonathan and that's Judy. Wife named them all with the same letter. She thought it was cute. I thought it was confusing. . ."

* * *

That night after Bud left, reeking again of aftershave, Jeff pulled his wife aside.

"Christina, I got to tell ya. I don't like leaving the house in the morning with you still here. And him." He nodded to the door from which their guest just exited. He rushed to add, "I trust you. Don't get me wrong. But something just smells of trouble."

"More than that awful aftershave?" she jested. Then, seeing her husband didn't smile, she continued, "He asked me if he should leave this morning." She wiped an invisible smudge from the kitchen countertop.

"Oh? And you said…?"

"It was his choice." She scrubbed a little harder.

269

Julie B Cosgrove

"Good God." His fist slammed next to her. It made her jump. He paced the room a few times. "People are talking. He's been here over two weeks."

"So?" She threw the scrubber in the sink, pivoting to look him in the eyes.

"Don't play naïve. You're too old." He waggled her finger at her.

"And don't you, Jeff Willis, think perhaps you should stand up for your wife, and your marriage, instead of listening to idle gossip?" She whisked past him and down the hall. She slammed the guest bathroom door for effect.

Christina ran the bathtub water, trying to ignore the lingering aftershave smell in the room. Or his brush and razor near the sink. Yes, Bud raised her blood pressure. Yes, she could kick Jeff at times, but lately he was trying. They had a quarter of a century together. They had a son. They had something worth preserving, or recovering. But, Bud made her heart leap. Secretly, she had to admit he'd always had.

Darn them both. Maybe she should leave and let them duke it out. Wait for the police call. Let them clean up the bloody mess and arrest whoever remained standing.

That cabin beckoned, except what would she say to the Owens? Angela had a guest room. Harriet did, too. But neither of them tolerated cats. She couldn't leave her babies and expect the men to clean their boxes or give them fresh water. Did she have any PTO time left? Could she take off?

Oh, what am I thinking? The woman slumped onto the edge of the tub and cried. Out of the corner of her tears she saw the door creep open and two size 11's

270

enter. She couldn't will herself to look up at her husband's face. He sat next to her on the narrow cold porcelain, reached behind her and turned off the water.

"Not this time, hon. You aren't crying alone." He softly said. "Come here. I want my wife back."

That did it. Darn him. Heck with Bud. She fell into her husband's chest and sobbed. After a few minutes she wiped he eyes with his shirt.

"This is becoming a habit, isn't it Jeff?" *So is cussing, even if only in my mind. I never used to do that.*

The third heartfelt talk in two months began, each in a way jumpstarted by Bud's presence. This one ended up in the tub amidst lemongrass bubbles, their clothes strewn on the floor.

"Any idea when our guest will be back?" Jeff played with the bubbles under her chin. "This could get a little awkward." He looked around the 1960's green and pink tile encased tub.

"Water's getting cold anyway. You hungry?" She stretched and grabbed a towel from the rack above their heads, stepped out, shook a bubbly foot, then wrapped the terrycloth around her. She opened the door to the cabinet and got her husband a towel.

Grabbing her clothes she slipped out. "See you in a minute," she called back through the door. "Grilled cheese okay?"

Later, they were curled up on the couch watching a cable movie when the front door creaked open. Boots resounded on the hardwood floors and stopped at the threshold to the den.

Jeff craned his head. "Hey, Bud. You have a good time?"

"Yes, Dad." The reply came, emphasizing the parental part mockingly. "What are you two still doing up?" But the afterglow on their faces answered his question. He cleared his throat. He'd also gotten his answer to the question posed in the kitchen the morning before.

"Avery's really nice. We had a good time. Went to her son's baseball game."

Christina didn't react. She coolly asked, "Who won?"

"The other team did. We consoled him with ice cream."

Jeff played with the ring on Christina's left hand. "Glad you had a good time, my friend," a 'by-the-way, so-did-we' was implied in his tone.

Their guest took the hint. "Well, goodnight, folks." He knew when to leave.

Jeff winked at Christina and nodded toward the hall bath. "Think it still smells like lemongrass in there?"

She reached up to brush his cheek with her lips. "I hope so."

Jeff's lips curled into a Cheshire Cat grin.

Chapter 38   Budding Romance

Her computer's calendar reminded Christina of her turn for Altar Guild. She called her team to meet on Saturday, usual time. Betty was out of town. That left just her and Mary Ellen. Feeling the awkwardness between them, she decided to keep it level. Show her how to do things, keep the conversation light. Mary Ellen obliged.

But whatever had begun to bud, pun intended, between the two old friends during the flood was obviously a distant memory of much ado about nothing in Bud's mind.

Bud actually turned out to be a wonderful houseguest. He was polite, cleaned up after himself, and Jeff seemed to finally enjoy his company. Some of the old friendship, briefly tarnished by an unresolved romance squelched once over thirty years ago and once a few days ago, now had returned shiny and like new. Christina was able to relax and actually enjoy having her old Bud around.

"Water under…" he had said. The bridge back to their friendship was solidified again, after all those

273

years. Glad they went through the process, Christina now began to understand why they both had needed to do that. A lot of healing had gone on under her roof over the past month.

Her and Jeff's marriage definitely lay on a better road. She put the mourning of her dad in perspective, and though she missed him and her mother as well, she felt they were finally resting in peace. She and Carrie discussed it on the phone, both realizing the first anniversary of her mother's death loomed right after Christina's fiftieth birthday in a few weeks.

"How do you feel about not having Mom around for your big birthday? I mean, are you okay?" Carrie asked.

"I am now. A few weeks ago, probably not. I am working through it."

"What? Turning fifty or not having Mom to arrange it all?"

"Both. And she would have, wouldn't she?" Christina chuckled. Leave it to Carrie to brighten the subject.

"Oh, yeah. Just like she did mine," her sister responded. That had been a gala event. Engraved invitations, navy on baby blue in a calligraphy font with a silver pre-tied bow in the crease. Catered appetizers from the posh new bistro, fully tended bar, chamber music quartet. Carrie would have preferred pepperoni pizza and beer with some Moody Blues or Dylan.

"You know, Jeff hasn't mentioned it," the younger sister replied, trying not to let her emotions get in the way. She folded towels, phone cocked on her shoulder. They had been left in the dryer. Not like

Focused

Avery to be absent minded. Christina hadn't noticed them for a few days, but an old damp wash cloth and extra fabric softener sheet while they flopped around in the dryer for ten minutes freshened them. "But he's been really swamped with something."

"He'll come through. So will Josh." Her elder sister advised. "How's it going with Bud?" Sudden switch of subject, a veer into lesser traffic. But Carrie's mind often took a side route.

"Bud seems to be less of a wounded puppy and more of the old Bud I always remembered. He seems more sure of himself and is laughing more." Christina reported.

"Good. I don't think that would work in my house." Her sister humphed.

"He and Jeff seem to be getting along, but I can't help but notice there's still a bit of tension. Maybe it 's just two males in the same territory."

"Yeah, and you are the territory."

Christina gasped. "Carrie!"

"So, tell me about this maid." Carrie dodged another oncoming collision in their conversation.

"My house never looked so clean. The girl works hard for her money, and even after several weeks, the job is still excellent. And, she's dating Bud."

Christina heard the phone clunk to the ground on her sister's end.

* * *

Avery was healing. Christina gave Bud some of the credit for that. Her anger over her husband's untimely and senseless death dissipated. She wrote to

275

his killer, now incarcerated in the State Pen, and also to his wife and kids. They were all victims of violence, Avery told her when she showed Christina the letter. The maid wanted her employer to preview it before she mailed it off. Christina admired her strength and told her so. She told her about her pastor and the lessons he learned by forgiving the drunk driver.

Sometimes Christina would find a Bible verse or a little note from Avery. She started leaving some for her to find. It became a game between them. A new version of an Easter egg hunt. A game of mutual love and respect between sisters in spirit, both recovering from losing someone dear. Their friendship blurred the lines between employer and employee. But there was a time to redraw it in the sand. And the time was now.

"You have to talk to her about this, you know." Jeff warned as he grabbed his ice tea and the remote. "Tomorrow."

"I know. I guess."

"You guess?" The sternness in his voice reminded her of the math teacher she endured in seventh grade with his demeaning, aloof, 'we've-been-over-this-so why-don't-you-know-it' tone.

"Okay. I'll broach the subject when she comes this week to clean." And enjoy it as much as getting a root canal. Christina picked up her stitchery and pretended to count the cross-stitches.

"Gooood," he drawled. A rustle of the evening paper ended the conversation in a hard period. Sarcasm dripped off the sports section as a footnote.

Focused

The next morning when she arrived, Christina prayerfully broached the subject they'd never discussed—Bud being there when Avery came to clean while she and Jeff were at work.

"What does Bud do when you're here?" She tried to make it sound like idle curiosity.

Avery didn't miss a beat. "Not anything you wouldn't approve of."

Christina felt immediately embarrassed. "Oh, that's not what I meant. I mean, I know you are doing your job. You do a great job."

"You have every right to ask. I am on your clock and he is your guest, and old friend."

"Avery, I am sorry. It's just, well, getting complicated."

The woman leaned on the kitchen counter and a grin etched across her cheeks. "I know."
Then she popped back into employee mode. "But it won't be for long. He's decided to leave."

Thud. The news hit the floor and shattered across Christina's mind. "He is? When?"

The woman looked at her employer with wide innocent eyes. "He didn't tell you?"

"No."

A voice sounded behind her. "Surprise."

He went over, and openly pecked Avery on the cheek.

Christina looked away. "I gotta get going," she muttered.

"I've got something in the works, Chris. I'll tell you to about it tonight. I am leaving your house, but not Allensville. Kinda getting to like the scenery here." He smiled at Avery.

Julie B Cosgrove

Avery blushed.

Christina left, purse and keys clenched in her hand and nausea in her throat.

At lunch her ears were still steaming. Why that man riled her nerves she'd never understand. And if he hurt Avery, she'd kill him, bud or no.

"I can't take it," she whined to Angela and Sandy as they walked to the deli down the street. People pushed pass them, everyone in a hurry to be somewhere else.

" 'Scuse you, Mister," Angela called back over her shoulder. "What ever happened to chivalry?"

Sandy stopped. Christina had also, several paces behind. She and Angela backtracked to their coworker who was looking in the window of a shop, seeing their rippled reflections grow bigger. "What ya see?'

Absentmindedly, Christina stared ahead into the darkened glass. "A big fat idiot. Me." Then she spun on her heels. Her nostrils flared. "Why can't my husband and my best friend share my life? And why can't he date my maid?" Five people stopped in their tracks and stared.

"Oh, boy" Angela reached in her purse and pulled out a twenty. "Sandy, you go get sandwich boxes. Egg salad if they have it. And baked chips. We'll be over there, on the bench." She grabbed Christina's elbow and dragged her towards the fountain in the park. One black wrought iron bench lay empty and waiting for three hineys to huddle in girl talk.

Focused

That evening, Bud had begun to fix dinner by the time Christina walked in the door. The house smelled clean. Avery's touch definitely lingered—on Bud's face as well, from the look of his grin. Christina set her keys down.

"What's this?" A bubbly aroma filled the kitchen when the oven door opened.

"Chicken Divan. Alice used to make it." He dug the casserole out of the depths of the dark speckled self-cleaning oven, his hands wrapped in a dish towel. Sizzling splatter drops of sauce sloshed over the sides of the casserole dish. Christina made a mental note to program the cleaning cycle to begin after they went to bed.

The garage door whirred and she heard Jeff's car engine. "Good," Bud nodded. "I can tell you both the good news."

Jeff set his keys on the hook by the door. He nodded at them. "What smells good?"

"Bud's cooking Chicken Divan. He has news." Christina raised her eyebrows in silent communication. Jeff nodded back.

"Table's all set. You both go on in. I'll bring it in there to serve in a minute." Bud wiped his hand on the dish towel stuck in his belt. He grabbed a serving spoon out of the drawer and handed it to Christina. "Here. Can ya take this?"

In the dining room, the table glistened with her grandmother's fine china . . . and her twenty year-old, slightly bent everyday stainless cutlery. "Oh, well, the guy tried."

"Maybe Avery helped him set it." Jeff sat at the head of the table and flipped his knife back and forth. "Exactly what is this about?"

His wife shrugged. "Haven't got a clue. Avery knows but I couldn't pry it out of her."

"So, you two talked, huh? Good girl." Jeff looked up and nodded. "We'll soon find out," he whispered. "Here comes the master chef."

Bud placed the casserole on the trivet and sat down, almost. Then he snapped his fingers and bounced back up like a Jack-in-the-box. "Rolls."

Jeff groaned. Christina kicked his shin under the table.

They waited patiently until Bud returned with a basket of bread, said Grace and motioned for them to hand over their plates. He scooped the fixings onto each, and passed them back before saying, "I found a job. Right here in Allensville."

Jeff froze, fork in mouth. Christina twisted the napkin in her lap with a forced wide-eyed smile. "Wow. Tell us about it."

Bud obliged—non-stop, for the next fifteen minutes. Avery's brother owned a rental shop two miles out of town towards the highway. His wife just had a baby and he needed more time with her. Business was picking up, so he needed a full time salesperson. One who knew about farming equipment, construction machinery and the like. Bud did.

"Good pay?" Jeff inquired, leaning back, arms crossed.

"Not bad, plus commission. Enough to squeak by. It'll grow. It's a franchise. Who knows, in a year or so, maybe I can open a branch of my own. This is closer to Maw and Paw than Houston, that's for sure."

"Less muggy, too." Christina piped in, trying to sound positive.

Bud nodded and put down his fork. "Here's the catch. I don't get paid until the fifteenth. Then I can get my own place. That's ten more days. Can you two put me up for that long?"

Jeff smirked. "You mean put up with you?" Another kick in the shin."Ouch!"

"Of course, Bud. We'd be happy to." Christina spoke to her friend, but eyed her husband. "Right, Jeff?"

Jeff yielded. "Sure. Just kidding, Bud. Happy to oblige. And congrats." He laid his napkin on the table, half stood and stretched his hand over the centerpiece. Male gesture of no-hard-feelings.

Bud shook it twice. None taken.

"I found an apartment just beyond the tracks heading west. One bedroom. It will be available in a week or so. They have to redo the carpet. The last owner evidently had an incontinent dog."

Christina looked at Jeff, who tried not to choke on his last bite. They both knew the complex he referred to.

"I put a deposit down today."

"Bud, get it back. The owner's got a bad rep," Jeff warned.

"New owner, Jeff." Bud held up a finger to correct him."I checked it out. Avery's brother, Tim, knows him. Went to school together. Anyway, he bought the place at auction. Foreclosure. He's fixed up the place. New appliances. Re-landscaped. Kicked out some of the deadbeats."

"Really?" Jeff leaned forward and crossed his elbows on the table. "I hadn't heard about that. Had you, hon?"

Christina shook her head.

"If I weekend manage, I get half the rent taken off. Figure I can do both for a while."

Jeff extended his hand. Bud took it and they shook . . again. "Good research, man. You've been busy."

Bud leaned back, chest puffed. "Didn't think I just laid around all day, did ya?"

Chapter 39   Mauve, of course

Jeff showed one of the apprentices named Tim how to calculate the amount of stair rail material needed for a local school's expansion. Then Midge buzzed him.

"That lady Harriet from your church's on the phone. Again."

"What?" Jeff took off his readers and rubbed his forehead. "Did she say why she's calling?" It was the third call in two days.

"It's about your wife's fiftieth birthday party? She has another question."

Jeff jumped for the phone to click off the speaker mode. "Put her through," he mumbled into the receiver. Then he eyed the apprentice with a "Can I have a minute?" look. The man nodded his head, rolled up the plans and left almost on tiptoe.

Jeff heard Harriet's nasal hello. He returned the greeting.

"I'm sorry to bother you at work again," she began. "I just need to know if you have an idea of how many invitations we need to send out. I am at the printer's now."

"Printers? You can't just get, you know, Hallmark cards?"

"Well, we could, I guess." Her voice sounded deflated, similar to his wallet if this kept up. The price of the cake alone made him swoon, much less the estimate on the flowers. Forty dollars apiece for the ten centerpieces and seventy-five dollars for the main table's arrangement. Thank goodness the credit card statement wouldn't get there before the big day. Christina would flip, and of course the surprise would be ruined.

Maybe if it's a success, she'd ignore the amount he spent. Well, not ignore, she'd never do that in a million decades, but chide him less. Like it or not, his only saving grace was going to be this woman so bent on spending it all on the other end of the line. The vise squeezed tighter around his temples. He felt trapped as a fly in a spider web. If he balked at costs, it might be interpreted he didn't think his wife was worth it, or that he didn't love her enough. *No sense struggling. I'll just get tangled more.* His thoughts returned to the high pitched voice on the other end.

"...but you see, if we order by 5 pm today, they will print the napkins for half price. That is, if we order the whole package, which includes the invites and guest book, and . . ."

Napkins. Right. Like I care. "Do what you think is best, Harriet. I'm guessing a hundred ought to do it since around sixty-five will be going out to the families at St. Martin's."

Focused

"That only leaves thirty-five others, Jeff. Her family, yours, her coworkers and friends there in Allensville. Oh, and childhood friends...is there anyone she keeps in touch with?"

Jeff steeled his jaw. Now was not the time or the place. Yet Harriet was one of his wife's dearest friends and had taken the bull by the horns. He'd been clueless without her advice. He inhaled his patience back into his tone of voice. "Her sister Carrie is coming up with that list at your suggestion. I haven't had the . . .Look, go with a hundred and fifty just in case." *It's only money.*

"Exactly my thoughts," Harriet's voice perked up with enthusiasm. Jeff could almost see her peacock feathers opening wide. The woman relished approval.

"You're a jewel, Harriet. Couldn't do this without you." He placated her, but meant it. He was about to hang up the phone when he heard —

"Do you think she'd like raspberry or chocolate filling in the cake? If you think chocolate there is still time for me to call the baker."

Jeff's chair squeaked with the added weight that had just plopped on his shoulder. Tim paced outside the office and he had a meeting in ten minutes. *Lord help me.* Then, to the well intentioned voice on the other end, "She loves both. You choose. I trust your judgment. Gotta go earn my keep so I can pay for all this." He chuckled for emphasis. "Take care Harriet, bye."

Jeff clicked the phone off just as he heard a "but" squeak out from the woman's end of the line. He felt like a horse's patoot but surely she grasped the concept that he worked for a living. He wasn't retired

285

like her husband Jake had been, God rest his soul. Jeff thought he now had an inkling why Jake had taken up golf so soon after he got the proverbial gold watch.

Harriet blinked the start of a tear from her eye and turned to the printing clerk. She gave a tight lipped, split second grin. "We'll go with hundred and fifty of each. Invitations and napkins. Oh, and the RSVP cards are included in the price, right?"

She called Bonnie's Bakery. Both she and the baker agreed on the raspberry. Clapping her cell phone back into a clam shape, she hummed as her high heels clicked on the downtown Allensville pavement. The cake decision accomplished, she felt more productive. She loved a mission. Ticking off the check marks on the to-do list in her brain, she dashed off to the next stop. She encountered the air conditioned blast that whooshed through the glass door of the florist's only to evaporate instantly in the late spring heat wave. Harriet mopped her brow with a crumpled Kleenex, oblivious to the trail of white wormy pieces it left on her forehead. Three smiles greeted her.

"Ladies. I just had the most frustrating conversation with Jeff. The man is clueless." She stuffed the Kleenex back into the front pocket of her purse as a rush of perfumes and shoulder bags descended upon her in sympathy.

"He's a man, Harriet. They are all." Marge pitter-pattered her back in sympathy. "Come see what they just got in. Irises. Won't those be lovely? And Maryanne says she'll give them to us for wholesale, just because it's Christina. Wipe your forehead again, dear," she said in the same breath but in a lower tone, "You have bits of Kleenex stuck to it."

Maryanne, the florist, looked up from twirling mauve and navy ribbons together into the tenth bow. "It is the least I can do. She brought us meals four times when Benjamin was out of work with that broken leg. Even did two loads of laundry for us."

Heads nodded. Each had a similar tale. Harriet sighed. "Well, he was at work. I know he's busy making the money to pay for this shin-dig."

"I'm sure Jeff didn't mean anything, dear." Another pitter-patter on the shoulder blades.

Harriet straightened her spine, letting the conversation slide down her backside and off into never, never land. "Well. Yes. Of course he didn't. I ordered the cake. Chocolate mocha with raspberry filling, white cream cheese icing and fresh raspberries and chocolate shavings sprinkled on top. Along with 'Happy 50th Christina' written in raspberry sauce, of course."

"Will there be any flowers on the cake? I love how Bonnie's makes those little frosted flowers," Marge hinted.

"Yes, I think. I 'm not sure. For your sixty-fifth next year, my dear, we'll make sure they are."

Marge suddenly lost sixty years as she giddily clapped her hands together and bounced in her orthopedic oxfords.

Harriet responded with her own pitter-patter on the shoulder, the St. Martin's women's friendship sign. Then, she turned back to the florist counter. "Maryanne, those are the perfect colors. Just look at how well they match the napkin sample. I have it in here somewhere."

Hands in bag, the woman sent keys, two lipsticks, breath mints, a comb, two curlers and three pens rolling across the counter to be snatched by eager helpers. At last she dug out the envelope with the crumpled example. Holding it up with pride, she crowed. "See? Mauve. Her favorite color, Jeff says."

"Like he would know." Marge sniffed.

"Well," Maryanne raised an eyebrow. "She decorated her new study in mauve and blue. She showed me the scraps left over from making the curtains. Go-orgeous. "The last word trilled for emphasis.

"Humph, you mean the room that Bud is now occupying? For how long now? Nearly a month? No wonder Jeff is so grouchy. My Bob would never allow one of my old beaus under our roof." Janice inserted.

"He has his eyes on Mary Ellen, not Christina, dear."

"Didn't you hear? He dumped her. Of all the nerve." Janice tapped her foot hard onto the florist's tiled floor.

"Well, she never wears mauve," Marge retorted, ignoring the turn in the conversation's direction. She held up the napkin to the light.

Maryanne put down the ribbon, not believing the incongruous comment. "Hon, haven't you ever noticed her nail polish? That's all she wears."

Chapter 40   Just Not That Way

Josh felt the buzz in his hip pocket. He peeked around the store for a pair of manager's eyes. Not spotting any, he turned his back to the counter and slipped out his Blackberry. It was his Dad. Weird. He never called. "Yeah, Dad. I'm at work. What's up? Mom okay?"

"Huh? Oh, yes, I guess. Haven't spoken with her yet today. Listen, we need to coordinate picking up folks from the airport. Can I count you in?"

"Sure. Text me and let me know who's arriving when and the Willis taxi service will be ready." He mimed a salute, then noticed Mandy strolling by, brow wrinkled. He pointed to the phone and mouthed the word "Dad". She nodded in recognition and craned her head in the direction of the floor manager.

"Mr. Stephens? Got a minute?" She dashed for the interception, glancing back with a wink. Josh gave her a thumb's up.

Josh turned back away from the counter. "Dad. Manager's on the floor. Gotta go. I'll call ya on break."

"No. Your Mom will be home. Call me tomorrow at work." What was one more interruption. Harriet would probably call at least six more times anyway, and probably Carrie.

"Okay. Bye."

"And Josh?"

"Yes, sir?" Josh tried to even his voice. His peripheral vision caught Mandy still discussing life in general with Mr. Stephens.

"Thanks."

"Dad. She is my mom. Talk tomorrow. Bye."

Jeff hung up his cell and stared at the traffic line in front of him. Double-strung beads of illuminated red pearls wound over the asphalt track in the evening dusk. Workers bull dozed rubble behind concrete pylons up ahead. They blocked the left lane for miles and would for the next eight to ten months, adding another lane to better accommodate the flow they now inhibited. Tax dollars at work. The congestions reminded him of his life. All the various pressures trying to cram into one lane called an eight hour day.

The weary exec snorted. More like ten to twelve hours. He couldn't remember the last time he only worked eight, except maybe on the weekends. Long hours away from his hearth and home, and her. His words to his son stung in the back of his throat. He hadn't talked to her yet today. How often their paths just crossed silently, routinely, a pattern worn over time. He remembered a time he couldn't wait to hear her voice on the other end of the phone. Had it been that long ago?

Not that he particularly relished the fact he put in the hours while his wife's old flame lulled around

Focused

the house. Well, maybe that wasn't fair. Evidently the man had some enterprising streak in him. Four more days and Bud would be in his own place. Two days later, the big event would commence. Jeff just hoped his marriage could hang on by the bare threads a few more days. Then, when his wife saw all he had done just for her, things would get better. He'd make sure of it.

The tension in her face had eased now that she had Avery to help out. That would keep getting better, if Bud didn't take Avery with him when he left. Well, at least Avery had shifted the guy's thoughts away from Christina. Right?

Jeff thrust his neck from side to side, looking for the familiar crackle then pop that would ease the tension which climbed up his shoulders into his cranium. Four more days. Then he'd be out of their hair, or so Jeff hoped. Surely Christina wouldn't be dashing over to decorate Bud's apartment the way she had Josh's. That was Avery's job. His neck tensed again, pleading for another good crack.

Jeff guessed he had to thank Bud for the wakeup call. His wife said she saw her life in a new perspective since her jaunt to the cabin and getting her new specs. Maybe it was catching. Seems her refocusing had made him do the same. Maybe Bud represented the lens cleaner for them both in God's good plan.

As the stream of paired red lights inched towards his exit, Jeff made a resolve. There'd be a lot more lemongrass moments from now on. More random acts of chores around the house, maid or no maid. And, more phone calls during the day just to say hi, I needed to hear your voice. It was time he wooed his wife again. He never should have stopped.

* * *

Christina leaned into the door jam, watching Bud pack. "Is there anything you need? Extra cups or dishes? We have some old mismatched stainless Jeff and Josh used to use when they went camping. It's not much, but. . ."

Her old friend's mouth curled on one side into a smirk. "Avery and I already went shopping. She has a membership at one of those mega discount stores. Got tons of deals. It's mostly in the trunk of her car right now or I'd show you."

"You two getting serious?" She bit her tongue, but it was too late, like closing the barn door after the horse already escaped. Bud stopped, his neck tucked into his chest as he folded another T-shirt. He laid it inside the suitcase and sat down on the bed. For a moment he looked out the window at nothing in particular. Christina hoisted herself onto the dresser with feminine grace, her legs dangled and crossed.

Bud 's steel blue eyes turned to peer into her face. "Would it upset you if we were?"

Would it? Christina slid off the dresser and moved to the window, leaning against the sill. His eyes moved with her. "No. Why?"

The baby blues narrowed. "Avery told me you two had a talk."

"Oh. Of course she did." Her left foot made a small circle across the hardwood floor, tracing an old paint stain that had seeped in from Josh's artsy elementary school days. She never could totally eradicate that spot. Nor had she wanted to. She raised her gaze to meet his.

A twinkle surfaced, spread across the azure eyes then slipped over the rest of his face. He got up and took two confident strides towards her. "Jealous?"

If she'd had something to pitch at him she would have. "No!" Christina crossed her arms across her chest, then dropped them again, conscious of the body language. Regrouping, she added, "Really, I'm not. It's just, well, not quite Kosher her working here and all."

Bud stepped back again, thumbs shoved in his jean pockets. "Nothing happened, Chris."

"It's none of my business, really. . ."

"Of course it is. You are paying her by the hour to clean, not be with me." He crossed his right leg over his left and leaned against the wall. James Dean pose. She dropped her eyes, breaking contact to find the paint stain again with her toe.

"I trust her. You. Both of you. I'm not your mother, Bud."

At that he reeled back his head and crowed with laughter. Over it she thought she heard the garage door opening. Jeff's home.

Bud wiped his eyes and sniffed. He looked at her as she moved to leave the room. "Chris." He reached for her hand.

"Yeah?" She turned to face him. A strand of hair stuck to her cheek.

"I love you." He drew closer. One tanned finger delicately pushed the lock of hair from her face and tucked it behind her ear.

The gesture sent a tingle through her to her core."I know. I love you, too."

"Just not in that way, right old friend?" The twinkle grew brighter now.

His hand felt warm and dry. She squeezed his knuckles and whispered. "Right."

Bud's jaw twitched. He let go."Then go tell your husband, 'Welcome home.' " He walked to the dresser, opened the drawer with a jerk and resumed his chore.

A momentary urge to thrust her arms under his and hold tight to him was pulverized by the sound of Jeff's boots coming down the hall.

Chapter 41 Fine

Bud called out. "Hey, Jeff. We're in here chatting while I pack. Join us."

Jeff shuffled into the room, leaning on the jam where twenty minutes earlier his wife's shoulder had been. "You leaving now? Thought you couldn't occupy until the first."

"Can't. Just did the laundry, so why not start packing the clothes while I'm at it. Spent all day doing it. Hate laundry."

"Uh, huh." Jeff commiserated. Christina saw the unsaid 'That's- why-we-have-women-in- our-lives. Sorry-you-don't- right-now' expression on his face.

Bud gave him a tight-lipped grin. Christina wanted to kick them both. But then again, she'd had that reaction often with these two. Men. She turned to inch past her husband, when he caught her arm.

"Hello?" He pecked her cheek. He smelled so familiar. The after affects of day-old aftershave with the scent of architectural ink and paper mingled with his natural maleness. It was like a soothing balm.

She patted his left love handle. "Hi, hon. How was your day?"

"Fine." A noncommittal shrug accompanied his response.

"Really?" She looked at him as his eyes quickly darted to the hall and to Precious sauntering down it. He pushed off and went to pick up the purring ball of fur. *Nauseating. But then again, maybe if I acted that glad to see him. . .*

Wait! Fine? When was the last time her husband had a fine day since being promoted? Something stank, more than Precious' just out of the cat box paws.

Christina watched as the cuddling pair headed for the den, and the recliner. Fine, indeed. He was up to something, and it didn't appear to be a non-existent church stage either.

Bud suddenly piped up. "Chris?"

"Hmm?" She craned her head back into the guest room, her would-be sanctuary. In four days it would be that again, for six weeks that is until her aunt arrived for the rest of the summer. She was researching for her latest book on little known Texas history tidbits and hoped to spend a good bit of her time in the Capitol archives. Christina hadn't had the chance to tell Jeff her Aunt Mildred invited herself, knowing her niece would never turn her down, or out, as the case may be. During her teen years when Christina and her mother locked horns over everything, Aunt Mildred had been her refuge. Ten years ago, after she lost her husband, she moved to Dayton to be with her grandkids. Christina admitted to herself she did miss having her nearby.

"I just wanted to let you know something. There's nothing going on between Avery and me. Never really was."

"Really?" Christina felt the egg sizzling on her face. She had just assumed, again. When would she learn to stop doing that? "I .. I . . ."

"Yeah, I know." He plopped onto the bed, silent for a moment tracing the suitcase stitches with the edge of his thumb. Then he admitted, "It's not like I didn't try. Actually thought we were headed down the right path. But she brought it to a screeching halt a few nights ago. She told me it had to do with something in the Bible about yoking."

"Yes, I know that passage."

"I didn't, which I guess was the problem. She politely explained I'm not enough of a practicing Christian for her tastes." A short chuckle did little to cover the hurt in his voice.

The blood poured out of Christina's heart for him. She rushed over, sat beside him and grasped his hand. Another rejection. His wife, Mary Ellen, Avery, and in a way, herself. "I'm so sorry." The words forced through her throat, clogged with sadness for her friend.

"Yeah. Well, the lady's wise. Besides, she is fifteen years younger than us. The thought of raising kids again, I don't know." Bud shook it off and winked.

Christina laughed. "Well, there is that."

* * *

Julie B Cosgrove

Down the hall, Jeff sat in his recliner with Precious purring on his lap. His eyes were on the weatherman's recap of the week's stats, but his fuming ears were tuned into the laughter coming from the guest room. He wanted his wife's attention, otherwise how else could he give her his? Maybe tonight it would be just the two of them. A cozy dinner of the delicious beef stew he smelled simmering in the crock pot. It could win ribbons if she ever entered it into a cook-off. He breathed in the aroma filtering into the den. His stomach growled in recognition and anticipation.

No, his day didn't go fine. But how could he tell his wife about all the interruptions caused by her best friend? The ones that almost made him late to the bid table and lose the job he had worked on the last fourteen days, calculating the pitch sale of his career. The pity party was in full swing so he let himself stay a while. Precious, however, noticed the added pressure to his petting. She leapt from his lap in search of one of the couch's throw pillows.

"Desert me, too?" He hissed. Fine.

* * *

Christina sauntered into the den shaking her head. "Ya know what Bud just told me?" she asked as she plopped on the couch, legs tucked under her.

Jeff mumbled a non-interested response, eyes fixed to the sports clip about the local high school's baseball loss of four to one. Christina turned to watch it as well. No sense carrying on a conversation with a mute stump. She picked up her mending basket, and settled in for a half hour of hem repair before dishing

298

out the stew that had been simmering in the crock pot all day.

"Bud? You eating with us or do you have plans?" She yelled back down the hall. Out of the corner of her eye she saw the stump shift in the recliner and the green glow of volume scale on the TV screen increase in level.

"Staying," came the response back down the hall to her couch perch. "Been smelling your stew all day. My stomach's been growling for two hours."

She swore she saw Jeff's eyes roll upwards. Fine, huh? She doubted it.

Chapter 42   What A Crock

Dinner was a silent affair, except for the sound of male slurping and Fat Cat's ID tag dinging against the bowl when Jeff offered him scraps. The vet specifically said no more table food for the overweight feline. Christina suspected Jeff did it just to get her goat, but she swallowed back the comments with her last piece of cornbread. The chiding could wait until Bud left the room.

As she got up to clear the dishes, Bud reached to pull out her chair for her. Jeff, her gallant knight in shining armor husband who should have made the gesture, kept his eyes on Fat Cat and patted his head before retrieving the bowl. The animal took two steps and then settled in for a marathon bath, just to show his gratitude, no doubt. Jeff made cooing sounds.

Christina couldn't stand it. She clunked the dishes in the sink and dashed down the hall to the master bedroom, slammed the door, and fell into a hump over her dressing table. Tears peppered her prayers for patience, understanding and control. Tears

301

for Bud and his perpetual broken heart, for Josh who no longer lived in that room, for Jeff and his job and the pressures and the load he carried, and for herself and the days that were no more.

Days before Josh graduated from high school when they shared in all of his activities and went to church together and seemed happy. Days when her mom and dad were alive, shivering in the bleachers with them watching Josh's soccer team score another goal. Days when Jeff stealthily slipped his hands over hers in public and his eyes twinkled with love. Maybe he was trying to recapture that feeling. Reignite the spark in lemongrass bubbles. She wanted that, too. Could they? Not with Bud in their face. Two more days. Did she feel glad, or sad, or both?

She shoved her fist into her mouth to stifle the sobs emitting from her throat. She didn't want Jeff or Bud, or even the cats, to know. Deep breaths. Expand the lungs and let in God's peace. She grabbed the last tissue from the box and blew her nose, then dabbed her eyes to remove the mascara smudges. The stew threatened to re-emerge in her throat in place of the sobs, so Christina got up and began to pace the room.

A barely audible tap on the door caught her off guard. She dashed into the bathroom and turned on the spigot before calling out, "Yes?"

"Don't mean to bother you. Just letting you know I am heading out for a bit." Bud's voice echoed into the bedroom.

Christina grabbed a hand towel and patted her face. Looking past his reflection in the medicine cabinet mirror she grinned. "Have fun." Then she turned away and pretended to place the towel back on the rack just so, dawdling until he got the message and left.

It worked. The boot steps headed out of the room and clumped down the hall, muffled by the two throw rugs. A few minutes later, they resumed down the hall then were silenced by the carpet in the den. She waited until she heard the male grumbles, some form of hospitable acknowledgement of each other's presence, then the front door close. The elephant on her chest left the room as well.

Shivering away in residual emotion, Christina went back to the kitchen through the formal living room and dining room, purposely avoiding the mute stump that would be sitting in the recliner in the den. To her surprise, the stump was bent over a sink of suds, sponging out the crock pot. Atonement flooded her heart.

Jeff looked up from his task, his expression veiled. "Hi."

"Hi. Thanks for doing that." She edged over to the sink and placed her palm on the small of his back. His muscles responded.

"No problem. You okay? Did you get sick or something? Flu bug's going around. . ."

"Jeff, I'm sorry."

"Me, too. It is because I fed Fat Cat?"

Christina laughed. How clueless men were. "No. Yes, maybe."

The look on Jeff's face confirmed she had only muddied the waters further.

"Bud and Avery broke up."

Jeff stopped drying the crock-pot lid. His eyes clouded over. "So?"

That was not the direction she wanted this conversation to go. "Why am I constantly focusing on Bud and not him?"

Jeff turned to her with his mouth open. "I have been wondering the same thing, if I'm the 'him' you're talking about."

She realized she'd expressed that last thought out loud. God opened her mouth and forced her thoughts out into the room.

He turned past her, brushed her shoulder and placed the crock pot back in the pantry.

Christina groaned. It was going to be a very long night. The stew had not been the only thing simmering a while. Well, she had prayed for patience. She pushed her glasses back up on the upper rim of her nose, slipped her arms around her husband's waist and nestled her head into his backbone.

"Talk time?" His voice vibrated through his back into her ear.

"Lemongrass?" she whispered, rising on tiptoes to kiss his neck.

"Sure, until we resolve this once and for all or prune up, whichever comes first." He tossed the dish towel towards the sink, grabbed her hand and led the way.

* * *

Bud stopped off at the Git-N-Go for a Lone Star Long Neck. Just one. Just enough to whet his whistle and shove the hurt back into his gut where it belonged. He understood Avery's objections. The brown glass bottle neck laced between his fingers emphasized their differences. She was a teetotaler, born and bred. He hadn't seen the inside of a church building in fifteen years until he'd come to stay with the Willises. Whoever said opposites attract was dead wrong.

Bud leaned against the door of his truck and twisted off the bottle cap. The first cold swig slid down his throat, numbing the lump lodged under his Adam's Apple. Much better.

Oil and water. That's what we are. She was just being friendly in that good Christian wanna-help-the-downtrodden kinda way. Just like Christina. He had, once again, misread the signals. Now he wondered if he should save face and turn down her brother's job offer.

But what good would that do? He'd signed a lease. He needed a job to pay the rent. Besides, he'd be good at it and there was nothing for him in Houston, or the Hill Country. Maybe if the new leaf turned over, Avery would see things differently.

He humphed. Never mind. That couldn't be his motivation. Perhaps a few months of women-less nights was the medicine he needed to cure this perpetual heartache.

Downing the last of the brew, he tossed it in the trash barrel on the side of the convenience store. The seat springs greeted his rear end with their usual squeak as he climbed into the truck's cab.

"I'll just stay away from all of them. Mary Ellen, Avery, Christina. . . and Jeff. Allensville is a good size town. We won't have to run into each other all the time," Bud said out loud in resolve.

Julie B Cosgrove

He thumped the dashboard of his truck in resolution. New life. New place. New job. Maybe he'd even scope out that little Bible Church down the road from the apartments. New habits.

He had to admit church going folk seemed accepting and friendly. At least they had been at St. Martin's. Might be the same down the way. He could make some good friends, the right sort of people to hang out with after work instead of heading for dingy pool halls and bars.

Driving to the hardware store for paint and supplies, he admitted to himself he'd miss Christina's cooking, especially that stew. He put a crock pot on his mental shopping list.

Maybe it would be okay to call her in a week or so after he got moved in, just for the recipe.

Chapter 43 Stop a Clock

Truth be told, Christina was relieved that nothing developed between Bud and Mary Ellen, or Bud and Avery, or Bud and anyone else in a skirt within a fifty mile radius. She didn't particularly relish the thought of every unattached woman she knew drooling over her old beau. It left her rather uncomfortable. She wasn't sure Harriet had been immune to the old Owens charm even though she carried a Medicare card in her wallet.

The next morning Bud met her in the kitchen. He looked at her then tilted his head towards the hall. "Everything okay?"

Christina turned her back to him and stirred her coffee. "Hmmm? Yes, just fine."

"It didn't seem that way last night..." His sentence was cut short by the sound of Jeff's boots coming down the hall. Bud leaned against the bar and uttered a simple "Morning."

Jeff returned the same greeting. He leaned over and brushed the air close to his wife's cheek with his lips. "I may be late tonight. Bob wants to go over this bid step by step. Don't worry. I'll grab food on the way home."

"Okay. Sure, hon. Have a good day." She patted his side.

"I'll try." He half-turned to his guest. "I suspect you'll be long gone before I get back, so, good to have you." The look in his eyes conveyed a territorial message enveloped in the Texas hospitality.

There was a nod and a slightly raised coffee cup as a reply. Christina didn't know whether to laugh at them or swat them both with the dishtowel. She watched Jeff exit through the back door.

"If my being here has caused you two any grief, I am sorry," Bud said after the door closed.

"It's nothing to do with you, Bud. Jeff's been under a lot of pressure with this promotion he got a while back. We'll get through it."

"You better. You two have the real thing, you know. Don't blow it."

She was about to say how could they after all these years, but bit her tongue before she spoke. Instead she mumbled that she wouldn't and headed down the hall to brush her teeth. She stopped halfway and then came back. "Bud, are you leaving today?"

"I need to, Chris. For all of our sakes."

"Why?" His response confused her.

"Let's just say I know when I've overstayed my welcome. Three's a crowd and I have crowded you two long enough. I called the landlord last night. He's letting me in early free of charge if I agree to paint the walls."

Focused

Christina smiled at her old friend. "Seems your mother's country wisdom has rubbed off on you finally."She swore he stuck out his tongue at her before he winked. "How'd Jeff know?"

"He was up when I got in last night, after I dropped off the paint at the new place and taped off the walls."

"What time was that? I didn't hear you come in?"

Bud shrugged and jammed his hands in his jean pockets. "Midnight, I guess, thereabouts."

"And Jeff was up? He came to bed with me . . .", she stopped. Too much information.

Bud took his hands out of his pockets. He scratched tiny splatters of paint off his knuckles. He looked like a little boy all alone in a huge cruel world.

"Keep in touch, alright?" She swallowed down the emotions with a gulp. His steps moved quietly towards her.

"Oh, heck, Chris. I will, I promise." His voice softened as he pulled her to him. His touch was that of a friend. It felt warm and welcomed. She held on tight. He nestled his face in her hair, his breath warm on her neck.

The back door opened.

"I forgot my..." Jeff's voice stopped cold. Without saying another word, he flipped open his cell phone and speed dialed his office.

"Midge? Tell Bob I just had something come up at home that needs my attention. I'll be in as soon as I can."

The next few seconds were shrouded in embarrassment, misunderstanding and not quite knowing what to say. Finally Bud took the high road.

"Look, man. We were just saying goodbye. It wasn't..."

Jeff stared at a spot on the floor and scratched his head with his cell phone. "Go pack, Bud. I need to talk to my wife."

Christina exploded. "No! You do not, Jeff Willis. Go to work. That's where I am headed. And when you want to act like an adult instead of a jealous hormonal teenager, let me know. Till then, I do NOT want to talk about it. Bud, goodbye. Good luck. " She grabbed her purse and slammed the door, knocking the clock off the wall.

The two men stared at the door then both dove for the clock, and missed. It smashed on the floor. The plastic face popped off. The batteries flew out and rolled under the cupboards. The two men watched it all helplessly. Suddenly Jeff burst out laughing. Bud stepped back and knitted his brows. "What?"

"Her anger could stop a clock." Jeff sputtered out.

Bud reared back his head and guffawed. The iciness melted into male companionship.

Jeff grabbed the dishtowel and wiped his eyes."Sorry, man."

"Hey, if that had been me, I'd have decked me." Bud shook his head. "I mean .. oh, hell's bells. You know."

Focused

"Yeah." Jeff motioned his head towards the garage door. "But how do I calm her down?"

Bud raised his hands in surrender and headed down the hall. "I'll set the burglar alarm when I leave."

"Okay." Jeff leaned to watch Bud exit, "But remember, I'm counting the silverware when I get home." A slight chuckle revealed his jest.

Bud's tongue in cheek expletive and reference to a physical impossibility didn't bear repeating.

Jeff laughed. He had to admit he liked the guy. Maybe they could all be friends from now on. They did have something in common, namely Christina. But Jeff definitely remained the Alpha Male in that circle. Bud represented no threat as long as he made sure he respected and loved his wife. In fact, he should thank the guy for reminding him he could always have competition if he took her for granted. Seems he had been doing so for way too long. After all, his bride had kept herself up pretty well over the years. When had he stopped noticing?

Speaking of, first things first. He needed to patch things up with her fast. Otherwise, the surprise would fall flat and all his plans would be for naught. He grabbed his cell phone, searched for the number. There. West Ave Florists. What had Bob said? Cover the bases, man.

* * *

Three hours later, Angela plopped a bouquet of peppermint carnations in a glass vase on Christina's desk. "What's the occasion this time? Another non-fight?"

311

Christina huffed into her bangs. "Maybe Jeff's funeral has just been postponed." She snatched the little card from the holder. It read—I'm an idiot. Please forgive me. Jeff.

Angela came around the desk to read over her shoulder. "Does this mean he's off the hook?"

"I honestly do not know. And I can't think about it now. I've used up half a roll of tape in this calculator and I can't get this account to balance." Christina stomped her foot, pushed her chair away and headed out the back door and down the hall to the restroom.

Sitting in the last stall prayed to stop the angst bubbling in her throat, then went outside for a breath of fresh air.

Her mountaintop experience seemed eons away. She had never felt lower in the valley of despair than now. Her emotions were spinning over her head like the cartoon stars when someone is conked on the noggin'. But they were not very bright and cheery.

She was angry with Jeff and hurt. How could he think she would even fathom the possibility of disregarding their vows? Even if Bud's attention tempted her, she'd never act on it.

She was angry at Bud for trying to make their friendship something more . . . twice.

But most of all she was angry at herself for almost wishing he would, then fearing he would, then chiding Jeff because he fell short of being some Hollywood rendition of the perfect loving husband, something no one could live up to no matter how hard they tried. Jeff was sorry he was an idiot. No, she was the idiot—again!

Focused

Lately she felt as if she was in a spin. First, she and Jeff were at each other's throats, then all sweet and smoochy, then back again. Maybe the old, dull, buried-in-a-rut doldrums had been better. *Get me off this roller coaster!*

Where were her new Godly eyes that she had been so determined to view everyone through? Had she changed at all?

She looked up to the sky. *Oh, God, why do you put up with me?* Why did Jeff, for that matter?

Christina brushed her frenzy aside and calmly returned to her desk, the calculator and her work. Angela had moved the vase to the worktable near the copier. She smiled and Christina mouthed a thank you back to her before she began to re-enter the numbers. Finally, the account balanced. Throughout the rest of the morning, she tried not to look at the flowers, lest she break down and cause a scene. Everyone picked up on the mood and gave her a wide berth.

At lunch Angela approached the subject from the side. "Want to talk about it or leave it?"

"Jeff's jealous of Bud."

"And that is just now dawning on you?"

"It all came out last night. I thought we had settled it. Then it all exploded again this morning. Then I exploded." Christina shrugged then bit into her turkey and no-fat mayo sandwich. It was not what she was hungry for. A double dip hot fudge sundae with chocolate and caramel syrup oozing down the sides and whipped cream stacked high as fluffy summer clouds - that's what she was hungry for.

"And he sends flowers to smooth it over." Angela's voice contained a bit of agitation.

313

Julie B Cosgrove

Christina immediately defended her man. "Hey, at least he's trying." She caught herself and noticed her friend's smirk. Angela coaxed her in and she fell, hook, line and sinker.

"Thanks." She said and threw a baked potato chip at Angela's lap.

Angela picked it up and chomped. "You're welcome," she mumbled.

At ten till five, Christina shut down her programs, picked up her purse and told everyone goodnight. She walked around the building the long way on purpose, letting the afternoon sun penetrate her back as she breathed in the scent of the honeysuckles dangling on the fence.

Each bloom was tethered together by a thin vine, wrapped through the linked fence in a graceful ballet. How she wanted to crawl in and cling with them. They existed without a care, receiving all they needed from God and releasing sweet fragrances in thanks. Instead she felt like it was her marriage that dangled. But this too would pass, even if it meant another tearful night.

For just a moment behind the wheel, she thought of heading west, again. But she couldn't run off to her hiding place every time things got bumpy. Especially since that was where Bud most likely headed if the stuff about his landlord had been a ruse, as she assumed. Instead Christina closed her eyes and rested her head on her knuckles which grasped the steering wheel in a death lock, begging them to guide the car homeward. She wanted her brain on auto pilot for a while. Just as it had been that day driving up to the cabin. Not feeling, just doing.

Then she asked God to get her there safely, enter the house with her and guide her mouth tonight above all other nights. She would face this battle. But first, she would thank her husband for the flowers.

God guided her mouth and Jeff's, too. She walked in, set her purse down and told him she was sorry, too.

"I just can't help these jealous feelings. There is a chemistry between you and Bud. Maybe it is because you shared a lot when you were kids, but. . ."

"Jeff, I love you. I married you, not him. There's always been a push-me, pull-you thing between us. We both knew it could never work in our teens. We know that now, too. You are the man I want."

"Really?" Jeff motioned her to the couch. "Convince me."

That night, they both slept on the couch.

A fragile peace returned and grew a bit stronger as each day went by. And nary a peep from Bud. When Avery came the next Thursday for their morning ritual of coffee and prayer, his name never came up in the conversation.

Chapter 44   Just Another Day

The calendar revealed the dreaded news. One day remained before her fiftieth birthday, something that Christina chose not to let bother her. She continued to keep her mind busy and avoided any discussion or hinting of the inauspicious day, unaware that actually made things easier for her co-workers and friends at church . . . and for Jeff.

As she leaned against the kitchen counter reading the email messages on her phone and sipping her second morning cup of coffee, Melinda from church called in a frantic voice saying that she just received a call from her mother and she might have to go out of town. Was there anyway Christina could fill in for her that weekend for altar duty?

She added in a breathless voice, "My partner Elaine can not meet until 11 a.m. because she's having her hair done and 10 a.m. was the only time slot she could get with her hairdresser."

"Sure, no problem. I'd be happy to do that. Then you can take the last week in June if that works out," Christina replied, a little down that her friend would ask her to do this on her 50ᵗʰ birthday. But, she corrected her emotion. This was about Melinda, not her. "I hope all goes well with your mom. Can we add her to the prayer list?"

Melinda anticipated her answer. "Father Rick already knows all about it. I'm sure he'll pass the word."

Christina hung up and told herself that Melinda was probably in a frenzy and in a few days it would dawn on her what she'd asked. Most likely, she would phone back apologizing profusely. Besides, Christina convinced herself, it might be a blessing to be busy that day so she would not ruminate over it all. Beats leaning over my dressing table mirror plucking gray hairs.

Just then, Jeff entered into the kitchen, briefcase gripped in one hand as the other grabbed the coffee pot. Since the explosion, a surface calm existed between them. Neither felt the desire for more "big talks". The days blended together with any residual angst shoved under the rug, filed away or hidden in the cupboard.

"I just got a huge scope review on Monday for a job that I just got the addendum on late yesterday. Looks like I am going to have to work on Saturday. Sorry, Babe, it just can't be helped." He blew the steam off the coffee cup. "I promise, we'll do something together later that evening. Okay?"

"We don't have to make plans set in stone," Christina shrugged.

"Hate to mention it, but yes we do. After all, it's a pretty big one coming up." He chortled and shook his finger at her, making her blush. She knew that was the exact affect he wanted.

"Jeff, it's just another day. Really. I don't want to make a big deal of it. And, "she added with emphasis as she poked his side, "No black balloons or banners in the yard, please!"

"But, hon . . ."

"Besides," she continued before he could continue, "We have spent so much on getting the TV fixed and my glasses.... and getting the stuff for my new study. Not to mention the new curtains you so graciously let me buy." She eyed him and smiled.

"You mean the sheets on clearance that you made into curtains in the room you really haven't been able to use until last week and in another week won't be able to use until your aunt leaves?"

Christina waved away the comment. "Really, that's present enough. I honestly do not want anything else. No fancy jewelry." She slapped his hand from reaching over and grabbing some of the bacon she drained on a paper towel. "AND, no black dress and veil. Please!"

"You sure?" he interrogated her.

"Absolutely, One hundred percent. Now go." She waved her hand towards the door.

He raised his hands in mock surrender. "I'm going."

"Wait." She handed him two pieces of bacon and a piece of buttered toast on a napkin. "Bacon's cooled off now."

"Thanks." He folded the napkin around the food and laid it in his briefcase.

"Don't get grease on the proposal." She brushed his cheek with a kiss."Try and have a good day."

"Yeah, right." Jeff gave her a nod and closed the door leading to the garage.

Christina pushed off the kitchen counter and headed down the hall for her final daily primping before heading out herself.

* * *

Jeff's heart skipped a beat, hoping she didn't mean what she'd said about no hoopla. He knew women often said the opposite of what they meant. He learned that one the first year they were married, the hard way.

Well, he wasn't about to change his plans, now. More than ever she deserved this, and he hoped it would be enough of a peace offering to make her forget the whole ordeal of the last month or so and put the Bud thing behind them once and for all.

Instead he popped his head back in and called back, "I'll take you out to dinner tomorrow night if you like. You just be thinking about where you would like to go and then call them if they require reservations, alright? Make it for, oh… say 7 p.m.? That ought to give me time to get home, shower and change." He heard her affirming reply as she walked down the hall.

He paused before he closed the door. "…And no fair picking the cafe or the diner. I want to take you someplace where I need to wear a coat and tie, got it?"

Focused

A laugh came from the direction of the bedroom. "Got it. I am recording this you know."

"Gotta run. See ya later," He added as he headed out the door, chomping on a piece of pilfered bacon left to drain on the counter.

* * *

Christina shook her head. The man was bent on trying. She knew Josh had to work on Saturday as well. Rinsing out her toothbrush, she reconciled herself to the fact she needed to do six loads of laundry that weekend anyway. It was no big deal. Ignoring the residual minty taste in her mouth, she grabbed the last piece of bacon and chewed on it as she plopped another piece of raisin bread in the toaster. Maybe nerves, but her stomach felt cavernous today.

"It's not like I'm a kid expecting a pizza party with balloons at the skating rink or something," she said to Fat Cat rubbing her calves. He obviously wanted bacon, not her. To the rest of the world, tomorrow was just another normal Saturday. Majority ruled.

She lumbered out the back door to head for work and another day in traffic. Joy, joy.

At work there was a small bouquet of cut flowers from the supermarket sitting on her desk and a Post It Note that said "Happy Birthday". It was signed by all her coworkers with a promise they would take her to lunch after payday.

"Thanks, ya'll," she sincerely replied. "You know how much I love their flowers at the Food Basket. They are always fresh and last for days. And carnations, too. They are my favorite." She stuck them in the vase left over from Jeff's bunch delivered after the fight. Or was it from the ones she got after her romp to the Hill Country? Or did it come from Sandy's anniversary bouquet? Or maybe when Angie's daughter sent her roses for taking care of the post tonsillectomy grandson? Lately, vases multiplied like rabbits under the break room sink. No matter.

A little before noon her boss brought in a pastry box of lemon squares, brownies and oatmeal raspberry bars. He plopped it on her desk and called back "Happy Birthday" as he went down the hall and ducked into his office.

Angela looked over at her and shook her head before returning to her computer screen. In a few moments they both sputtered out a laugh. Their boss never showed emotion. The fact that he had actually gone out and gotten the pastries was above and beyond. Christina really felt flattered by the effort.

So she got up and passed the box around, letting everyone take a piece. Then she let her teeth sink into the decadence of a double fudge brownie. Her taste buds acknowledged the dark chocolate chips and chocolate icing. She rolled her eyes into the back of her head and heaved a sigh. "Nirvana," She said with her mouth full.

"Better than...?" Angela asked.

"I wouldn't know," Christina responded, her mouth still savoring the chocolate on her taste buds.

"Not even when you had your old flame under your roof?" Sandy quipped.

"Definitely not then!"

Focused

"Right. Just when he was out of the house on dates with your maid." Angela crowed. "Your face has been glowing a bit lately, you know."

Christina threw her crumpled up napkin at Angela's desk and returned to her own little blinking cursor pointing at the bottom line of the Bronson's latest financial acquisition.

* * *

Jeff set his cell phone alarm for six in the morning. and put it under his pillow. That way he knew he would hear it and not disturb Christina. She requested they watch one of her favorite old tearjerker movies on TV last night and the darn thing hadn't ended until close to midnight.

He quickly showered and dressed as the coffee brewed. He had downed his cup and was out the door by 6:45 a.m., headed to the grocery store to get the last minute items, like ice. An hour later he was in the church parking lot waiting for someone who knew the alarm code to show up.

He plugged his cell into the car jack and dialed his son's number. Two rings, then a "Yeah?"

"Rise and shine. First plane full arrives in an hour."

A barely audible groan came over the airwaves. "I know, Dad. The alarm went off ten minutes ago. Okay?"

"Right. Sorry. Guess I'm nervous. I'm sitting here in the parking lot and nobody's here yet." He got out and closed his truck door.

323

"They will be. It'll all go great. Mom still has no clue?"

"She's not letting on if she does. The way she's been trying not to pout around the house, I don't think so."

Josh laughed. "I'll get to the Southwest terminal on time then get them checked in at the motel. See ya in a few hours."

* * *

Saturday arrived with the sun shining and the birds outside her bedroom window chirping, just like in the Disney movies. Zippity do-da, wonderful day. La, de, da. Christina grabbed her pillow, folded it over her eyes and groaned. She hated irony.

Chapter 45   The Prep

By 8 a.m., several of the ladies arrived. They began sweeping and mopping the Parish Hall. Their chattering filled the room. Harriet waved to Jeff to help her carry in the boxes of napkins, table cloths, serving pieces and an extra kitchen sink for all he knew. Betty arrived with the helium balloons and streamers while Elaine followed behind with the sheet cake from, where else but, Bonnie's Bakery.

The church's phone tree sent out reminders asking everyone to arrive by 10:15 so no stranglers would be coming late and give the surprise away. The mailed invitations included a three by five card and instructions which read: "On this card please write, or draw or depict some way that Christina has brightened up your life." It went on to explain they could add a photo or artwork or whatever they wanted. Announcements were placed two Sundays in a row in everyone's pew bulletins, except the Willis's.

Jeff borrowed and photocopied her address book so Jean could send invitations and cards to

Christina's family and friends outside of the parish. Fliers were rubber-banded onto the front door knobs of the neighbors and word of mouth spread throughout Allensville and neighboring Red Top.

All in all, Jean told Jeff that about one hundred-twenty-five people had RSVP'ed. He knew there would be plenty of food. These church ladies liked to cook. There were always leftovers. In fact, one of the volunteer firemen, Harry, stopped him in the store on Jeff's second run of the morning, this time for French vanilla and hazelnut coffee creamer. He suspected it was Harriet's way to keep him from getting underfoot.

"We sure are lookin' forward to a good meal later on from the St. Martin's women after your wife's shindig. Send all the leftovers our way and we'll take care of them."

Both men had laughed and patted each other's backs.

Jeff said, "I think it's such a tradition to send the leftovers to the firehouse after any church event that those women make extra on purpose."

"Be sure to wish her a good one from all of us on duty." Harry waved goodbye.

* * *

Jeff was already showered, dressed and long gone by the time Christina opened her eyes. She stared at the indention still left in the sheets, wishing he had woken her to kiss her good-bye.

Throwing off the covers, she sat up and stretched. I will not engage in a pity party. Christina

326

Focused

resolved to treat herself to her favorite breakfast of creamed eggs over toast, the traditional "what to do with all the hard boiled eggs in the Easter basket" breakfast she traditionally cooked for her family after Sunrise services.

While the boiled eggs were cooling in cold water, she whipped up the rue and added processed cheese, stirring it into a creamy cheddar sauce. She shelled and chopped up one egg and added it to the sauce along with cracked pepper and chopped chives. Viola. Served over toast points along with a cup of steaming Earl Grey tea and she felt pampered already. Her mood elevated. She would take the other eggs to work next Monday for her lunch.

Then the fifty year old took a long hot bubble bath with the last of the lemongrass. While soaking, she listened to one of her favorite classical music CDs. Oozing down into the fragrant, foamy water, she sighed and placed a warm damp washcloth over her eyes. The headache that crept into her temples dissipated.

The music ended. She lifted the washcloth and peeked out of the corner of her eye at the clock on the wall over the toilet. It read 10:15 a.m.

"I better hustle if I 'm going to make it to the church a little before 11a.m. to meet Elaine," she said to Precious crouching on the edge of the tub, her fluffy tail hovering micro-centimeters above the bubbles. Christina donned her St. Martin's T-shirt and her jeans. She always wore that shirt when working at the church because it gave her a little more credibility if she tripped the alarm and faced the police, again. She patted Fat Cat and dashed out the door.

Julie B Cosgrove

She stepped outside and immediately felt the heat. It was already up in the mid eighties and the weatherman had said it was supposed to top out at ninety-seven degrees today. She thought about going in and changing into her cut offs, but told herself that was a little too informal for church, even if she was just going to be vacuuming and setting up the altar. Besides, I've begun to get cellulite back there. Another sign I'm turning fifty.

By ten o'clock, while Christina soaked in her foamy bath, several women milled around and chatted in the kitchen. The Parish Hall was abuzz with people decorating, adding their cards to the photo album or signing the banner. Presents were stacked on the table where, a few weeks earlier, ones had been placed for the graduates. The Methodist Church half a block away graciously agreed to have everyone park in their lot and on the side streets so Christina wouldn't wonder what was going on when she pulled her car into St. Martin's property. She would just think the Methodists were having a wedding as she drove by their filled up parking lot. Bill, the Senior Warden, brought his golf cart to transport anyone who did not want to walk in the heat from the Methodist church to St Martin's.

* * *

Carrie and her daughter Beth, along with her husband, Carl and his wife Dawn and their daughter Melanie with her twins all came in a rented van. Her five living cousins and their families, her godmother, Jeff's parents, and her uncle and aunt were all driving

328

in as well. Coming in on planes were Carrie's other two kids, Jeff's two brothers and their families, seven friends from college, the youth minister she had known when she was in high school who had retired to Florida, and her old across the street neighbors who moved to Virginia to be nearer to their grandkids. George, their next-door neighbor and Bob volunteered to help Josh transport folk from the airport to the motel and then the church.

Several of the out-of-towners rented rooms in the same motel, deciding to make a weekend of the event. The motel gave them quite a group discount because the front desk manager remembered how Christina and her church friends helped him and his wife sort through the remains of their house a few years ago in the nearby town of Red Top. A tornado ravished it and fourteen others.

"She personally delivered sandwiches and water to us from the Red Cross two days in a row and brought us blankets and story books for the kids. Please, give this to her for me." He added an index card of his own to the pile to be delivered.

Carrie smiled back. "Of course. She'll be thrilled."

She left, marveling at how her sister always seemed to know what to do or say to help folks. Their mother had been that way, but she was never sure of her mother's motives. Had she been the philanthropist society woman or a real Christian woman of charity? She knew her sister Christina fell into the category of the latter.

* * *

Julie B Cosgrove

Jeff sat back for a moment observing the organized chaos for the woman he had spent more years of life with than without. He marveled at how, after he had bounced the idea off of Betty and Harriet one Sunday during the social hour, this event had blossomed. To think all these people added their own momentum, all more than willing to do something for his wife in return for all she'd been and done for them. It was like watching the Olympic torch being passed along the route, being exchanged hand after hand on the way to the opening ceremonies. He decided to stay out of the way, lest Harriet send him on one more unnecessary errand.

About 10:40 Father Rick noticed Jeff standing in the corner swinging his hands, clasping them in back and then in front.

He came over, patted him on the shoulder and said in his ear over the din of chattering, "It'll be just fine. Don't worry. Someone much larger and wiser is in charge of this, you know."

Jeff nodded back, his chest swelling with pride to know his wife was the recipient of all these good intentions poured out by so many folk.

"Yep, He is, Father. He knew what a wonderful woman Christina would turn into. I surely didn't when I proposed twenty-five years ago. I just knew she took my breath away." Jeff winked and wandered over to Janice who was motioning to him from across the room.

"Thanks. Can you help us put up the happy birthday banner? I think everyone has signed it now."

"Uh, except me," Jeff replied as clicked his pen. His signature made it number one hundred thirty-

Focused

four. As Janice and Elaine stood on chairs in stocking feet to tack it up, he and Father Rick gingerly held it in the middle. The ladies stretched and stuck the tacks into the columns that flanked the parish hall. A loud applause reverberated throughout the hall as the two jumped down and stood back to make sure it lay straight.

Delectable dishes were brought out in a parade from the kitchen like a bucket brigade. Betty created her famous punch — lime sherbet, ginger ale and pineapple juice with maraschino cherries floating in an ice ring of citrus slices. The light green froth slowly rose to the edge of the punch bowl as several children eagerly watched.

"None until she comes now, Okay?" Betty made an "uh-uh-uh" gesture at the pint-sized crowd.

"Aww, man." One little boy said. His mother came over quickly to grab his arm.

Fifteen tables, each seating eight, were corralled around the Hall, alternately decorated in blue and mauve, Christina's favorite colors, or so Jeff hoped, since those were the colors of her new study. Two long tables arranged to seat fourteen were at the head of the room to seat Christina and her immediate family. The centerpieces arrived. In each were carnations, irises, tea roses and daisies interlaced with baby's breath and ferns. Three staggered pillars clasped rose-scented votive candles and accents of mauve and blue ribbons completed the arrangements., As if on cue, the men started to light the votives.

Melinda opened a box of cocktail napkins Harriet just brought over. "Jeff, come look how they turned out." They were, of course, mauve with navy blue. Printed in cursive calligraphy read, *"Happy 50th, Christina June 9, 2009"*.

Harriet proudly spread them out around the cake. Jeff grinned and told her, "Thanks for ordering them." He held one up and nodded approval. "They came out great."

"I just hope Roger is taking notes. I'm turning fifty next year," Melinda giggled.

"Want me to put a bug in his ear?" Jeff bounced the ball back in her court.

Just then Josh whistled through his front teeth and yelled out "Okay everyone. Quiet!! She just pulled into the parking lot." Rustles and whispers could be heard as the crowd all gathered at the back of the Parish Hall. Jeff turned out the lights. They huddled in mass in the darkness.

Chapter 46 Plan Revealed

Christina got out of the car. She didn't see Elaine's minivan yet, or anyone else's vehicle for that matter. The fact that hers was the only one in the parking lot seemed a little strange. There were always cars on Saturdays — Sunday school teachers decorating their rooms, or the treasurer working on the computer, or someone running off copies of sheet music, or men mowing the grass.

Come to think of it, the grass is mowed. Oh well, it is the summer. They probably came early when it was cooler. Still, she did not cherish the idea opening the church and disarming the alarm alone.

She went to the side entrance near the kitchen. Digging in her purse for the keys, she set her purse on the stoop and took a deep breath. Come on Christina, you can do this. Don't let the darn thing intimidate you. Saying a quick prayer, she shoved the key into the dead bolt. It wasn't bolted? Someone must have forgotten to lock it. That meant the alarm was off.

Julie B Cosgrove

Instead of being concerned she chalked it up to Divine Providence.

She put the key in the regular lock, turned it and pushed the door open. Holding it open with her hip, she bent down to get her purse unknowingly showing her backside, spotlighted by the sunlight, to 134 pairs of eyes. Just as she turned around, the lights flashed on.

"SURPRISE!" Echoed from the rafters.

Christina squealed in terror and dropped her purse, scattering half of its contents across the floor as she grasped her chest. Everyone started to laugh, watching the crimson glow zip up her face. Children clapped with glee. Betty and Elaine skittered around the floor picking up keys, lipstick, a hairbrush, a drinking straw, pocket sized Kleenex, breath mints, an atomizer of cologne and the baby wipes she always carried just in case.

Slowly taking it all in, Christina spotted Jeff leaning against the wall grinning like the cat that ate the canary. He meandered over to her, chuckling. As he put his arm around her, Christina noticed her sister, brother . . . *Aunt Mildred, already? She wasn't due to come for weeks. And—oh my gosh—my old youth minister and next door neighbors I haven't seen in years.*

Hands to her mouth and pointing, she squealed again, then began to bounce up and down. Laughter echoed throughout the Parish Hall again as she ran to them, arms out, tears in her eyes. Soon hordes of people were gathered around her, hugging and kissing her and shaking her hand. There were so many people there. She felt overwhelmed. Each soul was a pleasant surprise.

334

Focused

Avery came forward, holding the hands of a boy and a girl, each with huge angelic eyes. The girl had two fingers in her mouth. Christina recognized them immediately from the pictures in Avery's wallet. She bent down to their level. "You must be Josh and Esther."

The little girl looked down at the ground and swung her mother's arm. Avery let go to hug her friend. Avery's Josh said, "Mom said it's your birthday. Is there cake?"

Avery looked embarrassed but laughed. "Josh, that's rude."

Christina laughed as well. Then she looked back down at little Josh. "I had the same question. Look on that table. I think there is and it looks yummy. Wanna go see?"

The boy nodded and grabbed her outstretched hand. "And I want you to meet my son in a moment. His name is Josh as well." She looked up to see where in the room her Josh stood. Then she noticed a dark haired, steel blue-eyed friend in the corner with his parents. The Owens maneuvered through the crowd to meet her halfway.

"Bud?"

"Sorry I hadn't called or anything. Had to go home and get Maw and Paw. You didn't think they'd miss this shindig, did ya?" Her old River Rat friend grinned. Father and son standing there together in ill-fitted suits, shaved and smiling their sparkling Owen smiles. Between them, they could light up a room. He leaned closer. "Water under?"

Christina nodded. "Water under." She hugged Dorothy.

Dorothy squeezed her hand. "We wouldn't miss your big day for the world. Fifty years. And to think we have known you through all of it. Bud done called and told us the minute Jeff told him all about it."

She looked puzzled as Bud winked. "Yes, Chris. All's cool between us. It was before I left that day. Right, Jeff?"

She felt Jeff next to her and her Josh on the other side. They pointed up and Christina saw the banner. The dam broke. Dropping little Josh's hand, she bawled like a baby. Immediately five tissues were rummaged out of purses and shoved towards her face.

Avery's Josh tugged on the other Josh's sleeve. "Why she's crying?"

The older and wiser Josh replied, " 'Cause women do that when they're happy."

"Weird."

Father and son, the two men in Christina's life guided her over to the cake on the table, with little Josh in tow. She eyed all the luscious dishes of food her friends prepared. "Oh that is so beautiful. Is that three bean salad and King Ranch casserole? Oh my! Betty's punch!" She continued to bounce on her feet like a three-year-old, clasping her hands. Little Josh bounced, too.

"That's what I admire about you, Christina." Father Rick's sermon-volume voice sang out. "You have never lost touch with your inner child."

Rounds of laughter sprung up again. Jeff waved his hands over his head.

"Quiet everyone. Let's give the lady of honor a moment to collect her wits and take this all in."

Focused

More laugher, then hums of voices and hushes could be heard as everyone strove to be quiet. Obediently, Christina eyed it all. She turned around, hands still clasped and said in a squeaky voice, "Why? All of you here. I can't believe…" Her tears swallowed her words.

"Hon, it's all for you," Jeff quietly replied. He waved his arm around the room. "I can't begin to tell you how many of your friends and family busted their britches putting this altogether. I just suggested it might be nice and off they went with the ball, handing it off and running for the goal post."

Josh came up and handed her the mauve colored album.

"Mom, this was Carrie's idea. She decorated the cover. It's for you. Most folks here have filled in cards with stories and best wishes. You can read it all later when it's quieter."

Applause broke out as she hugged her two men and her sister came forward.

"Actually, you know I commissioned it to be done. I have never had a creative bone in my body. Unlike my sister."

"It's wonderful of you, just the same." Christina carefully traced the design on the front of the cover as if it was spun glass. Lips quivering and tears flowing, she whispered "I just don't know what to say." She gingerly placed the album on the table, then hugged her sister.

"Watch out for the snake wrapped around your tire when you leave. I did that." Carl quipped and hugged her, too. That was at least the umpteenth time he'd reminded his younger sisters of the one time they'd gotten his goat, but good.

Christina leapt into Jeff's arms and gave him a big bear hug. He returned the favor, nestling his face in her hair. Josh hugged her from behind. A flash went off when her sister took a picture.

Aahhh's filtered throughout the Hall. Betty leaned over and whispered to Carrie, "I want a copy of that for the church yearbook."

Father Rick shoved a microphone in front of Christina and hooked the battery pack onto her jeans loop. Hushes went through the crowd. Christina suddenly became aware she was in T- shirt and jeans, everyone else in party clothes. She motioned her hands over her torso. "Father Rick, I 'm sorry."

"For what? No one shows up to clean the church in their Sunday best? Yes, we set that up, too. Everyone knows. How else were we going to get you here?"

Jeff whispered, "I brought you a change of clothes. They're in the Ladies if you want to step away for a moment."

"Why?" The confident Christina winked. "Everyone's already seen me. Sweet of you, but no thanks."

"That's my out of the goldfish bowl girl." He patted her on the back.

Then a little voice whined, "Can I have some punch now, Mommy?"

After the laugher abated, Christina managed to say a little louder "Thank y'all. Everyone. I can't believe y'all came." She began pointing to folks, and calling out names. "How can I ever..." her words caught in her throat again.

Father Rick stepped in front. "Travis wants some punch, so let us pray. The Lord be with you ..."

One hundred thirty-four voices responded, "And also with you."

He blessed the day, the woman and the food and declared the party officially started. A simultaneous "Amen" and a cheer resounded throughout the hall. The rush of feet began as folks milled around the tables of food they'd salivated over for the last twenty minutes before the honored guest's arrival.

An hour later, the cake was demolished, the punch bowl drained bone dry for the second time, and a good portion of the food sucked down. Christina made her way around to each table, chatted and hugged her friends—old and newer, coworkers and family.

Then Jeff led her to the love seat drug out from Father Rick's office for the occasion. Carl's twin grandkids took turns bringing her the prettily wrapped things to open.

Some people stood around on the floor, others pulled fold-out chairs around to watch as she opened each precious gift, read each card and passed them around for all to see. Then, Josh took the microphone and tapped into it. Everyone looked up and stopped what they were doing.

"Mom, I guess I just don't tell you enough how much I love you and how much you mean to me. And how much I appreciate all the things you do, and have done all my life. Even those times you yelled at me to do the dishes. Or to clean my plate or my room."

Julie B Cosgrove

Murmurs of laughter floated up through the rafters and back down to the microphone.

His speech continued and then others came up and began to tell an impromptu story of how Christina had helped them, or comforted them, or influenced them, or shown God's love to them. She sat there quietly listening, no longer able to emote, hands clutching the album.

Then very quietly, Barry, the youth minister, came forward with his guitar. Melinda, his wife, slipped in next to him and began to sing one of Christina's favorite contemporary hymn with her youthful angelic voice. It was "Surely the Presence of the Lord Is in This Place".

Christina wondered how the couple knew it was her favorite. She shot a glance upward and thanked the Informer, then let the melodic words flow through her soul. She could hear rush of the angel's wings and could see the glow on everyone's faces in the room, just as the lyrics said.

Her husband leaned over and whispered in her ear. "Want me to bribe them to sing hymn number 645 next?" That was the song in their hymnal called "The King of Love My Shepherd Is". Her Dad's favorite Irish hymn, it always brought tears to her eyes..

"No, make it 'Silent Night'," she parleyed back. That has been his Dad's favorite—the one he'd sung at every Christmas Eve Mass when Jeff was a child. It still caused Jeff to get misty-eyed.

"Truce." Her husband raised a mental white flag and kissed her cheek.

Chapter 48 Aftermath

That evening Christina sat curled up on the couch in the den with a steaming cup of Earl Grey and box of Kleenex next to her. She carefully flipped through her album nestled in her lap and one by one read the cards, looked at the artwork and cherished the old photos. Jeff canceled the reservations for dinner. They'd eaten so much at the party, they were still stuffed to the gills. Besides, a quiet evening at home seemed more in order.

"Are you sure you don't mind?" Christina asked.

"No, I don't. I 'm still full. That cake was way too good. Had three pieces."

"Hers always are. And so was the rest of the food." She puffed out her cheeks, indicating she too felt stuffed.

"I called. The restaurant has an opening next Saturday so we can go then. Besides, I think you'd much rather just sit here for now."

She grinned at him, tilting her head. "For now."

"And later, we'll lock the cats from the bedroom?" Jeff winked. Christina blushed. But for now he was satisfied to putter around or sit in the recliner and just watch her expressions. Every once in a while, she looked up to show him something and he nodded and grinned.

"Several more people who could not make the reception mailed back cards. Jean put them in an envelope." He reached in his jacket pocket. "She slipped these to me to give to you later. Guess this is later." He suspected they might need to buy another album for the overflow. Note to self. Find out where Carrie ordered the first one from, the one brimming with my wife's life.

Jeff noticed his wife's eyes were brimming again, too. She held up his card. He knew he could have talked until he was blue in the face about how much she meant to him and everyone else, that her life really did matter. He could tell her she represented her Lord to so many and always had as long as he'd known her. But without showing her, she would have waived it off. What better way to show her than what happened today. He hoped it thoroughly knocked her out of that "turning fifty" slump and dispelled all the unpleasantries of the past several months.

"After all, when I was in that I'm-turning-fifty sag, you snapped me out of it by throwing a kiddies' party in the backyard complete with clown, piñatas and Pin the Tail on the Donkey," He reminded her. "Pay backs are tough, girl."

342

Focused

Jeff never had a formal birthday party growing up because his parents could never afford it. She had knocked his socks off on his fiftieth. "You did good, hon."

Her tribute had turned out more wonderfully than he could have ever conceived it could, thanks to all the helping hands. Still, he admitted that he relished the thought of less calls while he was at work. The boss had been very understanding, but . . .

"Jeff?" her quiet voice said and he refocused his attention from an imaginary spot on the wall back to her face. He got up and walked over to her, hands in his pockets. She set the album down and patted the sofa cushion by her side. He plopped down on the couch, his arm around the back.

"Now do you get it?" he asked quietly. "Do you see how much you do for others as a second nature without even thinking about it? You are way too hard on yourself, Lady. You always have been. You keep looking at what you could have done better or should have done instead that you didn't do. I hate that 20/20 hindsight of yours."

She turned to face him more. Her eyes glistened with new tears.

He brushed a strand of hair from her brow and continued. "It's about time you see what you have done for me and everyone else. These index cards are proof of your worth. It hasn't been all you focusing on you. Not at all."

Jeff patted the album then sighed. "It's the blooms from the seeds of Christian kindness you have been sowing for as long as I have known you and before. After all, being a Christian is part of your nature as well as your name. It's about time you saw that. You do it well."

He leaned forward and picked up her tear-smudged glasses. Wiping them off on his pocket handkerchief, he held them up to the light. "You said these made you realize that you needed to focus on your life. But I don't think God gave you that message so you could take yourself out to the woodshed and mull over your shortcomings and mistakes."

Christina looked at her hands, her lips pressed together.

Jeff let out a sigh, and then continued. " Forget all of your past hurts and fears. He forgave you for those a long time ago, so it's time you forgave yourself. And while you're at it, please forgive me."

She opened her mouth to speak, but he put up his hands. "I know you were brought up to always be conscious of what others might think. Well, guess what? Your Mom was wrong. You let God take care of that, and you just keep opening your heart up to those He puts in your path. That's what you are best at. He gave you a sixth sense of knowing what people need before anyone else even has an inkling."

He slapped her hand mockingly and continued, "So quit putting yourself under the microscope and use these new glasses to look out there and see for me, too. Okay? I need your vision and guidance, too you know." He gently placed them back onto her face.

Grabbing a new Kleenex because the one in her hand was a twisted and tattered, Christina laid her head on her husband's shoulder and said, "I just don't know how to thank you."

Focused

Jeff pulled away, turned her towards him and laid his forehead against hers. She felt the warmth of him. That familiar warmth she thought she'd lost, now newly found.

"You ninny," He whispered with emotion, "That's the point. All your life, you already have."

Chapter 49   Rest in Peace

Around 3 a.m., she laid staring at the reflective patterns of the ash's branches as they danced on the ceiling of their bedroom in the moonlit night breeze. She felt exhausted, but not tired. Or was it the other way around?

"Heck if I know," she muttered to herself, sighed and slipped out of bed.

She tiptoed down the dark hall so as not to waken Jeff. Not that a marching band coming down the hall would. That man could sleep through an atomic bomb attack.

Christina sat on the back porch, reflecting over the day. She reeked of lemongrass, from the new bottle Jeff gave her, along with a pair of diamond stud earrings. His scent lingered on her as well like a cozy cloak.

She tried to find the words to tell her Lord she was so very sorry she had not seen things clearer much sooner, but her efforts fell short. It transformed into awed silence. She felt far too humbled, far too small to have her words reach to the heavens to someone so All Knowing and All Loving. But her faith assured her they did, even though she so often didn't deserve it.

Julie B Cosgrove

Her dad could finally rest in peace. She cherished his memory, the lessons he taught her and the love he had for her, but in her sorrow she'd almost lost the love of a good man, the one her dad had given her to at the altar twenty-five years ago. Her mom could rest as well. Up at the cabin, Christina finally saw her mother's inner wisdom. She also discovered how much she was like her mom, and found out that was Okay. God had blessed her with two good people as parents. They were not perfect. Certainly their kids had not turned out perfect. But heck, who was? Perfection was overrated.

Jeff 's words rang true. She was too hard on herself, and on him. "Guess you're never too old to learn, right?" she asked the marmalade cat rubbing against her back. She picked him up and nuzzled his fur. "Not mad because we locked you out, are you?"

The soft continuous purr let her know the answer. She gave the cat a squeeze and gently set him down, stroking his back.

With eyes closed, Christina returned to her prayer. She vowed to try better and then stopped herself. No, she did not have to try. The overwhelming guilt that she was just not doing enough to be a good person followed by the angst over what others might think— feelings she had lived with for way too long— dissipated for now.

She knew they would come back. She knew she would battle them the rest of her life. But she had that album now. It was proof God had worked through her after all. She had it as a weapon to dispel those negative thoughts when one of them raised their ugly head. Knowing she could dispel them, half the battle was already won.

She possessed new ways to see things now. When she allowed herself to be open to doing and seeing things His way, those were the times He blessed. The times which were celebrated today. Now she saw that, thanks to Jeff, Bud and all of her dear friends and family. All she could promise now to herself, to them and to her God was to keep on striving to concentrate less on herself so He could do more through her. After all, He died on the cross and sent His Spirit for just that reason.

Then she heard her husband's voice echoed by all the people who'd made up those cards, "...you already have." Words resounded in the heavens to be etched in her soul. God had used her all along in spite of her self-worrying, doubting, goldfish bowl making ways. God plopped her down into an American suburban lifestyle for a reason and He could darn well use her where He put her. After all, He was God.

Today she discovered that even through years of such a misconstrued view of her own self worth and others opinions of her, and in spite of her intentions or failings, He already had used her over and over. That was the best gift of all, though it took her fifty years to open it.

Fifty years old. It no longer seemed so daunting.

Christina pulled her knees to her chest and wrapped the hem of her nightgown around her bare feet. She rested her chin on her knees and interlaced her fingers under it. Then, she closed her eyes and just listened.

Julie B Cosgrove

There was always such a peace and calm in the stillness of the early morning. It almost seemed as if the sky was touchable and so was God. Tomorrow, life would start again with its joys, misunderstandings, heartbreaks and miracles. Now she knew He would see her through it.

All her life, He already had.

As long as Christ was her focus, everything else would work out. She would keep trying to make that her goal and not let life get in the way. And God would keep forgiving her when she didn't, as long as she came back with a contrite heart. Maybe that goldfish bowl had indeed smattered to smithereens.

A now-wiser Christina removed her new glasses from her nose and rubbed the tear spots off of them with the hem of her nightgown.

Somewhere in a nearby field a Chuck-wills-widow began to chirp out his song. She had never heard one here in Allensville. Up at the cabin, often. Not here.

A gentle warmth cascaded down her shoulders and relaxed the rest of her, including her mind. A small smile emerged on her lips. Was that bird calling out just for her benefit? Of course not. But the message was not lessened by that fact. God was here too, not just up on the river.

And where He was, there was love. And where love was … it was home.

* * *

350

Focused

Somewhere over the fields the bird stopped his song. He cocked his head as he listened to another one, not of a bird, but of a human lady.

It was a strange but pleasant, soft humming. It was the tune to "Surely the Presence of the Lord is in This Place".

ℭℨᕯ

Finally, brethren, whatever is true,
whatever is honorable, whatever is right,
whatever is pure, whatever is lovely,
whatever is of good repute,
if there is any excellence and
if anything is worthy of praise,
focus on things.

Philippians 4:8 (revised)

Synopsis from GROUNDED

Another Christina and Jeff adventure in Allensville
Coming in 2013 to Amazon and Kindle

A battered young black woman, a coworker of their son Josh, is thrust into Christina and Jeff's suburban empty-nest life as a tornado hits, leading both women to discover what it means to be grounded in God's protective love.

"Here's twenty. Yo' don't need mo' than that."

"Ray, what did you do? Where's the rest? Martin sent $500.00 this time." Shanice waved the stub under his nose. "He's my brother. He sent the check to me."

"I's got expenses." He leaned against the wall, confident, cocky.

"That money was mine!" She dug her toes into the tattered carpet in a futile effort to hang on to her emotions.

What's yours is mine 'cause yo' is mine."

"I am not yours. I am not anyone's," she yelled back, thrusting her fists against her thighs. The check stub crunched into a bow tie shape under her clenched fingers.

"Say what?" He replied with a stern look that froze her nerve. That is until he lunged and grabbed both her arms. An alarm went off in her head. She'd seen her Momma's boyfriends get like this.

"Don't you talk back to me, Girl."

"Shove it!" She jerked her hands up, pushed away and gulped an angry sob.

353

Julie B Cosgrove

That started it. She should've just kept quiet. The smack cracked her cheek and sent her sprawling onto the floor. Just where he had wanted her - vulnerable and dazed.

Shanice takes refuge in the apartment of a coworker, Josh Willis, son of Jeff and Christina. He leaves a cryptic message inviting his parents to his apartment, something he rarely does. Christina's maternal antenna raises.

Josh, dressed in cut offs and a T-shirt with no shoes, looked as if he had not bathed or shaved yet. "Hi Dad, Mom." He nodded and grabbed the cardboard box.

Setting it onto the hood of the car, he said "Thanks, this will help. . .But before you go in, there is something I need to tell you." A painful look clouded his blue eyes as he shaded them from the sun. "Can we sit by the pool?"

Christina shot Jeff an "I told you so" look.

Jeff responded with his hand on the small of her back and patted it twice.

"Let's not jump the gun, dear." He whispered in her ear as the followed their son.

The pool sat in a center courtyard. Three buildings, each housing six apartments, and the guest parking lot surrounded it. A chain link fence separated the lot from the courtyard and Josh balanced the cardboard box on one hip as he opened its gate to let his parents pass through. The stone in Cynthia's stomach grew into a boulder as she eyed Jeff and then began walking over to a grouping of plastic lawn chairs near the shallow end. They were slightly moldy and faded with age.

354

Grounded

The next moments of silence felt like an hour, as the parents stared at their son, seated, hands clasped between his knees, head down staring at an imaginary spot on the pebbled pavement. His brow knitted together.

Jeff sighed and crossed his leg over his thigh. He watched a plane glide along silently just above the horizon, leaving an ice trail that glistened in the Texas sun.

In her mind, Cynthia heard the Jeopardy tune.

"OK," Josh nodded, more to himself than them.

The break in the silence made them both jolt. Christina wiggled to the edge of her chair. Jeff uncrossed his leg.

"Here's the thing." Josh glanced up then back down to the pavement. "There is this, uh. . . . girl in my bed."

Jeff and Christina agree to let the young battered and bitter woman rent Josh's old room. The more they try to include her in their lives, the more she pulls away yet sends out signals she wants their help. Until through their love and prayers, she begins to bond, right when a tornado hits during the annual town fair, tearing the town and their lives apart.

Jeff and Christina spent the first few hours trying to help out at the fairground in any way they could. They began reuniting scouts with distressed, but relieved parents and praying with their neighbors who were waiting for medical help as the older scouts administered first aid. They did not even think of their house. Or maybe it was that they dared not to. It probably would have been more than they could handle. What was within their immediate eyesight was bad enough.

Julie B Cosgrove

As the family and the their neighbors try to assess the damage and move on, Christina can't help but notice some promising changes in her teen renter. As neighbor helps neighbor and an impromptu exchange starts up on the Town Hall grounds, in the midst of twisted and shattered buildings, an equally torn apart life just may be restored.

Therefore, put on the full armor of God, so that when the day of evil comes, you may be able to stand your ground, and after you have done everything, to stand."

Ephesians 6:13 NIV

356

Look for other works by Julie B Cosgrove

Available on Amazon.com in paperback, also in Kindle or Nook-

P.R.A.Y.I.N.G - Bringing Purpose and Power to Your Prayers
A step by step guide to a deeper, more purposeful conversation with the Almighty. Biblically backed techniques in this book will help surge power into your prayers as you focus on who you are and who God is. Discover how each of the letters in PRAYING represent a step towards making your prayer life richer—Praise, Recount His blessings, Atonement, Yielding to His will, Intercession, expressing your own Needs, giving God the Glory.

Song Notes - Devotionals from the Book of Psalms
Inside the pages of this book are ponderings, encouragements and an honest, fresh look at how the verses in the Psalms are just as pertinent today as they were when scribed centuries ago. A great bedside table book you can pick up and read whenever you want, however much you want.

What Can She Tell Us?
Ten lessons from un-named women in the New Testament and what happened when the Holy burst through into their domain. IN a 8x11 format, there is ample room for individual reflections and notes. Great Bible study for women, and men and youth as well. Bible passage for each 30-45 minute lesson is included in the text.

Plus . . .

And to be released March, 2012 by Abbott Press

Between the Window and the Door uses

examples taken from life and the people in the Bible who
also found themselves in "wait and see" situations. The
stories of Noah, Jonah, the young men in the fiery furnace,
and even Lazarus hold lessons for us about God's purpose
and how we are to react when God places us in transition.

Divided into eleven studies with reflective
questions, including the introduction, and with suggested
Bible passages from the Psalms as an appendix, this study is
perfect for teenagers, men and women as either a personal
study or as a group study. It is suitable for a weekend retreat
or in a Christian educational class setting. Each lesson can
be completed in 30-45 minutes, including time allotted for
discussion.

Coming Soon:

Hush in The Storm A suspense Novel

*Jen, a young widow floundering in the storm of
mourning, whose only lifeline is her humdrum job, is
thrust into a maze of deceit and intrigue by a
coworker named Tom. . . at the request of her late
husband, or so Tom says.*

For a sneak preview, go to
www.juliebcosgrove.com

More copies of this book may be purchased on Amazon.com

Note: If you purchased this book without a cover, that means it is likely stolen and neither the publisher, distributor nor the author received any monies for it.

Cross  Words
Press